HITCHCOCK SAYS,
"NO SEXISM IN SLAYING!"

Ghouls can be girls as well as boys, as far as Alfred Hitchcock is concerned. The hand that rocks the cradle can commit the most dastardly of acts, and those fingers protected by so many expensive lotions are as capable as Jack the Ripper's of being dipped in blood. Sweet lips can utter the most sinister of lies, those hours in the kitchen can cook up the most deadly of feasts, and above all, crime can and should always pay just as well for women as for men.

Equal wrongs for women take a giant step forward as Alfred Hitchcock sets his most fiendish femmes right alongside his most murderous males in a competition to the death in—

14 OF MY FAVORITES IN SUSPENSE

ALFRED HITCHCOCK PRESENTS

14

OF MY FAVORITES
IN SUSPENSE

A DELL BOOK

Published by
DELL PUBLISHING CO., INC.
1 Dag Hammarskjold Plaza
New York, New York 10017

Dell ® TM 681510, Dell Publishing Co., Inc.

The editor gratefully acknowledges the invaluable assistance
of Patricia O'Connell in the preparation of this volume.

Reprinted by arrangement with Random House, Inc.
Printed in Canada

Previous Dell Edition #F125
New Dell Edition
First printing—June 1976

ACKNOWLEDGMENTS

THE BIRDS, Daphne du Maurier. Reprinted by permission of Doubleday & Co., Inc., from "Kiss Me Again, Stranger," by Daphne du Maurier. Copyright, 1952, by Daphne du Maurier.

MAN WITH A PROBLEM, Donald Honig. Reprinted by permission of Ann Elmo Agency and H. S. D. Publications, Inc. This story first appeared in Alfred Hitchcock's Mystery Magazine. Copyright, 1958, by Donald Honig.

THEY BITE, Anthony Boucher. Reprinted by permission of Collins-Knowlton-Wing. Copyright, 1943, by Anthony Boucher. All rights reserved.

THE ENEMY, Charlotte Armstrong. Reprinted by permission of Coward-McCann, Inc. from "The Albatross," by Charlotte Armstrong. Copyright © 1957, by Charlotte Armstrong Lewi.

THE INEXPERIENCED GHOST, H. G. Wells. Reprinted by permission of the Executors of the Estate of H. G. Wells. From "Twelve Stories and a Dream," by H. G. Wells.

SENTENCE OF DEATH, Thomas Walsh. Reprinted by permission of the Author. Copyright, 1948, Curtis Publishing Company.

SPRING FEVER, Dorothy Salisbury Davis. Reprinted by permission of the Sterling Lord Agency. Copyright ©, 1952, by Dorothy Salisbury Davis.

THE CRATE AT OUTPOST 1, Matthew Gant. Reprinted by permission of the Sterling Lord Agency. Copyright ©, 1954, by Matthew Gant.

MY UNFAIR LADY, Guy Cullingford. Reprinted by permission of the Author and the American Literary Exchange. Copyright, 1958, by H. S. D. Publications, Inc.

NEW MURDERS FOR OLD, Carter Dickson. Reprinted by permission of William Morrow and Company, Inc., from "The Department of Queer Complaints," by Carter Dickson. Copyright, 1940, by William Morrow & Company, Inc.

TERRIFIED, C. B. Gilford. Reprinted by permission of the Author and Scott Meredith Literary Agency, Inc. Copyright, 1958, by H. S. D. Publications, Inc.

THE DUEL, Joan Vatsek. Reprinted by permission of Curtis Brown, Ltd. Copyright, 1959, by Mercury Press, Inc.

FOUR O'CLOCK, Price Day. Reprinted by permission of the Author. Copyright, 1958, by Price Day.

TOO MANY COINCIDENCES, Paul Eiden. Reprinted by permission of the Author and Scott Meredith Literary Agency, Inc. Copyright, 1958, by Fosdeck Publications, Inc.

CONTENTS

PREFACE 9

THE BIRDS Daphne du Maurier 13

MAN WITH A PROBLEM Donald Honig 49

THEY BITE Anthony Boucher 58

THE ENEMY Charlotte Armstrong 75

THE INEXPERIENCED GHOST H. G. Wells 108

SENTENCE OF DEATH Thomas Walsh 126

SPRING FEVER Dorothy Salisbury Davis 149

THE CRATE AT OUTPOST 1 Matthew Gant 180

MY UNFAIR LADY Guy Cullingford 190

NEW MURDERS FOR OLD Carter Dickson 206

TERRIFIED C. B. Gilford 230

THE DUEL Joan Vatsek 244

FOUR O'CLOCK Price Day 265

TOO MANY COINCIDENCES Paul Eiden 271

Preface

After spending a week end in the country, a friend of mine invariably sends his host a book. Recently it occurred to me that through television I have spent many Sunday evenings in your homes yet I have never thanked you properly. Ergo, this book. Of course I don't believe my friend charges for the books he sends, but no matter. It's the thought that counts.

Most prefaces soon become defensive, disintegrate into lengthy explanations of why certain stories have been chosen, and the anthologists quickly become apologists. The stories in this volume have only one reason for being here and that is explained in the title. I can only say that I like them. I very much hope that you will too.

A suspense story is not simply a Who-done-it. It might better be called a When's-he-gonna-do-it. I don't think I'm giving away any secrets when I tell you that in most of these stories somebody *does* do it. So don't say you haven't been warned.

There are those who say that the reading of a mystery or suspense story has a therapeutic value; cleansing one of his homicidal tendencies and allow- ing him to enjoy those crimes he has always wanted to commit but didn't because he lacked the get-up-and-go. If this is true, I think we have crimes to relieve every possible suppressed desire—or at least all the normal ones. I am confident that several of these cheerful little stories will put an end to the loose talk about truth being stranger than fiction.

I don't wish to spend too much time introducing these tales. I believe it was Henry James who observed, when speaking of prefatory pieces such as this, that when a work of creative literature is introduced to the reader at great length, when fiction is too carefully interpreted, explained and annotated, it is like having a dinner guest brought to the house by a policeman. This is the last thing I wish to do. I much prefer that you feel that this dinner guest to whom you are opening your home is a complete stranger and that there is no policeman within screaming distance.

And now, if you are anxious to curl up with a good book, perhaps we should be getting on. (My final parenthetical remark: the only things I know of that actually like to curl up with a good book are the silverfish in my basement.) When you begin reading, may I suggest you choose a time when you are alone in the house. If there are people there, get rid of them. The book is full of suggestions of how this can be accomplished. Now turn out all the lights you possibly can, look over the stories and take one before retiring. If you want to sample another, help yourself, but be careful. An overdose could be fatal. After all, this is a highly toxic book.

ALFRED J. HITCHCOCK

14
of My
Favorites
in Suspense

The Birds

DAPHNE DU MAURIER

On December the third the wind changed over-
night and it was winter. Until then the autumn had
been mellow, soft. The earth was rich where the
plow had turned it.

Nat Hocken, because of a wartime disability, had a
pension and did not work full time at the farm. He
worked three days a week, and they gave him the
lighter jobs. Although he was married, with chil-
dren, his was a solitary disposition; he liked best to
work alone.

It pleased him when he was given a bank to build
up, or a gate to mend, at the far end of the peninsula,
where the sea surrounded the farmland on either side.
Then, at midday, he would pause and eat the meat
pie his wife had baked for him and, sitting on the
cliff's edge, watch the birds.

In autumn great flocks of them came to the pen-
insula, restless, uneasy, spending themselves in
motion; now wheeling, circling in the sky; now
settling to feed on the rich, new-turned soil; but
even when they fed, it was as though they did so
without hunger, without desire.

Restlessness drove them to the skies again. Crying,

whistling, calling, they skimmed the placid sea and left the shore.

Make haste, make speed, hurry and begone; yet where, and to what purpose? The restless urge of autumn, unsatisfying, sad, had put a spell upon them, and they must spill themselves of motion before winter came.

Perhaps, thought Nat, a message comes to the birds in autumn, like a warning. Winter is coming. Many of them will perish. And like people who, apprehensive of death before their time, drive themselves to work or folly, the birds do likewise; tomorrow we shall die.

The birds had been more restless than ever this fall of the year. Their agitation more remarked because the days were still.

As Mr. Trigg's tractor traced its path up and down the western hills, and Nat, hedging, saw it dip and turn, the whole machine and the man upon it were momentarily lost in the great cloud of wheeling, crying birds.

Nat remarked upon them to Mr. Trigg when the work was finished for the day.

"Yes," said the farmer, "there are more birds about than usual. I have a notion the weather will change. It will be a hard winter. That's why the birds are restless."

The farmer was right. That night the weather turned.

The bedroom in the cottage faced east. Nat woke just after two and heard the east wind, cold and dry. It sounded hollow in the chimney, and a loose slate rattled on the roof. Nat listened, and he could hear the sea roaring in the bay. He drew the blanket round him, leaned closer to the back of his wife, deep in sleep. Then he heard the tapping on the window-pane. It continued until, irritated by the sound, Nat got out of bed and went to the window. He opened it; and as he did so something brushed his hand, jabbing at his knuckles, grazing the skin. Then he saw the flutter of wings and the thing was gone again, over the roof, behind the cottage.

It was a bird. What kind of bird he could not tell. The wind must have driven it to shelter on the sill.

He shut the window and went back to bed, but feeling his knuckles wet, put his mouth to the scratch. The bird had drawn blood.

Frightened, he supposed, bewildered, seeking shelter, the bird had stabbed at him in the darkness. Once more he settled himself to sleep.

Presently the tapping came again—this time more forceful, more insistent. And now his wife woke at the sound, and turning in the bed, said to him, "See to the window, Nat; it's rattling."

"I've already been to it," he told her. "There's some bird there, trying to get in."

"Send it away," she said. "I can't sleep with that noise."

He went to the window for the second time, and now when he opened it, there was not one bird on the sill but half a dozen; they flew straight into his face.

He shouted, striking out at them with his arms, scattering them; like the first one, they flew over the roof and disappeared.

He let the window fall and latched it.

Suddenly a frightened cry came from the room across the passage where the children slept.

"It's Jill," said his wife, roused at the sound.

There came a second cry, this time from both children. Stumbling into their room, Nat felt the beating of wings about him in the darkness. The window was wide open. Through it came the birds, hitting first the ceiling and the walls, then swerving in mid-flight and turning to the children in their beds.

"It's all right. I'm here," shouted Nat, and the children flung themselves, screaming, upon him, while in the darkness the birds rose, and dived, and came for him again.

"What is it, Nat? What's happened?" his wife called. Swiftly he pushed the children through the door to the passage and shut it upon them, so that he was alone in their bedroom with the birds.

He seized a blanket from the nearest bed, and using it as a weapon, flung it to right and left about him.

He felt the thud of bodies, heard the fluttering of wings; but the birds were not yet defeated, for again and again they returned to the assault, jabbing his hands, his head, their little stabbing beaks sharp as pointed forks.

The blanket became a weapon of defense. He wound it about his head, and then in greater darkness, beat at the birds with his bare hands. He dared not stumble to the door and open it lest the birds follow him.

How long he fought with them in the darkness he could not tell; but at last the beating of the wings about him lessened, withdrew; and through the dense blanket he was aware of light.

He waited, listened; there was no sound except the fretful crying of one of the children from the bedroom beyond.

He took the blanket from his head and stared about him. The cold gray morning light exposed the room.

Dawn and the open window had called the living birds; the dead lay on the floor.

Sickened, Nat went to the window and stared out across his patch of garden to the fields.

It was bitter cold, and the ground had all the hard, black look of the frost that the east wind brings. The sea, fiercer now with turning tide, whitecapped and steep, broke harshly in the bay. Of the birds there was no sign.

Nat shut the window and the door of the small bedroom and went back across the passage to his own room.

His wife sat up in bed, one child asleep beside her; the smaller one in her arms, his face bandaged.

"He's sleeping now," she whispered. "Something must have cut him; there was blood at the corners of his eyes. Jill said it was the birds. She said she woke up and the birds were in the room."

His wife looked up at Nat, searching his face for confirmation. She looked terrified, bewildered. He did not want her to know that he also was shaken, dazed almost, by the events of the past few hours.

"There are birds in there," he said. "Dead birds, nearly fifty of them."

He sat down on the bed beside his wife.

"It's the hard weather," he said. "It must be that; it's the hard weather. They aren't the birds, maybe, from around here. They've been driven down from upcountry."

"But Nat," whispered his wife, "it's only this night that the weather turned. They can't be hungry yet. There's food for them out there in the fields."

"It's the weather," repeated Nat. "I tell you, it's the weather."

His face, too, was drawn and tired, like hers. They stared at one another for a while without speaking.

Nat went to the window and looked out. The sky was hard and leaden, and the brown hills that had gleamed in the sun the day before looked dark and bare. Black winter had descended in a single night.

The children were awake now. Jill was chattering, and young Johnny was crying once again. Nat heard his wife's voice, soothing, comforting them as he went downstairs.

Presently they came down. He had breakfast ready for them.

"Did you drive away the birds?" asked Jill.

"Yes, they've all gone now," Nat said. "It was the east wind brought them in."

"I hope they won't come again," said Jill.

"I'll walk with you to the bus," Nat said to her.

Jill seemed to have forgotten her experience of the night before. She danced ahead of him, chasing the leaves, her face rosy under her pixy hood.

All the while Nat searched the hedgerows for the birds, glanced over them to the fields beyond, looked to the small wood above the farm where the rooks and jackdaws gathered; he saw none. Soon the bus came ambling up the hill.

Nat saw Jill onto the bus, then turned and walked

back toward the farm. It was not his day for work, but he wanted to satisfy himself that all was well. He went to the back door of the farmhouse; he heard Mrs. Trigg singing, the wireless making a background for her song.

"Are you there, missus?" Nat called.

She came to the door, beaming, broad, a good-tempered woman.

"Hullo, Mr. Hocken," she said. "Can you tell me where this cold is coming from? Is it Russia? I've never seen such a change. And it's going on, the wireless says. Something to do with the Arctic Circle."

"We didn't turn on the wireless this morning," said Nat. "Fact is, we had trouble in the night."

"Kiddies poorly?"

"No." He hardly knew how to explain. Now, in daylight, the battle of the birds would sound absurd.

He tried to tell Mrs. Trigg what had happened, but he could see from her eyes that she thought his story was the result of nightmare following a heavy meal.

"Sure they were real birds?" she said, smiling.

"Mrs. Trigg," he said, "there are fifty dead birds—robins, wrens, and such—lying low on the floor of the children's bedroom. They went for me; they tried to go for young Johnny's eyes."

Mrs. Trigg stared at him doubtfully. "Well, now," she answered. "I suppose the weather brought them; once in the bedroom they wouldn't know where they were. Foreign birds maybe, from that Arctic Circle."

"No," said Nat. "They were the birds you see about here every day."

"Funny thing," said Mrs. Trigg. "No explaining it, really. You ought to write up and ask the *Guardian*. They'd have some answer for it. Well, I must be getting on."

Nat walked back along the lane to his cottage. He found his wife in the kitchen with young Johnny.

"See anyone?" she asked.

"Mrs. Trigg," he answered. "I don't think she believed me. Anyway, nothing wrong up there."

"You might take the birds away," she said. "I daren't go into the room to make the beds until you do. I'm scared."

"Nothing to scare you now," said Nat. "They're dead, aren't they?"

He went up with a sack and dropped the stiff bodies into it, one by one. Yes, there were fifty of them all told. Just the ordinary, common birds of the hedgerow; nothing as large even as a thrush. It must have been fright that made them act the way they did.

He took the sack out into the garden and was faced with a fresh problem. The ground was frozen solid, yet no snow had fallen; nothing had happened in the past hours but the coming of the east wind. It was unnatural, queer. He could see the whitecapped seas breaking in the bay. He decided to take the birds to the shore and bury them.

When he reached the beach below the headland, he could scarcely stand, the force of the east wind was so strong. It was low tide; he crunched his way over the shingle to the softer sand and then, his back to the wind, opened up his sack.

He ground a pit in the sand with his heel, meaning

to drop the birds into it; but as he did so, the force of the wind lifted them as though in flight again, and they were blown away from him along the beach, tossed like feathers, spread and scattered.

The tide will take them when it turns, he said to himself.

He looked out to sea and watched the crested breakers, combing green. They rose stiffly, curled, and broke again; and because it was ebb tide, the roar was distant, more remote, lacking the sound and thunder of the flood.

Then he saw them. The gulls. Out there, riding the seas.

What he had thought at first were the whitecaps of the waves were gulls. Hundreds, thousands, tens of thousands.

They rose and fell in the troughs of the seas, heads to the wind, like a mighty fleet at anchor, waiting on the tide.

Nat turned; leaving the beach, he climbed the steep path home.

Someone should know of this. Someone should be told. Something was happening, because of the east wind and the weather, that he did not understand.

As he drew near the cottage, his wife came to meet him at the door. She called to him, excited. "Nat," she said, "it's on the wireless. They've just read out a special news bulletin. It's not only here, it's everywhere. In London, all over the country. Something has happened to the birds. Come listen; they're repeating it."

Together they went into the kitchen to listen to the announcement.

"Statement from the Home Office, at eleven A.M. this morning. Reports from all over the country are coming in hourly about the vast quantity of birds flocking above towns, villages, and outlying districts, causing obstruction and damage and even attacking individuals. It is thought that the Arctic air stream at present covering the British Isles is causing birds to migrate south in immense numbers, and that intense hunger may drive these birds to attack human beings. Householders are warned to see to their windows, doors, and chimneys, and to take reasonable precautions for the safety of their children. A further statement will be issued later."

A kind of excitement seized Nat. He looked at his wife in triumph. "There you are," he said. "I've been telling myself all morning there's something wrong. And just now, down on the beach, I looked out to sea and there were gulls, thousands of them, riding on the sea, waiting."

"What are they waiting for, Nat?" she asked.

He stared at her. "I don't know," he said slowly.

He went over to the drawer where he kept his hammer and other tools.

"What are you going to do, Nat?"

"See to the windows and the chimneys, like they tell you to."

"You think they would break in with the windows shut? Those wrens and robins and such? Why, how could they?"

He did not answer. He was not thinking of the robins and the wrens. He was thinking of the gulls.

He went upstairs and worked there the rest of the

morning, boarding the windows of the bedrooms, filling up the chimney bases.

"Dinner's ready." His wife called him from the kitchen.

"All right. Coming down."

When dinner was over and his wife was washing up, Nat switched on the one o'clock news. The same announcement was repeated, but the news bulletin enlarged upon it. "The flocks of birds have caused dislocation in all areas," said the announcer, "and in London the mass was so dense at ten o'clock this morning that it seemed like a vast black cloud. The birds settled on rooftops, on window ledges, and on chimneys. The species included blackbird, thrush, the common house sparrow, and as might be expected in the metropolis, a vast quantity of pigeons, starlings, and that frequenter of the London river, the black-headed gull. The sight was so unusual that traffic came to a standstill in many thoroughfares, work was abandoned in shops and offices, and the streets and pavements were crowded with people standing about to watch the birds."

The announcer's voice was smooth and suave; Nat had the impression that he treated the whole business as he would an elaborate joke. There would be others like him, hundreds of them, who did not know what it was to struggle in darkness with a flock of birds.

Nat switched off the wireless. He got up and started work on the kitchen windows. His wife watched him, young Johnny at her heels.

"What they ought to do," she said, "is to call the Army out and shoot the birds."

"Let them try," said Nat. "How'd they set about it?"

"I don't know. But something should be done. They ought to do something."

Nat thought to himself that "they" were no doubt considering the problem at that very moment, but whatever "they" decided to do in London and the big cities would not help them here, nearly three hundred miles away.

"How are we off for food?" he asked.

"It's shopping day tomorrow, you know that. I don't keep uncooked food about. Butcher doesn't call till the day after. But I can bring back something when I go in tomorrow."

Nat did not want to scare her. He looked in the larder for himself and in the cupboard where she kept her tins.

They could hold out for a couple of days.

He went on hammering the boards across the kitchen windows. Candles. They were low on candles. That must be another thing she meant to buy tomorrow. Well, they must go early to bed tonight. That was, if—

He got up and went out the back door and stood in the garden, looking down toward the sea.

There had been no sun all day, and now, at barely three o'clock, a kind of darkness had already come; the sky was sullen, heavy, colorless like salt. He could hear the vicious sea drumming on the rocks.

He walked down the path halfway to the beach. And then he stopped. He could see the tide had turned. The gulls had risen. They were circling, hundreds of them, thousands of them, lifting their wings against the wind.

It was the gulls that made the darkening of the sky.

And they were silent. They just went on soaring and circling, rising, falling, trying their strength against the wind. Nat turned. He ran up the path back to the cottage.

"I'm going for Jill," he said to his wife.

"What's the matter?" she asked. "You've gone quite white."

"Keep Johnny inside," he said. "Keep the door shut. Light up now and draw the curtains."

"It's only gone three," she said.

"Never mind. Do what I tell you."

He looked inside the tool shed and took the hoe.

He started walking up the lane to the bus stop. Now and again he glanced back over his shoulder; and he could see the gulls had risen higher now, their circles were broader, they were spreading out in huge formation across the sky.

He hurried on. Although he knew the bus would not come before four o'clock, he had to hurry.

He waited at the top of the hill. There was half an hour still to go.

The east wind came whipping across the fields from the higher ground. In the distance he could see the clay hills, white and clean against the heavy pallor of the sky.

Something black rose from behind them, like a smudge at first, then widening, becoming deeper. The smudge became a cloud; and the cloud divided again into five other clouds, spreading north, east, south, and west; and then they were not clouds at all but birds.

He watched them travel across the sky, within two or three hundred feet of him. He knew, from their speed, that they were bound inland; they had no business with the people here on the peninsula. They were rooks, crows, jackdaws, magpies, jays, all birds that usually preyed upon the smaller species, but bound this afternoon on some other mission.

He went to the telephone call box, stepped inside, lifted the receiver. The exchange would pass the message on. "I'm speaking from the highway," he said, "by the bus stop. I want to report large formations of birds traveling upcountry. The gulls are also forming in the bay."

"All right," answered the voice, laconic, weary.

"You'll be sure and pass this message on to the proper quarter?"

"Yes. Yes." Impatient now, fed up. The buzzing note resumed.

She's another, thought Nat. She doesn't care.

The bus came lumbering up the hill. Jill climbed out.

"What's the hoe for, Dad?"

"I just brought it along," he said. "Come on now, let's get home. It's cold; no hanging about. See how fast you can run."

He could see the gulls now, still silent, circling the fields, coming in toward the land.

"Look, Dad; look over there. Look at all the gulls."

"Yes. Hurry now."

"Where are they flying to? Where are they going?"

"Upcountry, I dare say. Where it's warmer."

He seized her hand and dragged her after him along the lane.

"Don't go so fast. I can't keep up."

The gulls were copying the rooks and the crows. They were spreading out, in formation, across the sky. They headed, in bands of thousands, to the four compass points.

"Dad, what is it? What are the gulls doing?"

They were not intent upon their flight, as the crows, as the jackdaws, had been. They still circled overhead. Nor did they fly so high. It was as though they waited upon some signal; as though some decision had yet to be given.

"I wish the gulls would go away." Jill was crying. "I don't like them. They're coming closer to the lane."

He started running, swinging Jill after him. As they went past the farm turning, he saw the farmer backing his car into the garage. Nat called to him.

"Can you give us a lift?" he said.

Mr. Trigg turned in the driver's seat and stared at them. Then a smile came to his cheerful, rubicund face. "It looks as though we're in for some fun," he said. "Have you seen the gulls? Jim and I are going to take a crack at them. Everyone's gone bird crazy, talking of nothing else. I hear you were troubled in the night. Want a gun?"

Nat shook his head.

The small car was packed, but there was room for Jill on the back seat.

"I don't want a gun," said Nat, "but I'd be obliged if you'd run Jill home. She's scared of the birds."

"Okay," said the farmer. "I'll take her home. Why don't you stop behind and join the shooting match? We'll make the feathers fly."

Jill climbed in, and turning the car, the driver sped up the lane. Nat followed after. Trigg must be crazy. What use was a gun against a sky of birds?

They were coming in now toward the farm, circling lower in the sky. The farm, then, was their target. Nat increased his pace toward his own cottage. He saw the farmer's car turn and come back along the lane. It drew up beside him with a jerk.

"The kid has run inside," said the farmer. "Your wife was watching for her. Well, what do you make of it? They're saying in town the Russians have done it. The Russians have poisoned the birds."

"How could they do that?" asked Nat.

"Don't ask me. You know how stories get around."

"Have you boarded your windows?" asked Nat.

"No. Lot of nonsense. I've had more to do today than to go round boarding up my windows."

"I'd board them now if I were you."

"Garn. You're windy. Like to come to our place to sleep?"

"No, thanks all the same."

"All right. See you in the morning. Give you a gull breakfast."

The farmer grinned and turned his car to the farm entrance. Nat hurried on. Past the little wood, past the old barn, and then across the stile to the remaining field. As he jumped the stile, he heard the whir of wings. A black-backed gull dived down at him from the sky. It missed, swerved in flight, and rose to

dive again. In a moment it was joined by others—
six, seven, a dozen.

Nat dropped his hoe. The hoe was useless. Cover-
ing his head with his arms, he ran toward the cot-
tage.

They kept coming at him from the air—noiseless,
silent, save for the beating wings. The terrible, flutter-
ing wings. He could feel the blood on his hands,
his wrists, upon his neck. If only he could keep them
from his eyes. Nothing else mattered.

With each dive, with each attack, they became
bolder. And they had no thought for themselves.
When they dived low and missed, they crashed,
bruised and broken, on the ground.

As Nat ran he stumbled, kicking their spent bodies
in front of him.

He found the door and hammered upon it with his
bleeding hands. "Let me in," he shouted. "It's Nat.
Let me in."

Then he saw the gannet, poised for the dive, above
him in the sky.

The gulls circled, retired, soared, one with another,
against the wind.

Only the gannet remained. One single gannet,
above him in the sky. Its wings folded suddenly to
its body. It dropped like a stone.

Nat screamed; and the door opened.

He stumbled across the threshold, and his wife
threw her weight against the door.

They heard the thud of the gannet as it fell.

His wife dressed his wounds. They were not deep.
The backs of his hands had suffered most, and his

wrists. Had he not worn a cap, the birds would have reached his head. As for the gannet—the gannet could have split his skull.

The children were crying, of course. They had seen the blood on their father's hands.

"It's all right now," he told them. "I'm not hurt."

His wife was ashen. "I saw them overhead," she whispered. "They began collecting just as Jill ran in with Mr. Trigg. I shut the door fast, and it jammed. That's why I couldn't open it at once when you came."

"Thank God the birds waited for me," he said. "Jill would have fallen at once. They're flying inland, thousands of them. Rooks, crows, all the bigger birds. I saw them from the bus stop. They're making for the towns."

"But what can they do, Nat?"

"They'll attack. Go for everyone out in the streets. Then they'll try the windows, the chimneys."

"Why don't the authorities do something? Why don't they get the Army, get machine guns?"

"There's been no time. Nobody's prepared. We'll hear what they have to say on the six o'clock news."

"I can hear the birds," Jill said. "Listen, Dad."

Nat listened. Muffled sounds came from the windows, from the door. Wings brushing the surface, sliding, scraping, seeking a way of entry. The sound of many bodies pressed together, shuffling on the sills. Now and again came a thud, a crash, as some bird dived and fell.

Some of them will kill themselves that way, he thought, but not enough. Never enough.

"All right," he said aloud. "I've got boards over the windows, Jill. The birds can't get in."

He went and examined all the windows. He found wedges—pieces of old tin, strips of wood and metal —and fastened them at the sides of the windows to reinforce the boards.

His hammering helped to deafen the sound of the birds, the shuffling, the tapping, and—more ominous —the splinter of breaking glass.

"Turn on the wireless," he said.

He went upstairs to the bedrooms and reinforced the windows there. Now he could hear the birds on the roof—the scraping of claws, a sliding, jostling sound.

He decided the whole family must sleep in the kitchen and keep up the fire. He was afraid of the bedroom chimneys. The boards he had placed at their bases might give way. In the kitchen they would be safe because of the fire.

He would have to make a joke of it. Pretend to the children they were playing camp. If the worst happened and the birds forced an entry by way of the bedroom chimneys, it would be hours, days perhaps, before they could break down the doors. The birds would be imprisoned in the bedrooms. They could do no harm there. Crowded together, they would stifle and die. He began to bring the mattresses downstairs.

At sight of them, his wife's eyes widened in apprehension.

"All right," he said cheerfully. "We'll all sleep together in the kitchen tonight. More cozy, here by the fire. Then we won't be worried by those silly old birds tapping at the windows."

He made the children help him rearrange the furniture, and he took the precaution of moving the dresser against the windows.

We're safe enough now, he thought. We're snug and tight. We can hold out. It's just the food that worries me. Food and coal for the fire. We've enough for two or three days, not more. By that time—

No use thinking ahead as far as that. And they'd be given directions on the wireless.

And now, in the midst of many problems, he realized that only dance music was coming over the air. He knew the reason. The usual programs had been abandoned; this only happened at exceptional times.

At six o'clock the records ceased. The time signal was given. There was a pause, and then the announcer spoke. His voice was solemn, grave. Quite different from midday.

"This is London," he said. "A national emergency was proclaimed at four o'clock this afternoon. Measures are being taken to safeguard the lives and property of the population, but it must be understood that these are not easy to effect immediately, owing to the unforeseen and unparalleled nature of the present crisis. Every householder must take precautions about his own building. Where several people live together, as in flats and hotels, they must unite to do the utmost that they can to prevent entry. It is absolutely imperative that every individual stay indoors tonight.

"The birds, in vast numbers, are attacking anyone

on sight, and have already begun an assault upon buildings; but these, with due care, should be impenetrable.

"The population is asked to remain calm.

"Owing to the exceptional nature of the emergency, there will be no further transmission from any broadcasting station until seven A.M. tomorrow."

They played "God Save the Queen." Nothing more happened.

Nat switched off the set. He looked at his wife. She stared back at him.

"We'll have supper early," suggested Nat. "Something for a treat—toasted cheese, eh? Something we all like."

He winked and nodded at his wife. He wanted the look of dread, of apprehension, to leave her face.

He helped with the supper, whistling, singing, making as much clatter as he could. It seemed to him that the shuffling and the tapping were not so intense as they had been at first, and presently he went up to the bedrooms and listened. He no longer heard the jostling for place upon the roof.

They've got reasoning powers, he thought. They know it's hard to break in here. They'll try elsewhere.

Supper passed without incident. Then, when they were clearing away, they heard a new sound, a familiar droning.

His wife looked up at him, her face alight.

"It's planes," she said. "They're sending out planes after the birds. That will get them. Isn't that gunfire? Can't you hear guns?"

It might be gunfire, out at sea. Nat could not tell.

Big naval guns might have some effect upon the gulls out at sea, but the gulls were inland now. The guns couldn't shell the shore because of the population.

"It's good, isn't it," said his wife, "to hear the planes?"

Catching her enthusiasm, Jill jumped up and down with Johnny. "The planes will get the birds."

Just then they heard a crash about two miles distant. Followed by a second, then a third. The droning became more distant, passed away out to sea.

"What was that?" asked his wife.

"I don't know," answered Nat. He did not want to tell her that the sound they had heard was the crashing of aircraft.

It was, he had no doubt, a gamble on the part of the authorities to send out reconnaissance forces, but they might have known the gamble was suicidal. What could aircraft do against birds that flung themselves to death against propeller and fuselage but hurtle to the ground themselves?

"Where have the planes gone, Dad?" asked Jill.

"Back to base," he said. "Come on now, time to tuck down for bed."

There was no further drone of aircraft, and the naval guns had ceased. Waste of life and effort, Nat said to himself. We can't destroy enough of them that way. Cost too heavy. There's always gas. Maybe they'll try spraying with gas, mustard gas. We'll be warned first, of course, if they do. There's one thing, the best brains of the country will be on it tonight.

Upstairs in the bedrooms all was quiet. No more scraping and stabbing at the windows. A lull in battle. The wind hadn't dropped, though. Nat could still hear it roaring in the chimneys. And the sea breaking down on the shore.

Then he remembered the tide. The tide would be on the turn. Maybe the lull in battle was because of the tide. There was some law the birds obeyed, and it had to do with the east wind and the tide.

He glanced at his watch. Nearly eight o'clock. It must have gone high water an hour ago. That explained the lull. The birds attacked with the flood tide.

He reckoned the time limit in his head. They had six hours to go without attack. When the tide turned again, around 1:20 in the morning, the birds would come back.

He called softly to his wife and whispered to her that he would go out and see how they were faring at the farm, see if the telephone was still working there so that they might get news from the exchange.

"You're not to go," she said at once, "and leave me alone with the children. I can't stand it."

"All right," he said, "all right. I'll wait till morning. And we can get the wireless bulletin then, too, at seven. But when the tide ebbs again, I'll try for the farm; they may let us have bread and potatoes."

His mind was busy again, planning against emergency. They would not have milked, of course, this evening. The cows would be standing by the gate, waiting; the household would be inside, battened behind boards as they were here at the cottage.

That is, if they had had time to take precautions.

Softly, stealthily, he opened the back door and looked outside.

It was pitch-dark. The wind was blowing harder than ever, coming in steady gusts, icy, from the sea.

He kicked at the step. It was heaped with birds. These were the suicides, the divers, the ones with broken necks. Wherever he looked, he saw dead birds. The living had flown seaward with the turn of the tide. The gulls would be riding the seas now, as they had done in the forenoon.

In the far distance on the hill, something was burning. One of the aircraft that had crashed; the fire, fanned by the wind, had set light to a stack.

He looked at the bodies of the birds. He had a notion that if he stacked them, one upon the other, on the window sills, they would be added protection against the next attack.

Not much, perhaps, but something. The bodies would have to be clawed at, pecked and dragged aside before the living birds gained purchase on the sills and attacked the panes.

He set to work in the darkness. It was queer. He hated touching the dead birds, but he went on with his work. He noticed grimly that every windowpane was shattered. Only the boards had kept the birds from breaking in.

He stuffed the cracked panes with the bleeding bodies of the birds and felt his stomach turn. When he had finished, he went back into the cottage and barricaded the kitchen door, making it doubly secure.

His wife had made him cocoa; he drank it thirstily.

He was very tired. "All right," he said, smiling, "don't worry. We'll get through."

He lay down on his mattress and closed his eyes.

He dreamed uneasily because, through his dreams, ran the dread of something forgotten. Some piece of work that he should have done. It was connected, in some way, with the burning aircraft.

It was his wife, shaking his shoulder, who awoke him finally.

"They've begun," she sobbed. "They've started this last hour. I can't listen to it any longer alone. There's something smells bad too, something burning."

Then he remembered. He had forgotten to make up the fire.

The fire was smoldering, nearly out. He got up swiftly and lighted the lamp.

The hammering had started at the windows and the door, but it was not that he minded now. It was the smell of singed feathers.

The smell filled the kitchen. He knew what it was at once. The birds were coming down the chimney, squeezing their way down to the kitchen range.

He got sticks and paper and put them on the embers, then reached for the can of kerosene.

"Stand back," he shouted to his wife. He threw some of the kerosene onto the fire.

The flame roared up the pipe, and down into the fire fell the scorched, blackened bodies of the birds.

The children waked, crying. "What is it?" asked Jill. "What's happened?"

Nat had no time to answer her. He was raking the bodies from the chimney, clawing them out onto the floor.

The flames would drive away the living birds from the chimney top. The lower joint was the difficulty though. It was choked with the smoldering, helpless bodies of the birds caught by fire.

He scarcely heeded the attack on the windows and the door. Let them beat their wings, break their backs, lose their lives, in the desperate attempt to force an entry into his home. They would not break in.

"Stop crying," he called to the children. "There's nothing to be afraid of. Stop crying."

He went on raking out the burning, smoldering bodies as they fell into the fire.

This'll fetch them, he said to himself. The draft and the flames together. We're all right as long as the chimney doesn't catch.

Amid the tearing at the window boards came the sudden homely striking of the kitchen clock. Three o'clock.

A little more than four hours to go. He could not be sure of the exact time of high water. He reckoned the tide would not turn much before half past seven.

He waited by the range. The flames were dying. But no more blackened bodies fell from the chimney. He thrust his poker up as far as it could go and found nothing.

The danger of the chimney's being choked up was over. It could not happen again, not if the fire was kept burning day and night.

I'll have to get more fuel from the farm tomorrow, he thought. I can do all that with the ebb tide. It can be worked; we can fetch what we need when the tide's turned. We've just got to adapt ourselves, that's all.

They drank tea and cocoa, ate slices of bread. Only half a loaf left, Nat noticed. Never mind, though; they'd get by.

If they could hang on like this until seven, when the first news bulletin came through, they would not have done too badly.

"Give us a smoke," he said to his wife. "It will clear away the smell of the scorched feathers."

"There's only two left in the packet," she said. "I was going to buy you some."

"I'll have one," he said.

He sat with one arm around his wife and one around Jill, with Johnny on his lap, the blankets heaped about them on the mattress.

"You can't help admiring the beggars," he said. "They've got persistency. You'd think they'd tire of the game, but not a bit of it."

Admiration was hard to sustain. The tapping went on and on; and a new, rasping note struck Nat's ear, as though a sharper beak than any hitherto had come to take over from its fellows.

He tried to remember the names of birds; he tried to think which species would go for this particular job.

It was not the tap of the woodpecker. That would be light and frequent. This was more serious; if it continued long, the wood would splinter as the glass had done.

Then he remembered the hawks. Could the hawks have taken over from the gulls? Were there buzzards now upon the sills, using talons as well as beaks? Hawks, buzzards, kestrels, falcons; he had forgotten the birds of prey. He had forgotten the gripping power of the birds of prey. Three hours to go; and while they waited, the sound of the splintering wood, the talons tearing at the wood.

Nat looked about him, seeing what furniture he could destroy to fortify the door.

The windows were safe because of the dresser. He was not certain of the door. He went upstairs; but when he reached the landing, he paused and listened.

There was a soft patter on the floor of the children's bedroom. The birds had broken through.

The other bedroom was still clear. He brought out the furniture to pile at the head of the stairs should the door of the children's bedroom go.

"Come down, Nat. What are you doing?" called his wife.

"I won't be long," he shouted. "I'm just making everything shipshape up here."

He did not want her to come. He did not want her to hear the pattering in the children's bedroom, the brushing of those wings against the door.

After he suggested breakfast, he found himself watching the clock, gazing at the hands that went so slowly around the dial. If his theory was not correct, if the attack did not cease with the turn of the tide, he knew they were beaten. They could not continue through the long day without air, without rest, without fuel.

A crackling in his ears drove away the sudden, desperate desire for sleep.

"What is it? What now?" he said sharply.

"The wireless," said his wife. "I've been watching the clock. It's nearly seven."

The comfortable crackling of the wireless brought new life.

They waited. The kitchen clock struck seven.

The crackling continued. Nothing else. No chimes. No music.

They waited until a quarter past. No news bulletin came through.

"We heard wrong," he said. "They won't be broadcasting until eight o'clock."

They left the wireless switched on. Nat thought of the battery, wondered how much power was left in the battery. If it failed, they would not hear the instructions.

"It's getting light," whispered his wife. "I can't see it but I can feel it. And listen! The birds aren't hammering so loud now."

She was right. The rasping, tearing sound grew fainter every moment. So did the shuffling, the jostling for place upon the step, upon the sills. The tide was on the turn.

By eight there was no sound at all. Only the wind. And the crackling of the wireless. The children, lulled at last by the stillness, fell asleep.

At half past eight Nat switched the wireless off.

"We'll miss the news," said his wife.

"There isn't going to be any news," said Nat. "We've got to depend upon ourselves."

He went to the door and slowly pulled away the barricades. He drew the bolts, and kicking the broken bodies from the step outside the door, breathed the cold air.

He had six working hours before him, and he knew he must reserve his strength to the utmost, not waste it in any way.

Food and light and fuel; these were the most necessary things. If he could get them, they could endure another night.

He stepped into the garden; and as he did so, he saw the living birds. The gulls had gone to ride the sea, as they had done before. They sought sea food and the buoyancy of the tide before they returned to the attack.

Not so the land birds. They waited, and watched.

Nat saw them on the hedgerows, on the soil, crowded in the trees, outside in the field—line upon line of birds, still, doing nothing. He went to the end of his small garden.

The birds did not move. They merely watched him.

I've got to get food, Nat said to himself. I've got to go to the farm to get food.

He went back to the cottage. He saw to the windows and the door.

"I'm going to the farm," he said.

His wife clung to him. She had seen the living birds from the open door.

"Take us with you," she begged. "We can't stay here alone. I'd rather die than stay here alone."

"Come on, then," he said. "Bring baskets and Johnny's pram. We can load up the pram."

They dressed against the biting wind. His wife put Johnny in the pram, and Nat took Jill's hand.

"The birds," Jill whimpered. "They're all out there in the fields."

"They won't hurt us," he said. "Not in the light."

They started walking across the field toward the stile, and the birds did not move. They waited, their heads turned to the wind.

When they reached the turning to the farm, Nat stopped and told his wife to wait in the shelter of the hedge with the two children. "But I want to see Mrs. Trigg," she protested. "There are lots of things we can borrow if they went to market yesterday, and—"

"Wait here," Nat interrupted. "I'll be back in a moment."

The cows were lowing, moving restlessly in the yard, and he could see a gap in the fence where the sheep had knocked their way through to roam unchecked in the front garden before the farmhouse.

No smoke came from the chimneys. Nat was filled with misgiving. He did not want his wife or the children to go down to the farm.

He went down alone, pushing his way through the herd of lowing cows, who turned this way and that, distressed, their udders full.

He saw the car standing by the gate. Not put away in the garage.

All the windows of the farmhouse were smashed. There were many dead gulls lying in the yard and around the house.

The living birds perched on the group of trees behind the farm and on the roof of the house. They were quite still. They watched him. Jim's body lay in the yard. What was left of it. His gun was beside him.

The door of the house was shut and bolted, but it

was easy to push up a smashed window and climb through.

Trigg's body was close to the telephone. He must have been trying to get through to the exchange when the birds got him. The receiver was off the hook, and the instrument was torn from the wall.

No sign of Mrs. Trigg. She would be upstairs. Was it any use going up? Sickened, Nat knew what he would find there.

Thank God, he said to himself, there were no children.

He forced himself to climb the stairs, but halfway up he turned and descended again. He could see Mrs. Trigg's legs protruding from the open bedroom door. Beside her were the bodies of black-backed gulls and an umbrella, broken. It's no use doing anything, Nat thought. I've only got five hours; less than that. The Triggs would understand. I must load up with what I can find.

He tramped back to his wife and children.

"I'm going to fill up the car with stuff," he said. "We'll take it home and return for a fresh load."

"What about the Triggs?" asked his wife.

"They must have gone to friends," he said.

"Shall I come and help you then?"

"No, there's a mess down there. Cows and sheep all over the place. Wait; I'll get the car. You can sit in the car."

Her eyes watched his all the time he was talking. He believed she understood. Otherwise she certainly would have insisted on helping him find the bread and groceries.

They made three journeys altogether, to and from the farm, before he was satisfied they had everything they needed. It was surprising, once he started thinking, how many things were necessary. Almost the most important of all was planking for the windows. He had to go around searching for timber. He wanted to renew the boards on all the windows at the cottage.

On the final journey he drove the car to the bus stop and got out and went to the telephone box.

He waited a few minutes, jangling the hook. No good, though. The line was dead. He climbed onto a bank and looked over the countryside, but there was no sign of life at all, nothing in the fields but the waiting, watching birds.

Some of them slept; he could see their beaks tucked into their feathers.

You'd think they'd be feeding, he said to himself, not just standing that way.

Then he remembered. They were gorged with food. They had eaten their fill during the night. That was why they did not move this morning.

He lifted his face to the sky. It was colorless, gray. The bare trees looked bent and blackened by the east wind.

The cold did not affect the living birds, waiting out there in the fields.

This is the time they ought to get them, Nat said to himself. They're a sitting target now. They must be doing this all over the country. Why don't our aircraft take off now and spray them with mustard gas? What are all our chaps doing? They must know; they must see for themselves.

He went back to the car and got into the driver's seat.

"Go quickly past that second gate," whispered his wife. "The postman's lying there. I don't want Jill to see."

It was a quarter to one by the time they reached the cottage. Only an hour to go.

"Better have dinner," said Nat. "Hot up something for yourself and the children, some of that soup. I've no time to eat now. I've got to unload all this stuff from the car."

He got everything inside the cottage. It could be sorted later. Give them all something to do during the long hours ahead.

First he must see to the windows and the door.

He went around the cottage methodically, testing every window and the door. He climbed onto the roof also, and fixed boards across every chimney except the kitchen's.

The cold was so intense he could hardly bear it, but the job had to be done. Now and again he looked up, searching the sky for aircraft. None came. As he worked, he cursed the inefficiency of the authorities.

He paused, his work on the bedroom chimney finished, and looked out to sea. Something was moving out there. Something gray and white among the breakers.

"Good old Navy," he said. "They never let us down. They're coming down channel; they're turning into the bay."

He waited, straining his eyes toward the sea. He was wrong, though. The Navy was not there. It was the gulls rising from the sea. And the massed flocks in the fields, with ruffled feathers, rose in formation from the ground and, wing to wing, soared upward to the sky.

The tide had turned again.

Nat climbed down the ladder and went inside the cottage. The family were at dinner. It was a little after two.

He bolted the door, put up the barricade, and lighted the lamp.

"It's nighttime," said young Johnny.

His wife had switched on the wireless once again. The crackling sound came, but nothing else.

"I've been all round the dial," she said, "foreign stations and all. I can't get anything but the crackling."

"Maybe they have the same trouble," he said. "Maybe it's the same right through Europe."

They ate in silence.

The tapping began at the windows, at the door, the rustling, the jostling, the pushing for position on the sills. The first thud of the suicide gulls upon the step.

When he had finished dinner, Nat planned, he would put the supplies away, stack them neatly, get everything shipshape. The boards were strong against the windows and across the chimneys. The cottage was filled with stores, with fuel, with all they needed for the next few days.

His wife could help him, and the children too. They'd tire themselves out between now and a quarter to nine, when the tide would ebb; then he'd tuck them down on their mattresses, see that they slept good and sound until three in the morning.

He had a new scheme for the windows, which was to fix barbed wire in front of the boards. He had brought a great roll of it from the farm. The nuisance was, he'd have to work at this in the dark, when the lull came between nine and three. Pity he had not thought of it before. Still, as long as the wife and kids slept—that was the main thing.

The smaller birds were at the windows now. He recognized the light tap-tapping of their beaks and the soft brush of their wings.

The hawks ignored the windows. They concentrated their attack upon the door.

Nat listened to the tearing sound of splintering wood, and wondered how many million years of memory were stored in those little brains, behind the stabbing beaks, the piercing eyes, now giving them this instinct to destroy mankind with all the deft precision of machines.

"I'll smoke that last cigarette," he said to his wife. "Stupid of me. It was the one thing I forgot to bring back from the farm."

He reached for it, switched on the crackling wireless.

He threw the empty packet onto the fire and watched it burn.

Man with a Problem

DONALD HONIG

With dull curiosity he watched the crowds gathering far below on the sidewalk. They had become a sea of bobbing upturned faces. It was rapidly increasing in size, swelling out into the street. The hurrying newcomers moved with insect-like briskness, drawn into the rest as if by magnetic tides. The traffic was beginning to back up with a cacophony of agitated horn sounds. It all looked very tiny and mysterious and incredible from twenty-six stories up. The sounds that reached him were faint, but the excitement in them unmistakable.

He was paying little heed to the startled, gasping faces that kept popping in and out of the window to gape or plead. First it had been a bellhop, staring with a disapproving look, crinkling his nose; then an elevator operator who in a hard gravelly voice had demanded to know what this was all about.

He looked at the elevator operator's face. "What do you think it is all about?" he asked calmly.

"You gonna jump?" the man asked, intrigued.

"Go away," the man on the ledge said irascibly and looked down at the streets. The traffic was still flowing quietly, undisturbed; he had not been noticed yet.

"You won't walk away from a jump like that," the elevator man growled as his head ducked in.

A moment later, the head of the assistant manager poked through the window, the curtains flying around his distinguished, clean-shaven, rather indignant face.

"I beg your pardon," the assistant manager said. The man waved him away.

"You're contemplating a very foolish thing," the assistant manager said, smug and comfortable in what he knew was unassailable logic.

The manager finally appeared, a fat red face that first looked down and then looked over at the man standing on the ledge, contemplating him for a moment.

"What are you doing out there?" the manager asked.

"I'm going to jump."

"Who are you? What's your name?"

"Carl Adams. And the reason why I'm doing this does not concern you."

"Think what you're doing, man," the manager said, his double chin trembling as he spoke, the strain of leaning forward out the window turning his face even redder.

"I've thought about it. Now go away and leave me alone."

The ledge was narrow, about eighteen inches in width. He stood between two windows, but there was no chance of reaching him from either of the windows. His back was against the wall, the bright sun falling full upon him. He had left his jacket inside.

His white shirt was open at the throat and he quite resembled a figure prepared for execution.

Successive heads kept poking through the window. They spoke quietly to him, addressing him as Mr. Adams. Some spoke to him condescendingly, as though they had already convinced themselves he was a paranoid. They identified themselves as a physician, various hotel officials, a clergyman.

"Why not come in and talk it over?" the clergyman asked gently.

"There's nothing left to say," Adams said.

"Do you want me to come out and guide you back through the window?"

"If you or anyone else steps out," Adams said tersely, "so help me I'll jump."

"Can't you tell us your problem?"

"No."

"How can we help you then?"

"You can't. Go away."

For a while no one came to the window. And then a policeman's head popped out, looking at him for a moment, rather cynically.

"Hey, fella," the policeman said.

Adams looked at him, studying his face. "What do you want?" he asked.

"They called me up from downstairs. Said there's a guy up here threatening to take a dive. You're not really going to jump, are you?"

"Yes."

"What do you want to do that for?"

"It's my nature to do spectacular things."

"Hey, you got a sense of humor," the policeman

said. He pushed his cap back on his head, sitting out on the window sill. "I like that. Want a cigarette?"

"No," Adams said.

The policeman shook a cigarette loose from his pack and lighted it. He inhaled deeply, expelling the smoke out into the sunshine where the wind snapped it up. "It's sure a pretty day, you know?'"

"A good day to die," Adams said, looking at him.

"You're pretty morbid, fella. You got a family?"

"No. Do you?"

"I've got a wife."

"Well, I have no one."

"That's too bad."

"Yes," Adams said. It wasn't so long ago that I did have a family, he thought. Only yesterday in fact. He had left the house in the morning to go to work and Karen had said good-by to him at the door (not kissed him, like she used to do; theirs was a kissless marriage now, but she was still his wife, he still loved only her, then and forever, would never give her the divorce, remained firm about that even though she said she would leave him eventually). And then he had come home at six o'clock and there was no wife any more, no love, nothing, only the empty bottle of sleeping pills and the note and the silent apartment . . . and Karen's body lying on the couch.

She had left the note on his pillow. It was written neatly, thoughtfully, explaining. Steve had told her he could not go away with her. Steve had deceived her. (It was that open, that blunt and brusque; she could mention Steve like that and he would know—

as he had known for months now. Once he had even
seen them together in a neighborhood cabaret.
There had been nothing surreptitious about it on her
part. She told him that their marriage was over,
spoke freely of Steve to him.)

He had gone out that night and walked the streets
until after midnight, come back to the house and
gone to sleep. He awoke that morning knowing im-
mediately that his mind had been made up, that he
was going to do this which he was now planning. He
walked to this part of town and checked into the
hotel, asking for a room near the top. He knew that
what would happen after that would happen nat-
urally, as a matter of course.

The streets were black with gaping, morbid,
curious people now. The police had forced the
throngs back, creating a great clearing directly
below, should he decide to jump. He could see the
firemen standing with their canvas life-net that
looked like a round black pancake, a red circle painted
in the center, but he knew that that could do nothing
for a body hurtling twenty-six floors. There was no
way his would-be rescuers could get at him. The
fire ladders did not reach that high. A cornice pro-
truding directly above him from the roof precluded
any rescue attempts from that quarter.

"This is useless, senseless," a man was saying to
him, his head leaning out of the window.

"You might think so," Adam said.

"Look, I'm a doctor," the man said earnestly. "I
can help you."

"In which ward?"

"No wards, Mr. Adams. I promise you."

"It's too late now."

"If you jump then it will be too late. Now there's still time."

"You'd better go and attend to somebody who needs you, doctor. I don't need you."

The doctor disappeared. Adams stared critically down at the crowds. Already he had the strange, singular feeling of apartness, the nearness of death having established the gulf between him and other men. He was different now, apart and alone. All those people down there waiting, waiting. They'll see something all right, he thought. And those men in the room, he could hear them jabbering, plotting, scheming, figuring ways of seducing his mind, probably making frantic phone calls to experts on the subject of suicide.

He looked around, a face was out the window, staring at him. It was the clergyman again, a round, concerned, sincere face.

"Is there anything we can do for you?" the clergyman asked.

"No," he said.

"Do you want to come in now?"

"You're wasting your time, father."

"I'm not wasting my time."

"Yes, you are. I'm not coming in."

"Do you want us to leave you alone to think?"

"Do as you please."

The clergyman's head disappeared. He was alone again. He watched the crowds, a soft amusement in his eyes now. The height did not bother him any longer, as it had when he had first stepped out onto the ledge. He felt close to the buildings that soared around him.

He wondered what intricate methods of rescue they were planning. Ropes, ladders, nets, dangling chairs. They would have to be very careful, he knew, because they were never quite certain what his state of mind was.

The policeman reappeared. Adams knew he would. He had been more responsive to him than any of the others and so the policeman would try again.

"You know, Adams," the officer said, sitting out on the window sill again, casually, "in a way you're doing me a favor."

"How's that?"

"Well, normally I'd be down there directing traffic. But because of you I'm up here taking it easy."

"Is that so?"

"That's so."

"You might just as well be up here. That traffic isn't moving anyway."

The policeman laughed. "That's right," he said. "Those people down there," he said with a gesture, "are expecting you to jump. They're looking forward to it."

Adams looked at him. "Looking forward to it?"

"Sure. They've made up their minds that you're going to jump and they want to see it. You going to disappoint them?"

Adams looked down, his eyes sweeping over the blocks and blocks of clustered people.

"You can't hear them up here," the policeman said, "but they're yelling for you to jump."

"Are they?"

"Uh-huh. They feel you owe them that for making them stand around here all afternoon."

"They're like a pack of hungry wolves," Adams said.

"That's right. Why give up your life just so they can have a thrill?" The policeman watched Adams' face, thought he detected a flicker of uncertainty. "Come on in," he said in a low, cajoling voice. "The hell with all those people."

"Maybe you're right," Adams said.

"Sure."

Adams wavered, his back coming away from the wall for a moment, then he fell back, covering his eyes for a second.

"What's the matter?" the policeman asked.

"I guess I'm a bit dizzy. Maybe you'd better give me a hand."

The policeman looked across the street, there were news photographers on the roof there, their cameras poised. It would make quite a picture for the morning papers.

"All right," the policeman said. "Hold on."

The crowd sent up a roar of thrill and terror when they saw the policeman climb out of the window and stand on the ledge, a few feet from the immobile man in the white shirt. They watched him edge along, carefully extending his hand.

Adams reached his hand toward the policeman's.

"I knew you would come up eventually," Adams said. "That's why I chose this place."

"What?" the policeman said, trying to maintain his balance on the narrow ledge.

"My name isn't Adams, Steve. Karen was my wife. Do you know that last night she . . ."

The terror spread over the policeman's face as he tried to draw back, but his hand was locked in the other's, and then there was a sudden lunge and sickening thrust and twist and as he began to topple softly out into space, toward the rising roar from the crowd, the last conscious thing he felt was the firm, hard hand gripping his like a vise.

They Bite

ANTHONY BOUCHER

There was no path, only the almost vertical ascent. Crumbled rock for a few yards, with the roots of sage finding their scanty life in the dry soil. Then jagged outcroppings of crude crags, sometimes with accidental footholds, sometimes with overhanging and untrustworthy branches of greasewood, sometimes with no aid to climbing but the leverage of your muscles and the ingenuity of your balance.

The sage was as drably green as the rock was drably brown. The only color was the occasional rosy spikes of a barrel cactus.

Hugh Tallant swung himself up on to the last pinnacle. It had a deliberate, shaped look about it— a petrified fortress of Lilliputians, a Gibraltar of pygmies. Tallant perched on its battlements and unslung his fieldglasses.

The desert valley spread below him. The tiny cluster of buildings that was Oasis, the exiguous cluster of palms that gave name to the town and shelter to his own tent and to the shack he was building, the dead-ended highway leading straightforwardly to nothing, the oiled roads diagraming the vacant blocks of an optimistic subdivision.

Tallant saw none of these. His glasses were fixed

beyond the oasis and the town of Oasis on the dry lake. The gliders were clear and vivid to him, and the uniformed men busy with them were as sharply and minutely visible as a nest of ants under glass. The training school was more than usually active. One glider in particular, strange to Tallant, seemed the focus of attention. Men would come and examine it and glance back at the older models in comparison.

Only the corner of Tallant's left eye was not preoccupied with the new glider. In that corner something moved, something little and thin and brown as the earth. Too large for a rabbit, much too small for a man. It darted across that corner of vision, and Tallant found gliders oddly hard to concentrate on.

He set down the bifocals and deliberately looked about him. His pinnacle surveyed the narrow, flat area of the crest. Nothing stirred. Nothing stood out against the sage and rock but one barrel of rosy spikes. He took up the glasses again and resumed his observations. When he was done, he methodically entered the results in the little black notebook.

His hand was still white. The desert is cold and often sunless in winter. But it was a firm hand, and as well trained as his eyes, fully capable of recording faithfully the designs and dimensions which they had registered so accurately.

Once his hand slipped, and he had to erase and redraw, leaving a smudge that displeased him. The lean, brown thing had slipped across the edge of his vision again. Going toward the east edge, he would swear, where that set of rocks jutted like the spines on the back of a stegosaur.

Only when his notes were completed did he yield

to curiosity, and even then with cynical self-reproach. He was physically tired, for him an unusual state, from this daily climbing and from clearing the ground for his shack-to-be. The eye muscles play odd nervous tricks. There could be nothing behind the stegosaur's armor.

There was nothing. Nothing alive and moving. Only the torn and half-plucked carcass of a bird, which looked as though it had been gnawed by some small animal.

It was halfway down the hill—hill in Western terminology, though anywhere east of the Rockies it would have been considered a sizable mountain—that Tallant again had a glimpse of a moving figure.

But this was no trick of a nervous eye. It was not little nor thin nor brown. It was tall and broad and wore a loud red-and-black lumberjacket. It bellowed "Tallant!" in a cheerful and lusty voice.

Tallant drew near the man and said, "Hello." He paused and added, "Your advantage, I think."

The man grinned broadly. "Don't know me? Well, I daresay ten years is a long time, and the California desert ain't exactly the Chinese rice fields. How's stuff? Still loaded down with Secrets for Sale?"

Tallant tried desperately not to react to that shot, but he stiffened a little. "Sorry. The prospector getup had me fooled. Good to see you again, Morgan."

The man's eyes had narrowed. "Just having my little joke." He smiled. "Of course you wouldn't have no serious reason for mountain-climbing around a glider school, now would you? And you'd kind of need fieldglasses to keep an eye on the pretty birdies."

"I'm out here for my health." Tallant's voice sounded unnatural even to himself.

"Sure, sure. You were always in it for your health. And come to think of it, my own health ain't been none too good lately. I've got me a little cabin way to hell-and-gone around here, and I do me a little prospecting now and then. And somehow it just strikes me, Tallant, like maybe I hit a pretty good lode today."

"Nonsense, old man. You can see—"

"I'd sure hate to tell any of them army men out at the field some of the stories I know about China and the kind of men I used to know out there. Wouldn't cotton to them stories a bit, the army wouldn't. But if I was to have a drink too many and get talkative-like—"

"Tell you what," Tallant suggested brusquely. "It's getting near sunset now, and my tent's chilly for evening visits. But drop around in the morning and we'll talk over old times. Is rum still your tipple?"

"Sure is. Kind of expensive now, you understand—"

"I'll lay some in. You can find the place easily—over by the oasis. And we . . . we might be able to talk about your prospecting, too."

Tallant's thin lips were set firm as he walked away.

The bartender opened a bottle of beer and plunked it on the damp-circled counter. "That'll be twenty cents," he said, then added as an afterthought, "Want a glass? Sometimes tourists do."

Tallant looked at the others sitting at the counter—

the red-eyed and unshaven old man, the flight sergeant unhappily drinking a Coke—it was after army hours for beer—the young man with the long, dirty trench coat and the pipe and the new-looking brown beard—and saw no glasses. "I guess I won't be a tourist," he decided.

This was the first time Tallant had had a chance to visit the Desert Sport Spot. It was as well to be seen around in a community. Otherwise people begin to wonder and say, "Who is that man out by the oasis? Why don't you ever see him any place?"

The Sport Spot was quiet that night. The four of them at the counter, two army boys shooting pool, and a half-dozen of the local men gathered about a round poker table, soberly and wordlessly cleaning a construction worker whose mind seemed more on his beer than on his cards.

"You just passing through?" the bartender asked sociably.

Tallant shook his head. "I'm moving in. When the army turned me down for my lungs I decided I better do something about it. Heard so much about your climate here I thought I might as well try it."

"Sure thing," the bartender nodded. "You take up until they started this glider school, just about every other guy you meet in the desert is here for his health. Me, I had sinus, and look at me now. It's the air."

Tallant breathed the atmosphere of smoke and beer suds, but did not smile. "I'm looking forward to miracles."

"You'll get 'em. Whereabouts you staying?"

"Over that way a bit. The agent called it 'the old Carker place.'"

Tallant felt the curious listening silence and frowned. The bartender had started to speak and then thought better of it. The young man with the beard looked at him oddly. The old man fixed him with red and watery eyes that had a faded glint of pity in them. For a moment Tallant felt a chill that had nothing to do with the night air of the desert.

The old man drank his beer in quick gulps, and frowned as though trying to formulate a sentence. At last he wiped beer from his bristly lips and said, "You wasn't aiming to stay in the adobe, was you?"

"No. It's pretty much gone to pieces. Easier to rig me up a little shack than try to make the adobe livable. Meanwhile, I've got a tent."

"That's all right, then, mebbe. But mind you don't go poking around that there adobe."

"I don't think I'm apt to. But why not? Want another beer?"

The old man shook his head reluctantly and slid from his stool to the ground. "No thanks. I don't rightly know as I—"

"Yes?"

"Nothing. Thanks all the same." He turned and shuffled to the door.

Tallant smiled. "But why should I stay clear of the adobe?" he called after him.

The old man mumbled.

"What?"

"They bite," said the old man, and went out shivering into the night.

The bartender was back at his post. "I'm glad he didn't take that beer you offered him," he said.

"Along about this time in the evening I have to stop serving him. For once he had the sense to quit."

Tallant pushed his own empty bottle forward. "I hope I didn't frighten him away?"

"Frighten? Well, mister, I think maybe that's just what you did do. He didn't want beer that sort of came, like you might say, from the old Carker place. Some of the old-timers here, they're funny that way."

Tallant grinned. "Is it haunted?"

"Not what you'd call haunted, no. No ghosts there that I ever heard of." He wiped the counter with a a cloth, and seemed to wipe the subject away with it.

The flight sergeant pushed his Coke bottle away, hunted in his pocket for nickels, and went over to the pinball machine. The young man with the beard slid onto his vacant stool. "Hope old Jake didn't worry you," he said.

Tallant laughed. "I suppose every town has its deserted homestead with a grisly tradition. But this sounds a little different. No ghosts, and they bite. Do you know anything about it?"

"A little," the young man said seriously. "A little. Just enough to—"

Tallant was curious. "Have one on me and tell me about it."

The flight sergeant swore bitterly at the machine.

Beer gurgled through the beard. "You see," the young man began, "the desert's so big you can't be alone in it. Ever notice that? It's all empty and there's nothing in sight, but there's always something moving over there where you can't quite see it. It's something very dry and thin and brown, only when you look around it isn't there. Ever see it?"

"Optical fatigue—" Tallant began.

"Sure. I know. Every man to his own legend. There isn't a tribe of Indians hasn't got some way of accounting for it. You've heard of the Watchers? And the twentieth-century white man comes along, and it's optical fatigue. Only in the nineteenth century things weren't quite the same, and there were the Carkers."

"You've got a special localized legend?"

"Call it that. You glimpse things out of the corner of your mind, same like you glimpse lean, dry things out of the corner of your eye. You encase 'em in solid circumstance and they're not so bad. That is known as the Growth of Legend. The Folk Mind in Action. You take the Carkers and the things you don't quite see and you put 'em together. And they bite."

Tallant wondered how long that beard had been absorbing beer. "And what were the Carkers?" he prompted politely.

"Ever hear of Sawney Bean? Scotland—reign of James First or maybe the Sixth, though I think Roughead's wrong on that for once. Or let's be more modern—ever hear of the Benders? Kansas in the 1870's? No? Ever hear of Procrustes? Or Polyphemus? Or Fee-fi-fo-fum?

"There are ogres, you know. They're no legend. They're fact, they are. The inn where nine guests left for every ten that arrived, the mountain cabin that sheltered travelers from the snow, sheltered them all winter till the melting spring uncovered their bones, the lonely stretches of road that so many passengers traveled halfway—you'll find 'em everywhere. All over Europe and pretty much in this country too before communications became what they are. Profitable business. And it wasn't just the profit. The Benders made money, sure; but that wasn't why they killed all their victims as carefully as a kosher butcher. Sawney Bean got so he didn't give a damn about the profit; he just needed to lay in more meat for the winter.

"And think of the chances you'd have at an oasis."

"So these Carkers of yours were, as you call them, ogres?"

"Carkers, ogres—maybe they were Benders. The Benders were never seen alive, you know, after the townspeople found those curiously butchered bodies. There's a rumor they got this far West. And the time checks pretty well. There wasn't any town here in the eighties. Just a couple of Indian families, last of a dying tribe living on at the oasis. They vanished after the Carkers moved in. That's not so surprising. The white race is a sort of super-ogre, anyway. Nobody worried about them. But they used to worry about why so many travelers never got across this stretch of desert. The travelers used to stop over at the Carkers, you see, and somehow they often never got any farther. Their wagons'd be found maybe fifteen miles beyond in the desert. Sometimes they found the bones, too, parched and white. Gnawed-looking, they said sometimes."

"And nobody ever did anything about these Carkers?"

"Oh, sure. We didn't have King James Sixth—only I still think it was First—to ride up on a great white horse for a gesture, but twice army detachments came here and wiped them all out."

"Twice? One wiping-out would do for most families." Tallant smiled.

"Uh-huh. That was no slip. They wiped out the Carkers twice because you see once didn't do any good. They wiped 'em out and still travelers vanished and still there were gnawed bones. So they wiped 'em out again. After that they gave up, and people detoured the oasis. It made a longer, harder trip, but after all—"

Tallant laughed. "You mean these Carkers were immortal?"

"I don't know about immortal. They somehow just didn't die very easy. Maybe, if they were the Benders —and I sort of like to think they were—they learned a little more about what they were doing out here on the desert. Maybe they put together what the Indians knew and what they knew, and it worked. Maybe Whatever they made their sacrifices to, understood them better out here than in Kansas."

"And what's become of them—aside from seeing them out of the corner of the eye?"

"There's forty years between the last of the Carker history and this new settlement at the oasis. And people won't talk much about what they learned here in the first year or so. Only that they stay away from that old Carker adobe. They tell some stories— The priest says he was sitting in the confessional one hot Saturday afternoon and thought he heard a penitent come in. He waited a long time and finally lifted the gauze to see was anybody there. Something was there, and it bit. He's got three fingers on his right hand now, which looks funny as hell when he gives a benediction."

Tallant pushed their two bottles toward the bartender. "That yarn, my young friend, has earned another beer. How about it, bartender? Is he always cheerful like this, or is this just something he's improvised for my benefit?"

The bartender set out the fresh bottles with great solemnity. "Me, I wouldn't've told you all that myself, but then he's a stranger, too, and maybe don't feel the same way we do here. For him it's just a story."

"It's more comfortable that way," said the young man with the beard, and took a firm hold on his beer bottle.

"But as long as you've heard that much," said the bartender, "you might as well— It was last winter, when we had that cold spell. You heard funny stories that winter. Wolves coming into prospectors' cabins just to warm up. Well, business wasn't so good. We don't have a license for hard liquor and the boys don't drink much beer when it's that cold. But they used to come in anyway because we've got that big oil burner.

"So one night there's a bunch of 'em in here—old Jake was here, that you was talking to, and his dog Jigger—and I think I hear somebody else come in. The door creaks a little. But I don't see nobody and the poker game's going and we're talking just like we're talking now, and all of a sudden I hear a kind of a noise like *crack!* over there in that corner behind the jukebox near the burner.

"I go over to see what goes and it gets away before I can see it very good. But it was little and thin and it didn't have no clothes on. It must've been damned cold that winter."

"And what was the cracking noise?" Tallant asked dutifully.

"That? That was a bone. It must've strangled Jigger without any noise. He was a little dog. It ate most of the flesh, and if it hadn't cracked the bone for the marrow it could've finished. You can still see the spots over there. The blood never did come out."

There had been silence all through the story. Now suddenly all hell broke loose. The flight sergeant let out a splendid yell and began pointing excitedly at the pinball machine and yelling for his pay-off. The construction worker dramatically deserted the poker game, knocking his chair over in the process, and announced lugubriously that these guys here had their own rules, see?

Any atmosphere of Carker-inspired horror was dissipated. Tallant whistled as he walked over to put a nickel in the jukebox. He glanced casually at the floor. Yes, there was a stain, for what that was worth.

He smiled cheerfully and felt rather grateful to the Carkers. They were going to solve his blackmail problem very neatly.

Tallant dreamed of power that night. It was a common dream with him. He was a ruler of the new American Corporate State that should follow the war; and he said to this man "Come!" and he came, and to that man "Go!" and he went, and to his servants "Do this!" and they did it.

Then the young man with the beard was standing

before him, and the dirty trench coat was like the robes of an ancient prophet. And the young man said, "You see yourself riding high, don't you? Riding the crest of the wave—the Wave of the Future, you call it. But there's a deep, dark undertow that you don't see, and that's a part of the Past. And the Present and even the Future. There is evil in mankind that is blacker even than your evil, and infinitely more ancient."

And there was something in the shadows behind the young man, something little and lean and brown.

Tallant's dream did not disturb him the following morning. Nor did the thought of the approaching interview with Morgan. He fried his bacon and eggs and devoured them cheerfully. The wind had died down for a change, and the sun was warm enough so that he could strip to the waist while he cleared land for his shack. His machete glinted brilliantly as it swung through the air and struck at the roots of the brush.

Morgan's full face was red and sweating when he arrived.

"It's cool over there in the shade of the adobe," Tallant suggested. "We'll be more comfortable." And in the comfortable shade of the adobe he swung the machete once and clove Morgan's full red sweating face in two.

It was so simple. It took less effort than uprooting a clump of sage. And it was so safe. Morgan lived in a cabin way to hell-and-gone and was often away on prospecting trips. No one would notice his absence for months, if then. No one had any reason to connect him with Tallant. And no one in Oasis would hunt for him in the Carker-haunted adobe.

The body was heavy, and the blood dripped warm on Tallant's bare skin. With relief he dumped what had been Morgan on the floor of the adobe. There were no boards, no flooring. Just the earth. Hard, but not too hard to dig a grave in. And no one was likely to come poking around in this taboo territory to notice the grave. Let a year or so go by, and the grave and the bones it contained would be attributed to the Carkers.

The corner of Tallant's eye bothered him again. Deliberately he looked about the interior of the adobe.

The little furniture was crude and heavy, with no attempt to smooth down the strokes of the ax. It was held together with wooden pegs or half-rotted thongs. There were age-old cinders in the fireplace, and the dusty shards of a cooking jar among them.

And there was a deeply hollowed stone, covered with stains that might have been rust, if stone rusted. Behind it was a tiny figure, clumsily fashioned of clay and sticks. It was something like a man and something like a lizard, and something like the things that flit across the corner of the eye.

Curious now, Tallant peered about further. He penetrated to the corner that the one unglassed window lighted but dimly. And there he let out a little choking gasp. For a moment he was rigid with horror. Then he smiled and all but laughed aloud.

This explained everything. Some curious individual had seen this, and from his account burgeoned the whole legend. The Carkers had indeed learned something from the Indians, but that secret was the art of embalming.

It was a perfect mummy. Either the Indian art had shrunk bodies, or this was that of a ten-year-old boy. There was no flesh. Only skin and bone and taut dry stretches of tendon between. The eyelids were closed; the sockets looked hollow under them. The nose was sunken and almost lost. The scant lips were tightly curled back from the long and very white teeth, which stood forth all the more brilliantly against the deep-brown skin.

It was a curious little trove, this mummy. Tallant was already calculating the chances for raising a decent sum of money from an interested anthropologist—murder can produce such delightfully profitable chance by-products—when he noticed the infinitesimal rise and fall of the chest.

The Carker was not dead. It was sleeping.

Tallant did not dare stop to think beyond the instant. This was no time to pause to consider if such things were possible in a well-ordered world. It was no time to reflect on the disposal of the body of Morgan. It was a time to snatch up your machete and get out of there.

But in the doorway he halted. There coming across the desert, heading for the adobe, clearly seen this time, was another—a female.

He made an involuntary gesture of indecision. The blade of the machete clanged ringingly against the adobe wall. He heard the dry shuffling of a roused sleeper behind him.

He turned fully now, the machete raised. Dispose of this nearer one first, then face the female. There was no room even for terror in his thoughts, only for action.

The lean brown shape darted at him avidly. He moved lightly away and stood poised for its second charge. It shot forward again. He took one step back, machete-arm raised, and fell headlong over the corpse of Morgan. Before he could rise the thin thing was upon him. Its sharp teeth had met through the palm of his left hand.

The machete moved swiftly. The thin dry body fell headless to the floor. There was no blood.

The grip of the teeth did not relax. Pain coursed up Tallant's left arm—a sharper, more bitter pain than you would expect from the bite. Almost as though venom—

He dropped the machete, and his strong white hand plucked and twisted at the dry brown lips. The teeth stayed clenched, unrelaxing. He sat bracing his back against the wall and gripped the head between his knees. He pulled. His flesh ripped, and blood formed dusty clots on the dirt floor. But the bite was firm.

His world had become reduced now to that hand and that head. Nothing outside mattered. He must free himself. He raised his aching arm to his face, and with his own teeth he tore at that unrelenting grip. The dry flesh crumbled away in desert dust, but the teeth were locked fast. He tore his lip against their white keenness, and tasted in his mouth the sweetness of blood and something else.

He staggered to his feet again. He knew what he must do. Later he could use cautery, a tourniquet, see a doctor with a story about a Gila monster—their heads grip, too, don't they?—but he knew what he must do now.

He raised the machete and struck again.

His white hand lay on the brown floor, gripped by the white teeth in the brown face. He propped himself against the adobe wall, momentarily unable to move. His open wrist hung over the deeply hollowed stone. His blood and his strength and his life poured out before the little figure of sticks and clay.

The female stood in the doorway now, the sun bright on her thin brownness. She did not move. He knew that she was waiting for the hollow stone to fill.

The Enemy

CHARLOTTE ARMSTRONG

They sat late at the lunch table and afterwards moved through the dim, cool, high-ceilinged rooms to the judge's library where, in their quiet talk, the old man's past and the young man's future seemed to telescope and touch. But at twenty minutes after three, on that hot, bright, June Saturday afternoon, the present tense erupted. Out in the quiet street arose the sound of trouble.

Judge Kittinger adjusted his pince-nez, rose, and led the way to his old-fashioned veranda from which they could overlook the tree-roofed intersection of Greenwood Lane and Hannibal Street. Near the steps to the corner house, opposite, there was a surging knot of children and one man. Now, from the house on the judge's left, a woman in a blue house dress ran diagonally toward the excitement. And a police car slipped up Hannibal Street, gliding to the curb. One tall officer plunged into the group and threw restraining arms around a screaming boy.

Mike Russell, saying to his host, "Excuse me, sir," went rapidly across the street. Trouble's center was the boy, ten or eleven years old, a tow-headed boy with tawny-lashed blue eyes, a straight nose, a fine brow. He was beside himself, writhing in the policeman's grasp. The woman in the blue dress was yammering at him. "Freddy! Freddy! Freddy!" Her voice simply did not reach his ears.

"You ole stinker! You rotten ole stinker! You ole nut!" All the boy's heart was in the epithets.

"Now, listen . . ." The cop shook the boy who, helpless in those powerful hands, yet blazed. His fury had stung to crimson the face of the grown man at whom it was directed.

This man, who stood with his back to the house as one besieged, was plump, half-bald, with eyes much magnified by glasses. "Attacked me!" he cried in a high whine. "Rang my bell and absolutely leaped on me!"

Out of the seven or eight small boys clustered around them came overlapping fragments of shrill sentences. It was clear only that they opposed the man. A small woman in a print dress, a man in shorts, whose bare chest was winter-white, stood a little apart, hesitant and distressed. Up on the veranda of the house the screen door was half open, and a woman seated in a wheel chair peered forth anxiously.

On the green grass, in the shade perhaps thirty feet away, there lay in death a small brown-and-white dog.

The judge's luncheon guest observed all this. When the judge drew near, there was a lessening of the noise. Judge Kittinger said, "This is Freddy Titus, isn't it? Mr. Matlin? What's happened?"

The man's head jerked. "I," he said, "did nothing to the dog. Why would I trouble to hurt the boy's dog? I try—you know this, Judge—I try to live in peace here. But these kids are terrors! They've made

this block a perfect hell for me and my family." The
man's voice shook. "My wife, who is not strong . . .
My step-daughter, who is a cripple . . . These kids are
no better than a slum gang. They are vicious! That
boy rang my bell and *attacked* . . . ! I'll have him up
for assault! I . . ."

The judge's face was old ivory and he was aloof
behind it.

On the porch a girl pushed past the woman in the
chair, a girl who walked with a lurching gait.

Mike Russell asked quietly, "Why do the boys
say it was you, Mr. Matlin, who hurt the dog?"

The kids chorused. "He's an ole mean . . ." "He's a
nut . . ." "Just because . . ." ". . . took Clive's hat
and . . ." ". . . chases us . . ." ". . . tries to put every-
thing on us." ". . . told my mother lies . . ." ". . . just
because . . ."

He is our enemy, they were saying; *he is our
enemy.*

"They . . ." began Matlin, his throat thick with
anger.

"Hold it a minute." The second cop, the thin one,
walked toward where the dog was lying.

"Somebody," said Mike Russell in a low voice,
"must do something for the boy."

The judge looked down at the frantic child. He
said, gently, "I am as sorry as I can be, Freddy." But
in his old heart there was too much known, and too
many little dogs he remembered that had already
died, and even if he were as sorry as he could be, he
couldn't be sorry enough. The boy's eyes turned,
rejected, returned. To the enemy.

Russell moved near the woman in blue, who pertained to this boy somehow. "His mother?"

"His folks are away. I'm there to take care of him,"
she snapped, as if she felt herself put upon by a crisis
she had not contracted to face.

"Can they be reached?"

"No," she said decisively.

The young man put his stranger's hand on the
boy's rigid little shoulder. But he too was rejected.
Freddy's eyes, brilliant with hatred, clung to the
enemy. Hatred doesn't cry.

"Listen," said the tall cop, "if you could hang onto
him for a minute—"

"Not I," said Russell.

The thin cop came back. "Looks like the dog got
poison. When was he found?"

"Just now," the kids said.

"Where? There?"

"Up Hannibal Street. Right on the edge of ole
Matlin's back lot."

"Edge of *my* lot!" Matlin's color freshened again.
"On the sidewalk, why don't you say? Why don't
you tell the truth?"

"We are! *We* don't tell lies!"

"Quiet, you guys," the cop said. "Pipe down,
now."

"Heaven's my witness, I wasn't even here!" cried
Matlin. "I played nine holes of golf today. I didn't
get home until . . . May?" he called over his shoulder.
"What time did I come in?"

The girl on the porch came slowly down, moving
awkwardly on her uneven legs. She was in her
twenties, no child. Nor was she a woman. She said in

a blurting manner, "About three o'clock, Daddy Earl. But the dog was dead."

"What's that, miss?"

"This is my step-daughter."

"The dog was dead," the girl said, "before he came home. I saw it from upstairs, before three o'clock. Lying by the sidewalk."

"You drove in from Hannibal Street, Mr. Matlin? Looks like you'd have seen the dog."

Matlin said with nervous thoughtfulness, "I don't know. My mind . . . Yes, I . . ."

"He's telling a lie!"

"Freddy!"

"Listen to that," said May Matlin, "will you?"

"She's a liar, too!"

The cop shook Freddy. Mr. Matlin made a sound of helpless exasperation. He said to the girl, "Go keep your mother inside, May." He raised his arm as if to wave. "It's all right, honey," he called to the woman in the chair, with a false cheeriness that grated on the ear. "There's nothing to worry about now."

Freddy's jaw shifted and young Russell's watching eyes winced. The girl began to lurch back to the house.

"It was my wife who put in the call," Matlin said. "After all, they were on me like a pack of wolves. Now, I—I *understand* that the boy's upset. But all the same, he cannot . . . He must learn . . . I will not have . . . I have enough to contend with, without this malice, this unwarranted antagonism, this persecution."

Freddy's eyes were unwinking.

"It has got to stop!" said Matlin almost hysterically.

"Yes," murmured Mike Russell, "I should think so." Judge Kittinger's white head, nodding, agreed.

"We've heard about quite a few dog-poisoning cases over the line in Redfern," said the thin cop with professional calm. "None here."

The man in the shorts hitched them up, looking shocked. "Who'd do a thing like that?"

A boy said boldly, "Ole Matlin would." He had an underslung jaw and wore spectacles on his snug nose. "I'm Phil Bourchard," he said to the cop. He had courage.

"We jist know," said another. "I'm Ernie Allen." Partisanship radiated from his whole thin body. "Ole Matlin doesn't want anybody on his ole property."

"Sure." "He doesn't want anybody on his ole property." "It was ole Matlin."

"It was. It was," said Freddy Titus.

"Freddy," said the housekeeper in blue, "now, you better be still. I'll tell your dad." It was a meaningless fumble for control. The boy didn't even hear it.

Judge Kittinger tried patiently. "You can't accuse without cause, Freddy."

"Bones didn't hurt his ole property. Bones wouldn't hurt anything. Ole Matlin did it."

"You lying little devil!"

"He's a liar!"

The cop gave Freddy another shake. "You kids found him, eh?"

"We were up at Bourchard's and were going down to the Titus house."

"And he was dead," said Freddy.

"*I* know nothing about it," said Matlin icily. "Nothing at all."

The cop, standing between, said wearily, "Any of you people see what coulda happened?"

"I was sitting in my backyard," said the man in shorts. "I'm Daugherty, next door, up Hannibal Street. Didn't see a thing."

The small woman in a print dress spoke up. "I am Mrs. Page. I live across on the corner, Officer. I believe I did see a strange man go into Mr. Matlin's driveway this morning."

"When was this, ma'am?"

"About eleven o'clock. He was poorly dressed. He walked up the drive and around the garage."

"Didn't go to the house?"

"No. He was only there a minute. I believe he was carrying something. He was rather furtive. And very poorly dressed, almost like a tramp."

There was a certain relaxing among the elders. "Ah, the tramp," said Mike Russell. "The good old reliable tramp. Are you sure, Mrs. Page? It's very unlikely."

But she bristled. "Do you think I am lying?"

Russell's lips parted, but he felt the judge's hand on his arm. "This is my guest, Mr. Russell . . . Freddy." The judge's voice was gentle. "Let him go, Officer. I'm sure he understands, now. Mr. Matlin was not even at home, Freddy. It's possible that this— er—stranger . . . Or it may have been an accident."

"Wasn't a tramp. Wasn't an accident."

"You can't know that, boy," said the judge, somewhat sharply. Freddy said nothing. As the officer slowly released his grasp, the boy took a free step backwards, and the other boys surged to surround him. There stood the enemy, the monster who killed and lied, and the grownups with their reasonable doubts were on the monster's side. But the boys knew what Freddy knew. They stood together.

"Somebody," murmured the judge's guest, "somebody's got to help the boy." And the judge sighed.

The cops went up Hannibal Street toward Matlin's back lot, with Mr. Daugherty. Matlin lingered at the corner talking to Mrs. Page. In the front window of Matlin's house the curtain fell across the glass.

Mike Russell sidled up to the housekeeper. "Any uncles or aunts here in town? A grandmother?"

"No," she said shortly.

"Brothers or sisters, Mrs. . . . ?"

"Miz Somers. No, he's the only one. Only reason they didn't take him along was it's the last week of school and he didn't want to miss."

Mike Russell's brown eyes suggested the soft texture of velvet, and they were deeply distressed. She slid away from their appeal. "He'll just have to take it, I guess, like everybody else," Mrs. Somers said. "These things happen."

He was listening intently. "Don't you care for dogs?"

"I don't mind a dog," she said. She arched her neck. She was going to call to the boy.

"Wait. Tell me, does the family go to church? Is there a pastor or a priest who knows the boy?"

"They don't go, far as I ever saw." She looked at him as if he were an eccentric.

"Then school. He has a teacher. What grade?"

"Sixth grade," she said. "Miss Dana. Oh, he'll be

okay." Her voice grew loud, to reach the boy and hint to him. "He's a big boy."

Russell said desperately, "Is there no way to telephone his parents?"

"They're on the road. They'll be in some time tomorrow. That's all I know." She was annoyed. "I'll take care of him. That's why I'm here." She raised her voice and this time it was arch and seductive. "Freddy, better come wash your face. I know where there's some chocolate cookies."

The velvet left the young man's eyes. Hard as buttons, they gazed for a moment at the woman. Then he whipped around and left her. He walked over to where the kids had drifted, near the little dead creature on the grass. He said softly, "Bones had his own doctor, Freddy? Tell me his name?" The boy's eyes flickered. "We must know what it was that he took. A doctor can tell. I think his own doctor would be best, don't you?"

The boy nodded, mumbled a name, an address. That Russell mastered the name and the numbers, asking for no repetition, was a sign of his concern. Besides, it was this young man's quality—that he listened. "May I take him, Freddy? I have a car. We ought to have a blanket," he added softly, "a soft, clean blanket."

"I got one, Freddy. . . ." "My mother'd let me . . ."

"I can get one," Freddy said brusquely. They wheeled, almost in formation.

Mrs. Somers frowned. "You must let them take a blanket," Russell warned her, and his eyes were cold.

"I will explain to Mrs. Titus," said the judge quickly.

"Quite a fuss," she said, and tossed her head and crossed the road.

Russell gave the judge a quick, nervous grin. He walked to the returning cops. "You'll want to run tests, I suppose? Can the dog's own vet do it?"

"Certainly. Humane officer will have to be in charge. But that's what the vet'll want."

"I'll take the dog, then. Any traces up there?"

"Not a thing."

"Will you explain to the boy that you are investigating?"

"Well, you know how these things go." The cop's feet shuffled. "Humane officer does what he can. Probably Monday, after we identify the poison, he'll check the drug stores. Usually, if it *is* a cranky neighbor, he has already put in a complaint about the dog. This Matlin says he never did. The humane officer will get on it Monday. He's out of town today. The devil of these cases, we can't prove a thing, usually. You get an idea who it was, maybe you can scare him. It's a misdemeanor all right. Never heard of a conviction myself."

"But will you explain to the boy . . . ?" Russell stopped, chewed his lip, and the judge sighed.

"Yeah, it's tough on a kid," the cop said.

When the judge's guest came back it was nearly five o'clock. He said, "I came to say goodbye, sir, and to thank you for the . . ." But his mind wasn't on the sentence and he lost it and looked up.

The judge's eyes were affectionate. "Worried?"

"Judge, sir," the young man said, *"must* they feed him? Where, sir, in this classy neighborhood is there an understanding woman's heart? I herded them to that Mrs. Allen. But she winced, sir, and she diverted them. She didn't want to deal with tragedy, didn't want to think about it. She offered cakes and Cokes and games."

"But my dear boy . . ."

"What do they teach the kids these days, judge? To turn away? Put something in your stomach. Take a drink. Play a game. Don't weep for your dead. Just skip it, think about something else."

"I'm afraid the boy's alone," the judge said gently, "but it's only for the night." His voice was melodious. "Can't be sheltered from grief when it comes. None of us can."

"Excuse me, sir, but I wish he *would* grieve. I wish he would bawl his heart out. Wash out that black hate. I ought to go home. None of my concern. It's a woman's job." He moved and his hand went toward the phone. "He has a teacher. I can't help feeling concerned, sir. May I try?"

The judge said, "Of course, Mike," and he put his brittle old bones into a chair.

Mike Russell pried the number out of the Board of Education. "Miss Lillian Dana? My name is Russell. You know a boy named Freddy Titus?"

"Oh, yes. He's in my class." The voice was pleasing.

"Miss Dana, there is trouble. You know Judge Kittinger's house? Could you come there?"

"What is the trouble?"

"Freddy's little dog is dead of poison. I'm afraid Freddy is in a bad state. There is no one to help him. His folks are away. The woman taking care of him," Mike's careful explanatory sentences burst into indignation, "has no more sympathetic imagination than a broken clothes pole." He heard a little gasp. "I'd like to help him, Miss Dana, but I'm a man and a stranger, and the judge . . ." He paused.

". . . is old," said the judge in his chair.

"I'm terribly sorry," the voice on the phone said slowly. "Freddy's a wonderful boy."

"You are his friend?"

"Yes, we are friends."

"Then could you come? You see, we've got to get a terrible idea out of his head. He thinks a man across the street poisoned his dog on purpose. Miss Dana, *he has no doubt!* And he doesn't cry." She gasped again. "Greenwood Lane," he said, "and Hannibal Street—the southeast corner."

She said, "I'll come. I have a car. I'll come as soon as I can."

Russell turned and caught the judge biting his lips. "Am I making too much of this, sir?" he inquired humbly.

"I don't like the boy's stubborn conviction." The judge's voice was dry and clear. "Any more than you do. I agree that he must be brought to understand. But . . ." the old man shifted in the chair. "Of course, the man, Matlin, is a fool, Mike. There is something solemn and silly about him that makes him fair game. He's unfortunate. He married a widow with a crippled child, and no sooner were they married than *she* collapsed. And he's not well off. He's encumbered with that enormous house."

"What does he do, sir?"

"He's a photographer. Oh, he struggles, tries his best, and all that; but with such tension, Mike. That poor misshapen girl over there tries to keep the house; devoted to her mother. Matlin works hard, is devoted, too. And yet the sum comes out in petty strife, nerves, quarrels, uproar. And certainly it cannot be necessary to feud with children."

"The kids have done their share of that, I'll bet," mused Mike. "The kids are delighted—a neighborhood ogre, to add the fine flavor of menace. A focus for mischief. An enemy."

"True enough." The judge sighed.

"So the myth is made. No rumor about ole Matlin loses anything in the telling. I can see it's been built up. You don't knock it down in a day."

"No," said the judge uneasily. He got up from the chair.

The young man rubbed his dark head. "I don't like it, sir. We don't know what's in the kids' minds, or who their heroes are. There is only the gang. What do you suppose it advises?"

"What could it advise, after all?" said the judge crisply. "This isn't the slums, whatever Matlin says." He went nervously to the window. He fiddled with the shade pull. He said suddenly, "From my little summerhouse in the backyard you can overhear the gang. They congregate under that oak. Go and eavesdrop, Mike."

The young man snapped to attention. "Yes, sir."

"I . . . think we had better know," said the judge, a trifle sheepishly.

The kids sat under the oak, in a grassy hollow. Freddy was the core. His face was tight. His eyes never left off watching the house of the enemy. The others watched him, or hung their heads, or watched their own brown hands play with the grass.

They were not chattering. There hung about them a heavy, sullen silence, heavy with a sense of tragedy, sullen with a sense of wrong, and from time to time one voice or another would fling out a pronouncement which would sink into the silence, thickening its ugliness.

The judge looked up from his paper. "Could you . . . ?"

"I could hear," said Mike in a quiet voice. "They are condemning the law, sir. They call it corrupt. They are quite certain that Matlin killed the dog. They see themselves as Robin Hoods, vigilantes defending the weak, the wronged, the dog. They think they are discussing justice. They are waiting for dark. They speak of weapons, sir—the only ones they have. B.B. guns, after dark."

"Great heavens!"

"Don't worry. Nothing's going to happen."

"What are you going to do?"

"I'm going to stop it."

Mrs. Somers was cooking supper when he tapped on the screen. "Oh, it's you. What do you want?"

"I want your help, Mrs. Somers. For Freddy."

"Freddy," she interrupted loudly, with her nose high, "is going to have his supper and go to bed his regular time, and that's all about Freddy. Now, what did you want?"

He said, "I want you to let me take the boy to my apartment for the night."

"I couldn't do that!" She was scandalized.

"The judge will vouch . . ."

"Now, see here, Mr. what's your name—Russell. This isn't my house and Freddy's not my boy. I'm responsible to Mr. and Mrs. Titus. You're a stranger to me. As far as I can see, Freddy is no business of yours whatsoever."

"Which is his room?" asked Mike sharply.

"Why do you want to know?" She was hostile and suspicious.

"Where does he keep his B.B. gun?"

She was startled to an answer. "In the shed out back. Why?"

He told her.

"Kid's talk," she scoffed. "You don't know much about kids, do you, young man? Freddy will go to sleep. First thing he'll know, it's morning. That's about the size of it."

"You may be right. I hope so."

Mrs. Somers slapped potatoes into the pan. Her lips quivered indignantly. She felt annoyed because she was a little shaken. The strange young man really had hoped so.

Russell scanned the street, went across to Matlin's house. The man himself answered the bell. The air in this house was stale, and bore the faint smell of old grease. There was over everything an atmosphere of struggle and despair. Many things ought to have been repaired and had not been repaired. The place was too big. There wasn't enough money, or strength. It was too much.

Mrs. Matlin could not walk. Otherwise, one saw, she struggled and did the best she could. She had a lost look, as if some anxiety, ever present, took about nine-tenths of her attention. May Matlin limped in and sat down, lumpishly.

Russell began earnestly, "Mr. Matlin, I don't know

how this situation between you and the boys began.
I can guess that the kids are much to blame. I
imagine they enjoy it." He smiled. He wanted to be
sympathetic toward this man.

"Of course they enjoy it." Matlin looked tri-
umphant.

"They call me the Witch," the girl said. "Pretend
they're scared of me. The devils. I'm scared of them."

Matlin flicked a nervous eye at the woman in the
wheel chair. "The truth is, Mr. Russell," he said in
his high whine, "they're vicious."

"It's too bad," said his wife in a low voice. "I think
it's dangerous."

"Mama, you mustn't worry," said the girl in an
entirely new tone. "I won't let them hurt you. No-
body will hurt you."

"Be quiet, May," said Matlin. "You'll upset her. Of
course nobody will hurt her."

"Yes, it is dangerous, Mrs. Matlin," said Russell
quietly. "That's why I came over."

Matlin goggled. "What? What's this?"

"Could I possibly persuade you, sir, to spend the
night away from this neighborhood—and depart
noisily?"

"No," said Matlin, raring up, his ego bristling,
"no, you cannot! I will under no circumstances be
driven away from my own home." His voice rose.
"Furthermore, I certainly will not leave my wife and
step-daughter."

"We could manage, dear," said Mrs. Matlin anx-
iously.

Russell told them about the talk under the oak, the
B.B. gun.

"Devils," said May Matlin, "absolutely. . . ."

"Oh, Earl," trembled Mrs. Matlin, "maybe we had all better go away."

Matlin, red-necked, furious, said, "We own this property. We pay our taxes. We have our rights. Let them! Let them try something like that! Then, I think, the law would have something to say. This is outrageous! I did not harm that animal. Therefore, I defy . . ." He looked solemn and silly, as the judge had said, with his face crimson, his weak eyes rolling.

Russell rose. "I thought I ought to make the suggestion," he said mildly, "because it would be the safest thing to do. But don't worry, Mrs. Matlin, because I—"

"A B.B. gun can blind," she said tensely.

"Or even worse," Mike agreed. "But I am thinking of the—"

"Just a minute," Matlin roared. "You can't come in here and terrify my wife! She is not strong. You have no right." He drew himself up with his feet at a right angle, his pudgy arm extended, his plump jowls quivering. "Get out," he cried. He looked ridiculous.

Whether the young man and the bewildered woman in the chair might have understood each other was not to be known. Russell, of course, got out. May Matlin hobbled to the door and as Russell went through it she said, "Well, you warned us, anyhow."

Russell plodded across the pavement again. Long enchanting shadows from the lowering sun struck aslant through the golden air and all the old houses were gilded and softened in their green setting. He moved toward the big oak. He hunkered down. The sun struck its golden shafts deep under the boughs. "How's it going?" he asked.

Freddy Titus looked frozen and still. "Okay," said Phil Bourchard with elaborate ease. Light on his owlish glasses hid the eyes.

Mike opened his lips, hesitated. Suppertime struck on the neighborhood clock. Calls, like chimes, were sounding.

" 'S my Mom," said Ernie Allen. "See you after."

"See you after, Freddy."

"Okay."

"Okay."

Mrs. Somers' hoot had chimed with the rest and now Freddy got up stiffly.

"Okay?" said Mike Russell. The useful syllables that take any meaning at all in American mouths asked, "Are you feeling less bitter, boy? Are you any easier?"

"Okay," said Freddy. The same syllables shut the man out.

Mike opened his lips. Closed them. Freddy went across the lawn to his kitchen door. There was a brown crockery bowl on the back stoop. His sneaker, rigid on the ankle, stepped over it. Mike Russell watched, and then, with a movement of his arms, almost as if he would wring his hands, he went up the judge's steps.

"Well?" The judge opened his door. "Did you talk to the boy?"

Russell didn't answer. He sat down.

The judge stood over him. "The boy . . . The enormity of this whole idea *must* be explained to him."

"I can't explain," Mike said. "I opened my mouth. Nothing comes out."

"Perhaps *I* had better . . ."

"What are you going to say, sir?"

"Why, give him the facts!"

"The facts are . . . the dog is dead."

"There are no facts that point to Matlin."

"There are no facts that point to a tramp, either. That's too sloppy, sir."

"What are you driving at?"

"Judge, the boy is more rightfully suspicious than we are."

"Nonsense," said the judge. "The girl saw the dog's body before Matlin came. . . ."

"There is no alibi for poison," Mike said sadly.

"Are you saying the man is a liar?"

"Liars," sighed Mike. "Truth and lies. How are those kids going to understand, sir? To that Mrs. Page, to the lot of them, truth is only a subjective intention. 'I am no liar,' sez she, sez he. 'I *intend* to be truthful. So do not insult me.' Lord, when will we begin? It's what we were talking about at lunch, sir. What you and I believe. What the race has been told and told in such agony, in a million years of bitter lesson. *Error,* we were saying. Error is the enemy."

He flung out of the chair. "We know that to tell the truth is not merely a good intention. It's a damned difficult thing to do. It's a skill, to be practiced. It's a technique. It's an effort. It takes brains. It takes watching. It takes humility and self-examination. It's a science and an art. Why don't we tell the *kids* these things? Why is everyone locked up in anger, shouting liar at the other side? Why don't they automatically know how easy it is to be, not wicked, but mistaken? Why is there this notion of violence? Because Freddy doesn't think to himself, 'Wait a minute. I might be wrong.' The habit isn't there. Instead, there are the heroes—the big-muscled, noble-hearted, gun-toting heroes, blind in a righteousness totally arranged by the author. Excuse me, sir."

"All that may be," said the judge grimly, "and I agree. But the police know the lesson. They—"

"They don't care."

"What?"

"Don't care enough, sir. None of us cares enough—about the dog."

"I see," said the judge. "Yes, I see. We haven't the least idea what happened to the dog." He touched his pince-nez.

Mike rubbed his head wearily. "Don't know what to do except sit under his window the night through. Hardly seems good enough."

The judge said simply, "Why don't you find out what happened to the dog?"

The young man's face changed. "What we need, sir," said Mike slowly, "is to teach Freddy how to ask for it. Just to ask for it. Just to want it." The old man and the young man looked at each other. Past and future telescoped. *"Now,"* Mike said. "Before dark."

Suppertime, for the kids, was only twenty minutes long. When the girl in the brown dress with the bare blond head got out of the shabby coupé, the gang was gathered again in its hollow under the oak. She went to them and sank down on the ground. "Ah, Freddy, was it Bones? Your dear little dog you wrote about in the essay?"

"Yes, Miss Dana." Freddy's voice was shrill and hostile. *I won't be touched!* it cried to her. So she said no more, but sat there on the ground, and presently she began to cry. There was contagion. The simplest thing in the world. First, one of the smaller ones whimpering. Finally, Freddy Titus, bending over. Her arm guided his head, and then he lay weeping in her lap.

Russell, up in the summerhouse, closed his eyes and praised the Lord. In a little while he swung his legs over the railing and slid down the bank. "How do? I'm Mike Russell."

"I'm Lillian Dana." She was quick and intelligent, and her tears were real.

"Fellows," said Mike briskly, "you know what's got to be done, don't you? We've got to solve this case."

They turned their woeful faces.

He said deliberately, "It's just the same as a murder. It is a murder."

"Yeah," said Freddy and sat up, tears drying. "And it was ole Matlin."

"Then we have to prove it."

Miss Lillian Dana saw the boy's face lock. He didn't need to prove anything, the look proclaimed. He knew. She leaned over a little and said, "But we can't make an ugly mistake and put it on Bones's account. Bones was a fine dog. That would be a terrible monument." Freddy's eyes turned, startled.

"It's up to us," said Mike gratefully, "to go after the real facts, with real detective work. For Bones's sake."

"It's the least we can do for him," said Miss Dana, calmly and decisively.

Freddy's face lifted.

"Trouble is," Russell went on quickly, "people get things wrong. Sometimes they don't remember straight. They make mistakes."

"Ole Matlin tells lies," said Freddy.

"If he does," said Russell cheerfully, "then we've got to *prove* that he does. Now, I've figured out a plan, if Miss Dana will help us. You pick a couple of the fellows, Fred. Have to go to all the houses around and ask some questions. Better pick the smartest ones. To find out the truth is very hard," he challenged.

"And then?" said Miss Dana in a fluttery voice.

"Then they, and you, if you will . . ."

"Me?" She straightened. "I'm a schoolteacher, Mr. Russell. Won't the police . . . ?"

"Not before dark."

"What are *you* going to be doing?"

"Dirtier work."

She bit her lip. "It's nosy. It's . . . not done."

"No," he agreed. "You may lose your job."

She wasn't a bad-looking young woman. Her eyes were fine. Her brow was serious, but there was the ghost of a dimple in her cheek. Her hands moved. "Oh, well, I can always take up beauty culture or something. What are the questions?" She had a pad of paper and a pencil half out of her purse, and looked alert and efficient.

Now, as the gang huddled, there was a warm sense of conspiracy growing. "Going to be the dickens of a job," Russell warned them. And he outlined some questions. "Now, don't let anybody fool you into taking a sloppy answer," he concluded. "Ask how they know. Get real evidence. But don't go to Matlin's—I'll go there."

"I'm not afraid of him." Freddy's nostrils flared.

"I think I stand a better chance of getting the answers," said Russell coolly. "Aren't we after the answers?"

Freddy swallowed. "And if it turns out . . . ?"

"It turns out the way it turns out," said Russell, rumpling the towhead. "Choose your henchmen. Tough, remember."

"Phil. Ernie." The kids who were left out wailed as the three small boys and their teacher, who wasn't a lot bigger, rose from the ground.

"It'll be tough, Mr. Russell," Miss Dana said grimly. "Whoever you are, thank you for getting me into this."

"I'm just a stranger," he said gently, looking down at her face. "But you are a friend and a teacher." Pain crossed her eyes. "You'll be teaching now, you know."

Her chin went up. "Okay, kids. I'll keep the paper and pencil. Freddy, wipe your face. Stick your shirt in, Phil. Now, let's organize. . . ."

It was nearly nine o'clock when the boys and the teacher, looking rather exhausted, came back to the judge's house. Russell, whose face was grave, reached for the papers in her hands.

"Just a minute," said Miss Dana. "Judge, we have some questions."

Ernie Allen bared all his heap of teeth and stepped forward. "Did you see Bones today?" he asked with the firm skill of repetition. The judge nodded. "How many times and when?"

"Once. Er—shortly before noon. He crossed my yard, going east."

The boys bent over the pad. Then Freddy's lips opened hard. "How do you know the time, Judge Kittinger?"

"Well," said the judge, "hm . . . let me think. I was looking out the window for my company and just then he arrived."

"Five minutes of one, sir," Mike said.

Freddy flashed around. "What makes you sure?"

"I looked at my watch," said Russell. "I was taught to be exactly five minutes early when I'm asked to a meal." There was a nodding among the boys, and Miss Dana wrote on the pad.

"Then I was mistaken," said the judge, thoughtfully. "It was shortly before one. Of course."

Phil Bourchard took over. "Did you see anyone go into Matlin's driveway or back lot?"

"I did not."

"Were you out of doors or did you look up that way?"

"Yes, I . . . When we left the table. Mike?"

"At two-thirty, sir."

"How do you know that time for sure?" asked Freddy Titus.

"Because I wondered if I could politely stay a little

longer." Russell's eyes congratulated Miss Lillian Dana. She had made them a team, and on it, Freddy was the How-do-you-know-for-sure Department.

"Can you swear," continued Phil to the judge, "there was nobody at all around Matlin's back lot then?"

"As far as my view goes," answered the judge cautiously.

Freddy said promptly, "He couldn't see much. Too many trees. We can't count that."

They looked at Miss Dana and she marked on the pad. "Thank you. Now, you have a cook, sir? We must question her."

"This way," said the judge, rising and bowing.

Russell looked after them and his eyes were velvet again. He met the judge's twinkle. Then he sat down and ran an eye quickly over some of the sheets of paper, passing each on to his host.

Startled, he looked up. Lillian Dana, standing in the door, was watching his face.

"Do you think, Mike . . . ?"

A paper drooped in the judge's hand.

"We can't stop," she challenged.

Russell nodded, and turned to the judge. "May need some high brass, sir." The judge rose. "And tell me, sir, where Matlin plays golf. And the telephone number of the Salvage League. No, Miss Dana, we can't stop. We'll take it where it turns."

"We must," she said.

It was nearly ten when the neighbors began to come in. The judge greeted them soberly. The Chief of Police arrived. Mrs. Somers, looking grim and uprooted in a crêpe dress, came. Mr. Matlin, Mrs. Page, Mr. and Mrs. Daugherty, a Mr. and Mrs. Baker, and Diane Bourchard, who was sixteen. They looked curiously at the tight little group, the boys and their blond teacher.

Last of all to arrive was young Mr. Russell, who slipped in from the dark veranda, accepted the judge's nod, and called the meeting to order.

"We have been investigating the strange death of a dog," he began. "Chief Anderson, while we know your department would have done so in good time, we also know you are busy, and some of us"—he glanced at the dark windowpane—"couldn't wait. Will you help us now?"

The chief said genially, "That's why I'm here. I guess." It was the judge and his stature that gave this meeting any standing. Naïve, young, a little absurd it might have seemed had not the old man sat so quietly attentive among them.

"Thank you, sir. Now, all we want to know is what happened to the dog." Russell looked about him. "First, let us demolish the tramp." Mrs. Page's feathers ruffled. Russell smiled at her. "Mrs. Page saw a man go down Matlin's drive this morning. The Salvage League sent a truck, to pick up rags and papers, which at ten-forty-two was parked in front of the Daughertys'. The man, who seemed poorly dressed in his working clothes, went to the toolroom behind Matlin's garage, as he had been instructed to. He picked up a bundle and returned to his truck. Mrs. Page," purred Mike to her scarlet face, "the man was there. It was only your opinion about him that proves to have been, not a lie, but an error."

He turned his head. "Now, we have tried to trace the dog's day and we have done remarkably well, too." As he traced it for them, some faces began to wear at least the ghost of a smile, seeing the little dog frisking through the neighborhood. "Just before one," Mike went on, "Bones ran across the judge's yard to the Allens' where the kids were playing ball. Up to this time no one saw Bones *above* Greenwood Lane or *up* Hannibal Street. But Miss Diane Bourchard, recovering from a sore throat, was not in school today. After lunch, she sat on her porch directly across from Mr. Matlin's back lot. She was waiting for school to be out, when she expected her friends to come by.

"She saw, not Bones, but Corky, an animal belonging to Mr. Daugherty, playing in Matlin's lot at about two o'clock. I want your opinion. If poisoned bait had been lying there at two, would Corky have found it?"

"Seems so," said Daugherty. "Thank God Corky didn't." He bit his tongue. "Corky's a show dog," he blundered.

"But Bones," said Russell gently, "was more like a friend. That's why we care, of course."

"It's a damned shame!" Daugherty looked around angrily.

"It is," said Mrs. Baker. "He was a friend of mine, Bones was."

"Go on," growled Daugherty. "What else did you dig up?"

"Mr. Matlin left for his golf at eleven-thirty. Now, you see, it looks as if Matlin couldn't have left poison behind him."

"I most certainly did not," snapped Matlin. "I have said so. I will not stand for this sort of innuendo, I am not a liar. You said it was a conference."

Mike held the man's eye. "We are simply trying to find out what happened to the dog," he said. Matlin fell silent.

"Surely you realize," purred Mike, "that, human frailty being what it is, there may have been other errors in what we were told this afternoon. There was at least one more.

"Mr. and Mrs. Baker," he continued, "worked in their garden this afternoon. Bones abandoned the ball game to visit the Bakers' dog, Smitty. At three o'clock the Bakers, after discussing the time carefully lest it be too late in the day, decided to bathe Smitty. When they caught him for his ordeal, Bones was still there. So, you see, Miss May Matlin, who says she saw Bones lying by the sidewalk *before three o'clock,* was mistaken."

Matlin twitched. Russell said sharply, "The testimony of the Bakers is extremely clear." The Bakers, who looked alike, both brown outdoor people, nodded vigorously.

"The time at which Mr. Matlin returned is quite well established. Diane saw him. Mrs. Daugherty, next door, decided to take a nap at five after three. She had a roast to put in at four-thirty. Therefore she is sure of the time. She went upstairs and from an upper window she, too, saw Mr. Matlin come home. Both witnesses say he drove his car into the garage at three-ten, got out, and went around the building to the right of it—*on the weedy side.*"

Mr. Matlin was sweating. His forehead was beaded. He did not speak.

Mike shifted papers. "Now, we know that the kids trooped up to Phil Bourchard's kitchen at about a quarter of three. Whereas Bones, realizing that Smitty was in for it, and shying away from soap and water like any sane dog, went up Hannibal Street at three o'clock sharp. He may have known in some doggy way where Freddy was. Can we see Bones loping up Hannibal Street, going *above* Greenwood Lane?"

"We can," said Daugherty. He was watching Matlin. "Besides, he was found above Greenwood Lane soon after."

"No one," said Mike slowly, "was seen in Matlin's back lot, except Matlin. Yet almost immediately after Matlin was there, the little dog died."

"Didn't Diane . . . ?"

"Diane's friends came at three-twelve. Their evidence is not reliable." Diane blushed.

"This—this is intolerable!" croaked Matlin. "Why *my* back lot?"

Daugherty said, "There was no poison lying around my place, I'll tell you that."

"How do you know?" begged Matlin. And Freddy's eyes, with the smudges under them, followed to Russell's face. "Why not in the street? From some passing car?"

Mike said, "I'm afraid it's not likely. You see, Mr. Otis Carnavon was stalled at the corner of Hannibal and Lee. Trying to flag a push. Anything thrown from a car on that block he ought to have seen."

"Was the poison quick?" demanded Daugherty. "What did he get?"

"It was quick. The dog could not go far after he got it. He got cyanide."

Matlin's shaking hand removed his glasses. They were wet.

"Some of you may be amateur photographers," Mike said. "Mr. Matlin, is there cyanide in your cellar darkroom?"

"Yes, but I keep it . . . most meticulously. . . ." Matlin began to cough.

When the noise of his spasm died, Mike said, "The poison was embedded in ground meat which analyzed, roughly, half beef and the rest pork and veal, half and half." Matlin encircled his throat with his fingers. "I've checked with four neighborhood butchers and the dickens of a time I had," said Mike. No one smiled. Only Freddy looked up at him with solemn sympathy. "Ground meat was delivered to at least five houses in the vicinity. Meat that *was* one-half beef, one-quarter pork, one-quarter veal, was delivered at ten this morning to Matlin's house."

A stir like an angry wind blew over the room. The Chief of Police made some shift of his weight so that his chair creaked.

"It begins to look . . ." growled Daugherty.

"Now," said Russell sharply, "we must be very careful. One more thing. The meat had been seasoned."

"Seasoned!"

"With salt. And with . . . thyme."

"Thyme," groaned Matlin.

Freddy looked up at Miss Dana with bewildered eyes. She put her arm around him.

"As far as motives are concerned," said Mike quietly, "I can't discuss them. It is inconceivable to me that any man would poison a dog." Nobody spoke. "However, where are we?" Mike's voice seemed to catch Matlin just in time to keep him from falling off the chair. "We don't know yet what happened to the dog." Mike's voice rang. "Mr. Matlin, will you help us to the answer?"

Matlin said thickly, "Better get those kids out of here."

Miss Dana moved, but Russell said, "No. They have worked hard for the truth. They have earned it. And if it is to be had, they shall have it."

"You know?" whimpered Matlin.

Mike said, "I called your golf club. I've looked into your trash incinerator. Yes, I know. But I want you to tell us."

Daugherty said, "Well? Well?" And Matlin covered his face.

Mike said gently, "I think there was an error. Mr. Matlin, I'm afraid, did poison the dog. But he never meant to, and he didn't know he had done it."

Matlin said, "I'm sorry . . . It's—I can't . . . She means to do her best. But she's a terrible cook. Somebody gave her those—those herbs. Thyme—thyme in everything. She fixed me a lunch box. I—couldn't stomach it. I bought my lunch at the club."

Mike nodded.

Matlin went on, his voice cracking. "I never . . . You see, I didn't even know it was meat the dog got.

She said—she told me the dog was already dead."

"And of course," said Mike, "in your righteous wrath, you never paused to say to yourself, 'Wait, what *did* happen to the dog?'"

"Mr. Russell, I didn't lie. How could I know there was thyme in it? When I got home, I had to get rid of the hamburger she'd fixed for me—I didn't want to hurt her feelings. She tries . . . tries so hard. . . ." He sat up suddenly. *"But what she tried to do today,"* he said, with his eyes almost out of his head, *"was to poison me!"* His bulging eyes roved. They came to Freddy. He gasped. He said, "Your dog saved my life!"

"Yes," said Mike quickly, "Freddy's dog saved your life. You see, your step-daughter would have kept trying."

People drew in their breaths. "The buns are in your incinerator," Mike said. "She guessed what happened to the dog, went for the buns, and hid them. She was late, you remember, getting to the disturbance. And she did lie."

Chief Anderson rose.

"Her mother . . ." said Matlin frantically, "her mother . . ."

Mike Russell put his hand on the plump shoulder. "Her mother's been in torment, tortured by the rivalry between you. Don't you think her mother senses something wrong?"

Miss Lillian Dana wrapped Freddy in her arms. "Oh, what a wonderful dog Bones was!" she covered the sound of the other voices. "Even when he died, he saved a man's life. Oh, Freddy, he was a wonderful dog."

And Freddy, not quite taking everything in yet, was released to simple sorrow and wept quietly against his friend. . . .

When they went to fetch May Matlin, she was not in the house. They found her in the Titus's back shed. She seemed to be looking for something.

Next day, when Mr. and Mrs. Titus came home, they found that although the little dog had died, their Freddy was all right. The judge, Russell, and Miss Dana told them all about it.

Mrs. Titus wept. Mr. Titus swore. He wrung Russell's hand. ". . . for stealing the gun . . ." he babbled.

But the mother cried, ". . . for showing him, for teaching him. . . . Oh, Miss Dana, oh, my dear!"

The judge waved from his veranda as the dark head and the blond drove away.

"I think Miss Dana likes him," said Ernie Allen.

"How do you know for sure?" said Freddy Titus.

The Inexperienced Ghost

H. G. WELLS

The scene amidst which Clayton told his last story comes back very vividly to my mind. There he sat, for the greater part of the time, in the corner of the authentic settle by the spacious open fire, and Sanderson sat beside him smoking the Broseley clay that bore his name. There was Evans, and that marvel among actors, Wish, who is also a modest man. We had all come down to the Mermaid Club that Saturday morning, except Clayton, who had slept there overnight—which indeed gave him the opening of his story. We had golf until golfing was invisible; we had dined, and we were in that mood of tranquil kindliness when men will suffer a story. When Clayton began to tell one, we naturally supposed he was lying. It may be that indeed he was lying—of that the reader will speedily be able to judge as well as I. He began, it is true, with an air of matter-of-fact anecdote, but that we thought was only the incurable artifice of the man.

"I say!" he remarked, after a long consideration of the upward rain of sparks from the log that Sanderson had thumped, "you know I was alone here last night?"

"Except for the domestics," said Wish.

"Who sleep in the other wing," said Clayton. "Yes. Well—" He pulled at his cigar for some little time as though he still hesitated about his confidence. Then he said, quite quietly, "I caught a ghost!"

"Caught a ghost, did you?" said Sanderson. "Where is it?"

And Evans, who admires Clayton immensely and has been four weeks in America, shouted, *"Caught a ghost, did you, Clayton? I'm glad of it! Tell us all about it right now."*

Clayton said he would in a minute, and asked him to shut the door.

He looked apologetically at me. "There's no eavesdropping of course, but we don't want to upset our very excellent service with any rumours of ghosts in the place. There's too much shadow and oak panelling to trifle with that. And this, you know, wasn't a regular ghost. I don't think it will come again— ever."

"You mean to say you didn't keep it?" said Sanderson.

"I hadn't the heart to," said Clayton.

And Sanderson said he was surprised.

We laughed, and Clayton looked aggrieved. "I know," he said, with the flicker of a smile, "but the fact is it really *was* a ghost, and I'm as sure of it as I am that I am talking to you now. I'm not joking. I mean what I say."

Sanderson drew deeply at his pipe, with one reddish eye on Clayton, and then emitted a thin jet of smoke more eloquent than many words.

Clayton ignored the comment. "It is the strangest thing that has ever happened in my life. You know

I never believed in ghosts or anything of the sort, before, ever; and then, you know, I bag one in a corner: and the whole business is in my hands."

He meditated still more profoundly and produced and began to pierce a second cigar with a curious little stabber he affected.

"You talked to it?" asked Wish.

"For the space, probably, of an hour."

"Chatty?" I said, joining the party of the sceptics.

"The poor devil was in trouble," said Clayton, bowed over his cigar-end and with the very faintest note of reproof.

"Sobbing?" someone asked.

Clayton heaved a realistic sigh at the memory. "Good Lord!" he said; "yes." And then, "Poor fellow! yes."

"Where did you strike it?" asked Evans, in his best American accent.

"I never realised," said Clayton, ignoring him, "the poor sort of thing a ghost might be," and he hung us up again for a time, while he sought for matches in his pocket and lit and warmed to his cigar.

"I took an advantage," he reflected at last.

We were none of us in a hurry. "A character," he said, "remains just the same character for all that it's been disembodied. That's a thing we too often forget. People with a certain strength or fixity of purpose may have ghosts of a certain strength and fixity of purpose—most haunting ghosts, you know, must be as one-idea'd as monomaniacs and as obstinate as mules to come back again and again. This poor creature wasn't." He suddenly looked up rather queerly, and his eye went round the room. "I say it," he said, "in all kindliness, but that is the plain truth of the case. Even at the first glance he struck me as weak."

He punctuated with the help of his cigar.

"I came upon him, you know, in the long passage. His back was towards me and I saw him first. Right off I knew him for a ghost. He was transparent and whitish; clean through his chest I could see the glimmer of the little window at the end. And not only his physique but his attitude struck me as being weak. He looked, you know, as though he didn't know in the slightest whatever he meant to do. One hand was on the panelling and the other fluttered to his mouth. Like—*so!*"

"What sort of physique?" said Sanderson.

"Lean. You know that sort of young man's neck that has two great flutings down the back, here and here—so! And a little meanish head with scrubby hair and rather bad ears. Shoulders bad, narrower than the hips; turndown collar, ready-made short jacket, trousers baggy and a little frayed at the heels. That's how he took me. I came very quietly up the staircase. I did not carry a light, you know—the candles are on the landing table and there is that lamp—and I was in my list slippers, and I saw him as I came up. I stopped dead at that—taking him in. I wasn't a bit afraid. I think that in most of these affairs one is never nearly so afraid or excited as one imagines one would be. I was surprised and interested. I thought, 'Good Lord! Here's a ghost at last! And I haven't believed for a moment in ghosts during the last five-and-twenty years.'"

"Um," said Wish.

"I suppose I wasn't on the landing a moment before he found out I was there. He turned on me sharply, and I saw the face of an immature young man, a weak nose, a scrubby little moustache, a feeble chin. So for an instant we stood—he looking over his shoulder at me—and regarded one another. Then he seemed to remember his high calling. He turned round, drew himself up, projected his face, raised his arms, spread his hands in approved ghost fashion—came towards me. As he did so his little jaw dropped, and he emitted a faint, drawn-out 'Boo.' No, it wasn't—not a bit dreadful. I'd dined. I'd had a bottle of champagne, and being all alone, perhaps two or three—perhaps even four or five—whiskies, so I was as solid as rocks and no more frightened than if I'd been assailed by a frog. 'Boo!' I said. 'Nonsense. You don't belong to *this* place. What are you doing here?'

"I could see him wince. 'Boo—oo,' he said.

"'Boo—be hanged! Are you a member?' I said; and just to show I didn't care a pin for him I stepped through a corner of him and made to light my candle. 'Are you a member?' I repeated, looking at him sideways.

"He moved a little so as to stand clear of me, and his bearing became crestfallen. 'No,' he said, in answer to the persistent interrogation of my eye; 'I'm not a member—I'm a ghost.'

"'Well, that doesn't give you the run of the Mermaid Club. Is there anyone you want to see, or anything of that sort?' And doing it as steadily as possible for fear that he should mistake the carelessness of whisky for the distraction of fear, I got my candle alight. I turned on him, holding it. 'What are you doing here?' I said.

"He had dropped his hands and stopped his booing, and there he stood, abashed and awkward, the ghost of a weak, silly, aimless young man. 'I'm haunting,' he said.

" 'You haven't any business to,' I said in a quiet voice.

" 'I'm a ghost,' he said, as if in defence.

" 'That may be, but you haven't any business to haunt here. This is a respectable private club; people often stop here with nursemaids and children, and, going about in the careless way you do, some poor little mite could easily come upon you and be scared out of her wits. I suppose you didn't think of that?'

" 'No, sir,' he said, 'I didn't.'

" 'You should have done. You haven't any claim on the place, have you? Weren't murdered here, or anything of that sort?'

" 'None, sir; but I thought as it was old and oak-panelled—'

" 'That's *no* excuse.' I regarded him firmly. 'Your coming here is a mistake,' I said, in a tone of friendly superiority. I feigned to see if I had my matches, and then looked up at him frankly. 'If I were you I wouldn't wait for cock-crow—I'd vanish right away.'

"He looked embarrassed. 'The fact *is,* sir—' he began.

" 'I'd vanish,' I said, driving it home.

" 'The fact is, sir, that—somehow—I can't.'

" 'You *can't?*'

" 'No, sir. There's something I've forgotten. I've been hanging about here since midnight last night, hiding in the cupboards of the empty bedrooms and things like that. I'm flurried. I've never come haunting before, and it seems to put me out.'

" 'Put you out?'

" 'Yes, sir. I've tried to do it several times, and it doesn't come off. There's some little thing has slipped me, and I can't get back.'

"That, you know, rather bowled me over. He looked at me in such an abject way that for the life of me I couldn't keep up quite the high hectoring vein I had adopted. 'That's queer,' I said, and as I spoke I fancied I heard someone moving about down below. 'Come into my room and tell me more about it,' I said. 'I didn't, of course, understand this,' and I tried to take him by the arm. But, of course, you might as well have tried to take hold of a puff of smoke! I had forgotten my number, I think; anyhow, I remember going into several bedrooms—it was lucky I was the only soul in that wing—until I saw my traps. 'Here we are,' I said, and sat down in the armchair; 'sit down and tell me all about it. It seems to me you have got yourself into a jolly awkward position, old chap.'

"Well, he said he wouldn't sit down; he'd prefer to flit up and down the room if it was all the same to me. And so he did, and in a little while we were deep in a long and serious talk. And presently, you know, something of those whiskies and sodas evaporated out of me, and I began to realise just a little what a thundering rum and weird business it was that I was in. There he was, semi-transparent—the proper conventional phantom and noiseless except for his ghost of a voice—flitting to and fro in that nice, clean, chintz-hung old bedroom. You could see the gleam of the copper candlesticks through him, and the lights on the brass fender, and the corners of the framed engravings on the wall, and there he was telling me all about this wretched little life of his that had recently ended on earth. He hadn't a particularly honest face, you know, but being transparent, of course, he couldn't avoid telling the truth."

"Eh?" said Wish, suddenly sitting up in his chair.

"What?" said Clayton.

"Being transparent—couldn't avoid telling the truth—I don't see it," said Wish.

"*I* don't see it," said Clayton, with inimitable assurance. "But it *is* so, I can assure you nevertheless. I don't believe he got once a nail's breadth off the Bible truth. He told me how he had been killed—he went down into a London basement with a candle to look for a leakage of gas—and described himself as a senior English master in a London private school when that release occurred."

"Poor wretch!" said I.

"That's what I thought, and the more he talked the more I thought it. There he was, purposeless in life and purposeless out of it. He talked of his father and mother and his schoolmaster, and all who had ever been anything to him in the world, meanly. He had been too sensitive, too nervous; none of them had ever valued him properly or understood him, he said. He had never had a real friend in the world, I think; he had never had a success. He had shirked games and failed examinations. 'It's like that with some people,' he said; 'whenever I got into the examination-room or anywhere everything seemed to go.' Engaged to be married of course—to another over-sensitive person, I suppose—when the indiscretion with the gas escape ended his affairs. 'And where are you now?' I asked. 'Not in—?'

"He wasn't clear on that point at all. The impression he gave me was of a sort of vague, intermediate state, a special reserve for souls too non-existent for anything so positive as either sin or virtue. *I* don't know. He was much too egotistical and unobservant to give me any clear idea of the kind of place, kind of country, there is on the Other Side of Things. Wherever he was, he seems to have fallen in with a set of kindred spirits: ghosts of weak Cockney young men, who were on a footing of Christian names, and among these there was certainly a lot of talk about 'going haunting' and things like that. Yes—going haunting! They seemed to think 'haunting' a tremendous adventure, and most of them funked it all the time. And so primed, you know, he had come."

"But really!" said Wish to the fire.

"These are the impressions he gave me, anyhow," said Clayton modestly. "I may, of course, have been in a rather uncritical state, but that was the sort of background he gave to himself. He kept flitting up and down, with his thin voice going—talking, talking about his wretched self, and never a word of clear, firm statement from first to last. He was thinner and sillier and more pointless than if he had been real and alive. Only then, you know, he would not have been in my bedroom here—if he *had* been alive. I should have kicked him out."

"Of course," said Evans, "there *are* poor mortals like that."

"And there's just as much chance of their having ghosts as the rest of us," I admitted.

"What gave a sort of point to him, you know, was the fact that he did seem within limits to have found himself out. The mess he had made of haunting had depressed him terribly. He had been told it would be a 'lark'; he had come expecting it to be a 'lark,' and here it was, nothing but another failure added to his record! He proclaimed himself an utter out-and-out failure. He said, and I can quite believe it, that he had never tried to do anything all his life that he hadn't made a perfect mess of—and through all the wastes of eternity he never would. If he had had sympathy, perhaps— He paused at that, and stood regarding me. He remarked that, strange as it might seem to me, nobody, not anyone, ever, had given him the amount of sympathy I was doing now. I could see what he wanted straight away, and I determined to head him off at once. I may be a brute, you know, but being the Only Real Friend, the recipient of the confidences of one of these egotistical weaklings, ghost or body, is beyond my physical endurance. I got up briskly. 'Don't you brood on these things too much,' I said. 'The thing you've got to do is to get out of this—get out of this sharp. You pull yourself together and *try*.' 'I can't,' he said. 'You try,' I said, and try he did."

"Try!" said Sanderson. *"How?"*

"Passes," said Clayton.

"Passes?"

"Complicated series of gestures and passes with the hands. That's how he had come in and that's how he had to get out again. Lord! what a business I had!"

"But how could *any* series of passes—" I began.

"My dear man," said Clayton, turning on me and putting a great emphasis on certain words, "you want *everything* clear. I don't know *how*. All I know is that you *do*—that *he* did, anyhow, at least. After a fearful time, you know, he got his passes right and suddenly disappeared."

"Did you," said Sanderson slowly, "observe the passes?"

"Yes," said Clayton, and seemed to think. "It was tremendously queer," he said. "There we were, I and this thin vague ghost, in that silent room, in this silent, empty inn, in this silent little Friday-night town. Not a sound except our voices and a faint panting he made when he swung. There was the bed-room candle, and one candle on the dressing-table alight, that was all—sometimes one or other would flare up into a tall, lean, astonished flame for a space. And queer things happened. 'I can't,' he said; 'I shall never—!' And suddenly he sat down on a little chair at the foot of the bed and began to sob and sob. Lord! what a harrowing whimpering thing he seemed!

" 'You pull yourself together,' I said, and tried to pat him on the back, and . . . my confounded hand went through him! By that time, you know, I wasn't nearly so—massive as I had been on the landing. I got the queerness of it full. I remember snatching back my hand out of him as it were, with a little thrill, and walking over to the dressing-table. 'You pull yourself together,' I said to him, 'and try.' And in order to encourage and help him I began to try as well."

"What!" said Sanderson, "the passes?"

"Yes, the passes."

"But—" I said, moved by an idea that eluded me for a space.

"This is interesting," said Sanderson, with his finger in his pipe-bowl. "You mean to say this ghost of yours gave way—"

"Did his level best to give away the whole confounded barrier? *Yes.*"

"He didn't," said Wish; "he couldn't. Or you'd have gone there too."

"That's precisely it," I said, finding my elusive idea put into words for me.

"That *is* precisely it," said Clayton, with thoughtful eyes upon the fire.

For just a little while there was silence.

"And at last he did it?" said Sanderson.

"At last he did it. I had to keep him up to it hard, but he did it at last—rather suddenly. He despaired, we had a scene, and then he got up abruptly and asked me to go through the whole performance, slowly, so that he might see. 'I believe,' he said, 'if I could *see* I should spot what was wrong at once.' And he did. '*I* know,' he said. 'What do you know?' said I. '*I* know," he repeated. Then he said, peevishly, 'I *can't* do it, if you look at me—I really *can't;* it's been that, partly, all along. I'm such a nervous fellow that you put me out.' Well, we had a bit of an argument. Naturally I wanted to see; but he was as obstinate as a mule, and suddenly I had come over as tired as a dog—he tired me out. 'All right,' I said, '*I* won't look at you,' and turned towards the mirror, on the wardrobe, by the bed.

"He started off very fast. I tried to follow him by looking in the looking-glass, to see just what it was had hung. Round went his arms and his hands, so, and so, and so, and then with a rush came to the last gesture of all—you stand erect and open out your arms—and so, don't you know, he stood. And then he didn't! He didn't! He wasn't! I wheeled round from the looking-glass to him. There was nothing! I was alone, with the flaring candles and a staggering mind. What had happened? Had anything happened? Had I been dreaming? . . . And then, with an absurd note of finality about it, the clock upon the landing discovered the moment was ripe for striking *one*. So!—Ping! And I was as grave and sober as a judge, with all my champagne and whisky gone into the vast serene. Feeling queer, you know—confoundedly *queer*! Queer! Good Lord!"

He regarded his cigar-ash for a moment. "That's all that happened," he said.

"And then you went to bed?" asked Evans.

"What else was there to do?"

I looked Wish in the eye. We wanted to scoff, and there was something, something perhaps in Clayton's voice and manner, that hampered our desire.

"And about these passes?" said Sanderson.

"I believe I could do them now."

"Oh!" said Sanderson, and produced a pen-knife and set himself to grub the dottel out of the bowl of his clay.

"Why don't you do them now?" said Sanderson, shutting his pen-knife with a click.

"That's what I'm going to do," said Clayton.

"They won't work," said Evans.

"If they do—" I suggested.

"You know, I'd rather you didn't," said Wish, stretching out his legs.

"Why?" asked Evans.

"I'd rather he didn't," said Wish.

"But he hasn't got 'em right," said Sanderson, plugging too much tobacco into his pipe.

"All the same, I'd rather he didn't," said Wish.

We argued with Wish. He said that for Clayton to go through those gestures was like mocking a serious matter. "But you don't believe—?" I said. Wish glanced at Clayton, who was staring into the fire, weighing something in his mind. "I do—more than half, anyhow, I do," said Wish.

"Clayton," said I, "you're too good a liar for us. Most of it was all right. But that disappearance . . . happened to be convincing. Tell us it's a tale of cock and bull."

He stood up without heeding me, took the middle of the hearthrug, and faced me. For a moment he regarded his feet thoughtfully, and then for all the rest of the time his eyes were on the opposite wall, with an intent expression. He raised his two hands slowly to the level of his eyes and so began. . . .

Now, Sanderson is a Freemason, a member of the lodge of the Four Kings, which devotes itself so ably to the study and elucidation of all the mysteries of Masonry past and present, and among the students of this lodge Sanderson is by no means the least. He followed Clayton's motions with a singular interest in his reddish eye. "That's not bad," he said, when it was done. "You really do, you know, put things together, Clayton, in a most amazing fashion. But there's one little detail out."

"I know," said Clayton. "I believe I could tell you which."

"Well?"

"This," said Clayton, and did a queer little twist and writhing and thrust of the hands.

"Yes."

"That, you know, was what *he* couldn't get right," said Clayton. "But how do *you*—?"

"Most of this business, and particularly how you invented it, I don't understand at all," said Sanderson, "but just that phase—I do." He reflected. "These happen to be a series of gestures—connected with a certain branch of esoteric Masonry— Probably you know. Or else— *How?*" He reflected still further. "I do not see I can do any harm in telling you just the proper twist. After all, if you know, you know; if you don't, you don't."

"I know nothing," said Clayton, "except what the poor devil let out last night."

"Well, anyhow," said Sanderson, and placed his churchwarden very carefully upon the shelf over the fireplace. Then very rapidly he gesticulated with his hands.

"So?" said Clayton, repeating.

"So," said Sanderson, and took his pipe in hand again.

"Ah, *now*," said Clayton, "I can do the whole thing—right."

He stood up before the waning fire and smiled at

us all. But I think there was just a little hesitation in his smile. "If I begin—" he said.

"I wouldn't begin," said Wish.

"It's all right!" said Evans. "Matter is indestructible. You don't think any jiggery-pokery of this sort is going to snatch Clayton into the world of shades. Not it! You may try, Clayton, so far as I'm concerned, until your arms drop off at the wrists."

"I don't believe that," said Wish, and stood up and put his arm on Clayton's shoulder. "You've made me half believe in that story somehow, and I don't want to see the thing done."

"Goodness!" said I, "here's Wish frightened!"

"I am," said Wish, with real or admirably feigned intensity. "I believe that if he goes through these motions right he'll *go*."

"He'll not do anything of the sort," I cried. "There's only one way out of this world for men, and Clayton is thirty years from that. Besides. . . . And such a ghost! Do you think—?"

Wish interrupted me by moving. He walked out from among the chairs and stopped beside the table and stood there. "Clayton," he said, "you're a fool."

Clayton, with a humorous light in his eyes, smiled back at him. "Wish," he said, "is right and all you others are wrong. I shall go. I shall get to the end of these passes, and as the last swish whistles through the air, Presto!—this hearthrug will be vacant, the room will be blank amazement, and a respectably dressed gentleman of fifteen stone will plump into the world of shades. I'm certain. So will you be. I decline to argue further. Let the thing be tried."

"No," said Wish, and made a step and ceased, and Clayton raised his hands once more to repeat the spirit's passing.

By that time, you know, we were all in a state of tension—largely because of the behaviour of Wish. We sat all of us with our eyes on Clayton—I, at least, with a sort of tight, stiff feeling about me as though from the back of my skull to the middle of my thighs my body had been changed to steel. And there, with a gravity that was imperturbably serene, Clayton bowed and swayed and waved his hands and arms before us. As he drew towards the end one piled up, one tingled in one's teeth. The last gesture, I have said, was to swing the arms out wide open, with the face held up. And when at last he swung out to this closing gesture I ceased even to breathe. It was ridiculous, of course, but you know that ghost-story feeling. It was after dinner, in a queer, old shadowy house. Would he, after all—?

There he stood for one stupendous moment, with his arms open and his upturned face, assured and bright, in the glare of the hanging lamp. We hung through that moment as if it were an age, and then came from all of us something that was half a sigh of infinite relief and half a reassuring *"No!"* For visibly—he wasn't going. It was all nonsense. He had told an idle story, and carried it almost to conviction, that was all! . . . And then in that moment the face of Clayton changed.

It changed. It changed as a lit house changes when its lights are suddenly extinguished. His eyes were suddenly eyes that were fixed, his smile was frozen on his lips, and he stood there still. He stood there, very gently swaying.

That moment, too, was an age. And then, you know, chairs were scraping, things were falling, and we were all moving. His knees seemed to give, and he fell forward, and Evans rose and caught him in his arms. . . .

It stunned us all. For a minute I suppose no one said a coherent thing. We believed it, yet could not believe it. . . . I came out of a muddled stupefaction to find myself kneeling beside him, and his vest and shirt were torn open, and Sanderson's hand lay on his heart. . . .

Well—the simple fact before us could very well wait our convenience; there was no hurry for us to comprehend. It lay there for an hour; it lies athwart my memory, black and amazing still, to this day. Clayton had, indeed, passed into the world that lies so near to and so far from our own. And he had gone thither by the only road that mortal man may take. But whether he did indeed pass there by that poor ghost's incantation, or whether he was stricken suddenly by apoplexy in the midst of an idle tale—as the coroner's jury would have us believe—is no matter for my judging; it is just one of those inexplicable riddles that must remain unsolved until the final solution of all things shall come. All I certainly know is that, in the very moment, in the very instant, of concluding those passes, he changed, and staggered, and fell down before us—dead!

Sentence of Death

THOMAS WALSH

Item One, the grimmest and most important item, was the body of a respectable middle-aged pharmacist named Carl Sawyer. Item Two, the usual emotional item, was an attractive blond woman, apparently his widow, who was sobbing hysterically over him when Cochran and McReynolds arrived from the precinct house. Item Three—which, to Cochran and McReynolds, explained everything at first glance and completely—was a rifled cash register. Item Four, the familiar professional headache, was a store crowded with excited and talkative neighbors.

It appeared at first that every one of these people was quite willing to furnish Cochran with detailed and significant information; it developed later, when he had attended to the necessary elimination, that just four of them had actually seen anything. Mrs. Sawyer and a chance customer named Ellen Morison had witnessed the shooting; two others—a husband and wife—glimpsed a man who sprinted out of the drugstore immediately afterward, and raced away in a car which he had parked thirty or forty feet distant, in heavy shadow. This couple agreed, however, on one or two distinguishing facts about the car; and Ellen Morison, a slim and alert young girl with brown hair, intelligent dark eyes and a sensible if excited voice, described the man.

She informed Cochran that fifteen or twenty minutes ago, when she had entered the drugstore, the man had been standing in front of Mr. Sawyer. They were so close together, just a bit left of the cash register, that at first she had taken him for a friend of Mr. Sawyer, and had assumed that Mr. Sawyer was chatting with him; then the man had turned quickly, apparently in panic, looked at her quickly, fired twice at Mr. Sawyer and slapped his left hand out and down at the cash register. It was her opinion that the man was about twenty-eight years old, perhaps older; that he had blond hair, a slim build and a very sharp, narrow jaw. She seemed to be breathless and considerably upset at this time, which was quite natural, but because she remembered the right things about the man—not too many of these, just the striking and obvious details— Cochran was inclined to accept her as perhaps the most dependable witness.

The married couple, who had observed the man from the side and in motion, were the only people who had seen the car. They described it to Cochran as either a black or a dark blue sedan with a dented fender—the right rear fender. One of them thought that the man had been wearing a brown suit and brown shoes; the other, that he had on slacks and a gray sports jacket. They both declared, like Ellen Morison, that the man had been hatless. They both remembered the blond hair.

McReynolds, in the meantime, had attempted first to compose Mrs. Sawyer and then to question her. Both attempts failed. She did not appear to understand who McReynolds was or what he wanted; she would just shake her head dumbly and blindly at him, as if she were still in a condition of severe shock. Cochran left her alone. He was sure then that they wanted a man of a certain age, build and complexion; one who owned or who had access to a cheap sedan with a dented fender; who had a gun; and who, in all likelihood, had also a police record.

He and McReynolds set out to locate this man. They checked pictures and records downtown; they settled on a few possible suspects; they rounded up and detained four of these; and then, two days later, Mrs. Sawyer picked one of the four immediately and hysterically from a line-up.

The married couple supported Mrs. Sawyer's identification, even though, in Cochran's opinion, they could not be half so sure of it as they insisted they were. Ellen Morison would not corroborate. She was the only witness who had impressed Cochran to any extent, and she admitted now that the man they showed her looked something, not too much, like the man who had shot the druggist. She was not prepared to swear that he was the man . . . or that he was not. She told Cochran uncomfortably that she remembered the other man as being older and taller. This one—

She shook her head. McReynolds became impatient with her; Cochran, who suspected that bereaved women like Mrs. Sawyer, after and because of their bereavement, often hit out at the first convenient and likely target, reserved judgment on the identification and went out to do some routine checking.

He discovered these facts: The man Mrs. Sawyer had identified—a tough and surly young truck helper named Johnny Palica, who had a couple of minor arrests to his discredit—lived with a brother-in-law who owned a cheap black sedan. On the night in question, last Thursday, Johnny Palica had been permitted to use the sedan, which had a couple of deep scrapes on the back fender, and had kept it out from early evening until after midnight. Just driving around, he admitted uneasily to Cochran; he had his girl with him. What did anyone do when he had his girl with him? He kept to himself, didn't he? Well, then—

The girl corroborated his story—only the girl. She was not an impressive or disinterested witness. There were still three people who identified Johnny Palica —who, indeed, were more certain of him now than they had been previously—and two of these people also identified the brother-in-law's car. There was another witness, Ellen Morison, who could not seem to make up her mind definitely about him. It was a shaky defense, very badly handled, and the jury convicted. After the conviction, which made the death sentence mandatory, Cochran began to avoid McReynolds for some reason; and then one afternoon he discovered suddenly, with a shock of acute physical discomfort, that McReynolds was beginning also to avoid him.

Each of them knew that an identification made under circumstances of great excitement and tension was not always trustworthy. And apparently each of them, because of a highly developed instinct in such matters, disliked this one. They did not discuss it with each other—it was not their province—but they did not forget about it either. Then March came, and on March fifth, at half past two in the afternoon, Cochran received a phone call which for some time, and in an uneasy and illogical manner, he had been anticipating.

"You remember the Morison girl?" McReynolds asked him, quiet enough about it—perhaps too quiet. "The one who couldn't make up her mind about this Johnny Palica?"

"Who?" Cochran said. But, of course, he remembered her immediately; he pretended not to because he did not want McReynolds to get any ideas about him. "No. I don't seem to— Wait a minute. That one?" He rubbed his mouth carefully. "What's the matter now? What's up?"

McReynolds said stolidly, "Big news. She just told me that Palica isn't the guy. She claims she's positive. You better hustle around here, Ray. I think we're in trouble."

So Cochran got a cab for himself. He found McReynolds and Ellen Morison in an upstairs room at the precinct house, with a busy and impatient young man named Wilson who was somebody unimportant on the district attorney's staff; and he was informed by Wilson that last night, outside a tavern on Third Avenue, Miss Morison saw—or thought she saw—the man who had actually murdered Carl Sawyer. She was positive about him, Wilson added dryly, because he had turned his head and glanced at her exactly the way he had glanced at her that night in the drugstore. She did not think that he had recognized her.

When she came back five or ten minutes afterward with a policeman, he was gone. A bartender in the tavern remembered him. Unfortunately, however, the bartender was unable to furnish any useful information about him. That seemed to be it, Wilson said. A long silence followed.

Cochran was waiting for McReynolds to break it; McReynolds, who looked a bit pale and haggard that afternoon, appeared to be waiting for Cochran.

At last Cochran said, "Well," uncertainly, and sat down on a corner of the desk with his hat pushed back, his lips pursed and his palms on his knees.

"Exactly," said the district attorney's man, as if Cochran had made a very shrewd and penetrating remark. "The whole thing is almost childishly simple. Last night Miss Morison happened to see someone who bore a superficial resemblance to our friend Palica. So immediately—"

Cochran said, "We never found the gun."

"Granted. I wish we had too. But when we've been able to convince a jury without it, I don't see—"

McReynolds said suddenly, angrily and pugnaciously, as if the words burst out of him, "Wait a minute now. Me and Cochran are responsible for him; not you, mister. And I've kind of been sweating a little blood over it lately, if that means anything. I don't like this thing. I never did."

He went that far. Cochran—they were boosting each other along now—took his right palm from his knee, turned it over, examined it and decided to go a bit further.

Cochran said, "I've seen nervous and hysterical women like Mrs. Sawyer identify cops who were just put into a line-up to fill it out. Sure, that married couple agreed with her; witnesses like them always go along with the first person who makes up her mind. I kind of agree with Mac here. Let's talk this over."

Ellen Morison, who appeared nervous but determined, glanced at him and said quietly, "Thank you. I'm beginning to feel better. I testified at the trial that the man who shot Mr. Sawyer—the man I'm telling you I saw outside that tavern last night— seemed to be older and thinner, and a lot taller, than the man you arrested. I was treated then as if I didn't know what I was talking about. I wasn't sure, or I told myself that I wasn't sure. But now I am. And now I want something done about it."

The man from the district attorney's office stopped looking annoyed and angry, and started looking concerned and worried. More discussion ensued; then it was decided that the first thing to do, if they wanted a reasonable standard of comparison, was to give Ellen Morison another and longer look at Johnny Palica. The lieutenant, who had been careful enough to disassociate himself entirely from this interview, was called in. The lieutenant phoned downtown, and then downtown made arrangements with a Captain Mooney.

At half past eight the next morning, Cochran and the girl drove up to—to that place, as Cochran had begun to think of it, very uneasily—and found Mooney waiting for them. They shook hands and conferred briefly; then Mooney glanced sidewise, without much facial expression, at Ellen Morison, and conducted them out of the visitors' room and into a corridor which had high barred windows.

They went by two men who were dressed in the uniform of prison guards; they stopped in front of a steel door which was unlocked from within, and they waited for several moments, even though they had Mooney with them, in front of another door just beyond the first, and quite as massive and powerful looking, until the one through which they had been admitted was closed and locked.

Afterward there were more doors, more prison guards, more corridors, and finally a courtyard and another and rather isolated building. When they entered that building, Cochran, who did not have to be told what it was, touched his lips in a nervous and delicate manner with his tongue. He did not look at Ellen Morison. He did not make any attempt to speak to her.

They stopped presently outside a room. It was this kind of room. It had yellow composition walls and a brown baseboard. It had a cheap oak table with a soiled blotter on it and a clean ash tray; it had two chairs, one window and one powerful ceiling lighting fixture. In this room there was a peculiar but unmistakable sort of presence waiting for Cochran. He knew why; he and McReynolds were chiefly responsible for it. He entered.

Ellen Morison, who was not to talk to Johnny Palica, but only to observe him through a grille concealed in the outside door at normal eye level, remained in the hall; but Captain Mooney entered behind Cochran, glanced at him and went out through another exit. Almost as soon as Cochran was left alone, the harsh light in the room and the intense stillness made him restless and uncomfortable. Several minutes passed; to Cochran they seemed to pass with extreme slowness. Then there were steps in the inside corridor, and Cochran jabbed his hands into his hip pockets, turned and braced himself, at least physically, for this.

Mooney came in. "All right now," Mooney said, in the simplest and most matter-of-fact tone. "In here, Johnny. You remember Ray Cochran, don't you?"

Cochran spoke the first words that came into his head. "Sure," Cochran said, his lips feeling like wet flour. "Sure, he does. . . . Come on in and sit down, fella. How've you been?"

He had intended to shake hands here, but he stopped awkwardly after starting the gesture, because Johnny Palica did not appear to recognize him. Because of that, and of what it meant, the tone which Cochran had decided to employ—official, authoritative, but not unfriendly—became, after the first moment or two, a shabby and ridiculous pretense. There was no necessity for it. Johnny Palica was whiter, quieter and much more nervous than Cochran remembered; and as soon as he recognized Cochran, he made a desperate and pathetic attempt to ingratiate himself.

There was no more toughness or defiance in him. He was well broken. Not by Mooney, not by a couple of months' imprisonment, but by a certain idea and a certain date which Cochran and McReynolds had arranged for him. He grinned anxiously, and when it seemed that Cochran was not going to respond to the grin, he widened it in a slow, clumsy manner, with much effort.

"Fine," he said. "I'm okay, Mr. Cochran. I'm—
You got some news?"

It was the first time he had ever addressed Cochran
by that title; it was a small thing, and it was intoler-
able. Cochran began to sweat at the same time, be-
cause he had been warned by Mooney not to excite
Johnny Palica and not to tell him anything about
the girl until they had one or two definite facts to
go on; he muttered that there didn't seem to be
anything new in this thing, not yet. Headquarters,
he added, just thought Johnny Palica might want to
go over his story about that night again. If he did—

He did. He nodded violently. So Cochran put a
couple of questions to him, the answers to which he
and McReynolds had already checked, in so far as
was humanly possible, months ago; and then Coch-
ran pretended to listen intently to what Johnny
Palica said to him, and even checked everything off,
detail by detail, in a pocket notebook. "Sure, sure,"
Cochran muttered, even when the words had no
particular application to what had preceded them.
That was another thing, he'd add huskily, which he
and McReynolds would check right away. They'd
talk to Johnny Palica's girl, of course. And they'd go
back carefully over the whole affair. They'd—

He would have done anything, said anything,
promised anything, to get out of that room quickly,
to remove himself from the way in which Johnny
Palica kept watching him. As if he wanted help and
reassurance from somewhere, Cochran thought
savagely; not as if he expected it; as if he just wanted
it. And then, when Mooney concluded the interview,
when Cochran picked up his coat and mumbled

something hearty and cheerful and got out of there, it was worse than before. In the outside hall, Ellen Morison was waiting for him.

She was quite pale, her eyes looked extremely odd, and apparently she did not want to talk to Cochran any more than Cochran wanted to talk to her. All she did was to shake her head at him. Of course, Cochran thought, she meant that he and McReynolds had the wrong man in here. That— He turned away from her. He did not ask himself whether she was right about Johnny Palica; before he had half completed his turn something much worse had happened to him. He felt it.

Later that afternoon, McReynolds also appeared to feel it. He did not discuss the thing logically with Cochran; he just nodded a couple of times, swallowed once, got his hat and drove over with Cochran to interview Mrs. Sawyer.

They discovered that something had happened to her, too, because she was no longer a pink and cunning little woman with demure blue eyes and fluffy gold hair. She had aged noticeably; and by gradual degrees, as Cochran talked to her, she became withdrawn, bitter, nervous and finally hysterical again.

She was still sure that it was Johnny Palica who had murdered her husband; now, Cochran reflected hopelessly, hatred and loneliness had done their usual sort of job on her. So he and McReynolds did not tackle the two supporting witnesses; that was useless unless and until they had first shaken Mrs. Sawyer. That evening McReynolds went downtown and started rechecking the files for another picture and description that might approximate Johnny Palica's;

and at almost the same hour Cochran and Ellen Morison established a vigil over on Third Avenue, outside the Shamrock tavern.

They would park there, in Cochran's coupé, for five or six hours a night—the late hours—and for seven nights a week. They would stay there until half past one in the morning, with elevated trains rumbling overhead monotonously, with March wind lashing at them, and then Cochran would drive the girl home and go home himself after a cup of coffee somewhere. But he would not sleep any too well—the coffee, perhaps, or perhaps other things. He would remain restless for a while, doze again, and then rouse suddenly with the conviction in him that someone had been shouting his name just now, at an infinite distance, but quite clearly. He never managed to hear the voice—not as sound—but at the same time he recognized it, and in the end it came to have its own sort of existence for him.

He knew what it wanted from Mr. Cochran. He knew that much the first time it happened to him, and every time afterward, but he could not do anything helpful because, if there was going to be any appeal made on the basis of new evidence, he and McReynolds needed this other man. They could not find him. They could not imagine how to find him. They had twelve weeks at first, and then ten, and then eight, and then six. But nothing came up, either at headquarters or outside the Shamrock tavern.

Occasionally, after his end had dried up on him, McReynolds spent a couple of uncomfortable hours with them, but for the rest of the time Cochran and the girl had no company but themselves. At that period Cochran could have described the girl well, at least partially, although he himself did not seem to retain any personal or individual impression of her. She had dark hair, of which at times he had a vague sort of recollection, and the softness and delicacy around the mouth which had never been particularly attractive to him in other girls. He liked her all right, but he did not think about her as he had thought about one or two other girls. There was no opportunity. On those endless and monotonous evenings they rarely conversed at length because the appalling significance of their watch made ordinary conversation nearly impossible; and yet, despite that, they achieved a kind of intimacy which would have seemed very new and unusual to Cochran if he had been in any position to consider it.

Every so often, instead of just sitting there and waiting for the right man to show up, she worried him by attempting to force a resemblance between the person they wanted and some unimportant client of the Shamrock tavern. And so once, in their sixth week, he explained impersonally to her that it was rather silly to get excited about this, because the only thing they could use here was patience and more patience and again patience. You couldn't rush these things, Cochran said. You waited them out. They generally came to some sort of conclusion in the long run.

But she noticed at once that Cochran did not commit himself, here and now, as to the sort of conclusion they were going to reach outside the Sham-

rock tavern. She sat back in her corner of the seat
and then glanced at him.

She said, "I suppose they do. Only this time"—she
put her lips together for a moment—"they simply
have to work out in the right way. Not that I'm dis-
couraged about anything; I can't make myself be-
lieve for one minute that a mistake like this, a cruel
and vicious mistake, is going to be—well, permitted.
We'll find him. You wait and see."

"I hope we do," Cochran said. But when he looked
out at Third Avenue—shabby, rain-swept, deserted,
watery yellow light spilling across the black pave-
ment in front of the tavern—he felt heavily de-
pressed. "We've got a chance, anyway."

She said, with a confidence that surprised Coch-
ran, "Oh, we've got more than that . . . much more.
Things don't happen that way. If they did, there
wouldn't be much point to the whole mess."

"Maybe there isn't," Cochran said.

"Of course that's silly," Ellen Morison said. She
was very calm about it. "Or out-and-out horrible.
We've just got to believe that certain things are true
and important. If we don't—"

"What things?" Cochran asked; it was the first
discussion that had interested him even slightly.
"You name a couple. I'd like to find out about them."

So it was that, of all subjects, they began arguing
the most profound and imponderable one. They
would argue it from exactly opposed viewpoints—not
with the technical skill and finish of philosophers,
but from each of their individual accumulations of
judgment, experience and intuition. If she knew

half the things he knew, Cochran would say darkly, or if she understood half the facts about the uglier side of human nature, she wouldn't talk so much about this or that being permitted or else not permitted. Things happened; that was all you could say about them.

She was earnest at first, and then irritated, and then scornful, but, of course, she never convinced Cochran. What he did admit—reluctantly and not to her—was that it might be pretty comforting to see this as Ellen Morison saw it, to believe in reasons for things, to be sure that someone, somewhere, was keeping an eye peeled in Ray Cochran's direction or Johnny Palica's.

An idea of that kind would have provided him with some useful insulation. He admitted so much, again privately; and then, little by little, and very stubbornly, he became a bit weaker in regard to his own arguments, and a bit more responsive in regard to hers. Friday night at about half past ten, he had just declared that perhaps people did achieve happier and more useful lives when they shared Ellen Morison's belief, and not his, but that didn't prove anything at all, as Cochran saw it. True was true. And if—

A man who did not resemble Johnny Palica at all parked in front of them and went into the Shamrock tavern. Cochran glanced at him and dismissed him, but Ellen Morison froze up, made some sort of breathlessly inarticulate sound and grabbed at Cochran.

He got out of the car slowly, his heart thumping.

He said, "All right. You stick here. We don't want him to know anything about you yet. I'll be back as soon as I get a better look at him." Then he walked around the front of the coupé and into the tavern . . . and went numb.

The man whom Ellen Morison had just identified for him was at least four inches taller than Johnny Palica, noticeably older, noticeably stouter; there was, apart from his blond hair, not even the slightest physical similarity between them. *What is this?* Cochran asked himself very quietly. Something broke in him. He strode back to the coupé to that girl, but what he felt for her at this moment was a mixture of cold rage and ferocious contempt.

Did she understand, Cochran demanded thickly, what she had been doing for the last six weeks to him and McReynolds? Did she have any idea of how she had put them up on the rack, and kept them there, and twisted the wheel night after night until each of them was just about out of his head?

She looked very pale and excited, but not as if she understood what he was talking about.

"What's the matter?" she said. She was still breathless. "Why don't you— He's the man, Cochran! I know he is! Do you think I could ever—"

"Then where's the mistake?" Cochran almost shouted at her. He began pounding his fist, with an impression of infinite restrained force, against the roof of the car. "How did anybody ever take this guy for Palica? You kept telling us all along that they looked like each other. That's the thing we were going to spring on everybody. That's all we had."

"But he does!" She pushed her head out anxiously at him. "Of course, he's grown that mustache. That's what you—"

Cochran spun away from her, maddened; then he got into the car blindly, closed the door, cradled his arms in front of him on the steering wheel and laid the right side of his face against them. That way he did not have to so much as look at her.

"He grew too," Cochran said. His voice hated her. "He grew four inches. Me and McReynolds were the dumbheads; all along the district attorney's office had you down for just what you were. We figured you knew what you were talking about. We were stupid enough to go through hell because somebody like you—"

She faltered out several jerky sentences. Why was he talking like this? Hadn't they waited together for the man all these weeks? And now wasn't he in their hands?

Cochran would not answer her. The only clear idea in his mind was that if this man had looked like Johnny Palica, they might have got the witnesses to admit confusion and perhaps error. This way no one —not Mrs. Sawyer, not the married couple, not the district attorney's office—would even consider him. So—

The girl shook him again. Then she whispered painfully, "Listen, Cochran. Will you please, please listen to me? I tell you—"

The man came out of the Shamrock tavern, had a bit of trouble in starting his car—Cochran would scarcely have noticed him otherwise—and pulled out into Third Avenue. After a few moments, Cochran

—a good, careful cop—turned on his ignition and pulled into Third Avenue after him. They drove north. By now, of course, Cochran was following him more by training and dogged instinct than because of any remaining hope in this angle. He still hated the girl; he still felt that she had first argued with him, and then convinced him, and then—most shameful of all—got him almost ready to believe Ray Cochran was something a lot more significant than an ordinary precinct detective who had been instructed to straighten something out, and who had torn himself into little pieces because he was unable to manage it. Always merry and bright, Cochran thought savagely, that was the ticket. There were reasons for everything—oh, sure! Good and logical reasons, if you were stupid enough to understand what they were. If—

Twice she attempted to speak to him; twice Cochran would not listen to her. Then the sedan in front of him turned into a side street that seemed hazily familiar. He followed. He saw, halfway along this street, an apartment house which was also vaguely familiar to him, and then, when the sedan parked in front of it, he recognized that building with a complete and paralyzing shock.

He whispered something. He drove past the sedan, past the man who was ringing a bell in the apartment vestibule, and parked several houses away. He noticed without hate, with a complete detachment, that Ellen Morison was looking white, scared and miserable. What was the matter with her now? Cochran asked himself. What was she—

He got her out of the car. He told her where to

phone McReynolds, and what to tell him; then he moved back carefully to the sedan which he had followed up here from the Shamrock tavern. All his thoughts had become quick, sharp and decisive. His heart had begun to thump heavily again. An old car with a new paint job, Cochran saw now; no marks on it. Of course. Not so much as a scratch on the rear fender. But he and McReynolds would find the shop where that paint job had been put on, and where the right rear fender had been hammered out; and then, Cochran told himself grimly, he'd get that married couple to identify this sedan if he had to knock their heads together.

He left the sedan and secluded himself in a dim hallway just down the street from it. The girl came back, and Cochran waved her over imperatively to him, but he did not bother with explanations because he had very little time or attention for her at that moment. He got out two cigarettes and smoked them in extraordinarily long draughts; then McReynolds and a couple of precinct men cruised past him in a department car. Cochran whistled twice. McReynolds stopped.

They discussed matters for a moment or two, Cochran explaining why he was up here, McReynolds grasping the explanation almost immediately. After that the precinct men went around to the rear entrance and to the fire escapes, and Cochran and McReynolds entered the apartment house after ringing a bell on the top floor—which was not the floor they wanted. They went up two flights, rapidly. They each took deep breaths. Then Cochran rang a bell on that landing, and after some delay the door was open about three inches and Cochran put a palm against it, shoved and walked in.

The blond man with the dinky little mustache was in there. Cochran walked up to him, gave him a very tight, ugly smile, and hit him. Cochran hit him very hard, and for no apparent reason at all. He just felt that way. He felt fine. At the same moment, McReynolds did what he was supposed to do. McReynolds took care of Mrs. Sawyer.

Of course, after the event it was all obvious. Then Cochran told himself that he and McReynolds should have paid much more attention to the story Ellen Morison had told them. Hadn't she said that when she entered the drugstore, Mr. Sawyer and the holdup man were standing and talking together like old friends? And hadn't Mrs. Sawyer got all excited and hysterical when he and McReynolds had gone back to question her as to how sure she was about Johnny Palica? What should have been at least indicated then was that she could be making some attempt to cover up the real killer, and that, consequently, she herself might be involved in the murder.

It was also clear that Ellen Morison had walked in at just the wrong moment. Mrs. Sawyer and her masculine friend had thought up a perfectly simple and effective method through which to rid themselves of a husband who was getting along in years, and who owned a profitable business. They had attempted to arrange everything so that Mrs. Sawyer, who was supposed to be the only close witness, would describe a man to the police who did not resemble the gentleman friend in any respect; and then Ellen Morison had appeared just when the gentleman friend had nerved himself up to it, and had got himself into so much of a panic that he was unable to postpone it.

And so, on that first night, Mrs. Sawyer had pretended grief and horror, and had refused to understand McReynolds' questions, because it was necessary for her to learn as quickly as possible what Ellen Morison remembered about the man. If she had differed too much with the girl's description, which was fairly accurate, she might have started Cochran and McReynolds nosing around; and so she agreed with it, and identified Johnny Palica.

She did that to cover herself, obviously, and to keep the police busy on another angle. And then the married couple supported her identification, and Johnny Palica was unable to prove his whereabouts, and everything had begun to work out very nicely for Mrs. Sawyer and her friend. Until he had done the one thing he should never have done—until he had visited Mrs. Sawyer at home, very late at night, in the same apartment house where Cochran and McReynolds had questioned her weeks ago.

As soon as Cochran had recognized the apartment house, he had asked himself the natural question: What connection was there between this man and an attractive little woman like Mrs. Sawyer? Only one answer had seemed at all feasible. It explained immediately why Mrs. Sawyer had identified Johnny Palica, and why Ellen Morison had refused to identify him. Now Cochran was unable to understand why he had never considered that particular aspect before; and even after McReynolds and the other two men had got Mrs. Sawyer and her masculine friend

—screaming at each other, blaming each other—
into the department car and had started downtown
with them, the whole thing continued to exasperate
Cochran as the evidence of a colossal personal stupid-
ity.

"Because in something like this we always check
on the wife or husband," he insisted to Ellen Morison,
who was still waiting downstairs for him. "Always!
We'd have done it this time if you hadn't been there
to back up her story. But when you saw the whole
thing happen just in front of you— Well, how were
we going to question it? What for? It wasn't reason-
able."

"But I suppose this is," Ellen Morison said. She
looked very tired and miserable. "Now everything's
fine. If those two make you ashamed of the whole
human race, that doesn't matter at all. It's just—"
Her mouth twisted. "Get me away from here, Coch-
ran, please. I'm scared. I don't want to hear anything
else about this. All I—"

She began shivering. Cochran soothed her. There
was a perspective you attained in such matters, Coch-
ran said; the one important thing was that you did
not permit an event of this nature to throw you off
balance, to make you cynical, to— He stopped, there;
he remembered suddenly that not too long ago he
had been arguing a similar question from another
position. Ah, forget it, he thought angrily. Who un-
derstood why things like this happened the way they
did? Who wanted to? He could go this far with
Ellen Morison—they worked out pretty well fre-
quently. They had worked out now, hadn't they?

It did not strike him at once that he had gone

much further with her than he had ever gone with anyone else. When it did strike him, he decided that perhaps there was some sort of significance there. He got her into the car and patted her hand tentatively and murmured to her. On other nights, Cochran decided, and under different conditions, they could argue the verities, but just now he would have to be very firm and sensible about this.

He was. He started the car and got her away from there. They drove aimlessly at first, with Cochran very quiet and reassuring with her, and then he took her home and went home himself. He slept fourteen hours with nothing disturbing him, not even the garbage trucks or the morning traffic, and when he woke up at last, he discovered that he felt fine and comfortable, and that he was thinking about Ellen Morison. *Say,* Cochran thought slowly, *what is this?* But he knew. He knew almost as soon as the question completed itself.

Spring Fever

DOROTHY SALISBURY DAVIS

Sarah Shepherd watched her husband come down the stairs. He set his suitcase at the front door, checked his watch with the hall clock, and examined beneath his chin in the mirror. There was one spot he sometimes missed in shaving. He stepped back and examined himself full length, frowning a little. He was getting paunchy and not liking it. That critical of himself, how much more critical of her he might be. But he said nothing either in criticism or compliment, and she remembered, uncomfortably, doing all sorts of stunts to attract his eye: coy things —more becoming a girl than a woman of fifty-five. She did not feel her twelve years over Gerald . . . most of the time. Scarcely aware of the movement, she traced the shape of her stomach with her finger-tips.

Gerald brought his sample spice kit into the living-room and opened it. The aroma would linger for some time after he was gone. "There's enough wood, dear, if it gets cold tonight," he said. "And I wish you wouldn't haul things from the village. That's what delivery trucks are for . . ." He numbered his solicitudes as he did the bottles in the sample case, and with the same noncommittal attention.

As he took the case from the table, she got up and went to the door with him. On the porch he hesitated a moment, flexing his shoulders and breathing deeply. "On a morning like this I almost wish I drove a car."

"You could learn, Gerald. You could reach your accounts in half the time, and . . ."

"No, dear. I'm quite content with my paper in the bus, and in a town a car's a nuisance." He stooped and brushed her cheek with his lips. "Hello there!" he called out as he straightened up.

Her eyes followed the direction in which he had called. Their only close neighbor, a vegetable and flower grower, was following a plow behind his horse, his head as high as the horse's was low, the morning wind catching his thatch of gray hair and pointing it like a shock of wheat.

"That old boy has the life," Gerald said. "When I'm his age that's for me."

"He's not so old," she said.

"No. I guess he's not at that," he said. "Well, dear, I must be off. Till tomorrow night, take care of yourself."

His step down the road was almost jaunty. It was strange that he could not abide an automobile. But not having one was rather in the pattern. A car would be a tangible link between his life away and theirs at home. Climbing into it of an evening, she would have a feeling of his travels. The dust would rub off on her. As it was, the most she had of him away was the lingering pungency of a sample spice kit.

When he was out of sight she began her household chores—the breakfast dishes, beds, dusting. She had brought altogether too many things from the city. Her mother had left seventy years' accumulation in the old house, and now it was impossible to lay a book on the table without first moving a figurine, a vase, a piece of delft. Really the place was a clutter of bric-a-brac. Small wonder Gerald had changed toward her. It was not marriage that had changed him —it was this house, and herself settling in it like an old Buddha with a bowl of incense in his lap.

A queer thing that this should occur to her only now, she thought. But it was not the first time. She was only now finding a word for it. Nor had Gerald always been this remote. Separating a memory of a particular moment in their early days, she caught his eyes searching hers—not numbering her years, as she might think were he to do it now, but measuring his own worth in her esteem.

She lined up several ornaments that might be put away, or better, sold to a junkman. But from the line-up she drew out pieces of which she had grown especially fond. They had become like children to her, as Gerald made children of the books with which he spent his evenings home. Making a basket of her apron she swept the whole tableful of trinkets into it.

Without a downward glance, she hurried them to the ash-box in the backyard. Shed of them, she felt a good deal lighter, and with the May wind in her face and the sun gentle, like an arm across her shoulders, she felt very nearly capersome. Across the fence the jonquils were in bloom, and the tulips, nodding like fat little boys. Mr. Joyce had unhitched the horse. He saw her then.

"Fine day this morning," he called. He gave the horse a slap on the rump that sent him into the pasture, and came to the fence.

"I'm admiring the flowers," she said.

"Lazy year for them. Two weeks late they are."

"Is that a fact?" Of course it's a fact, she thought. A silly remark, and another after it: "I've never seen them lovelier, though. What comes out next?"

"Snaps, I guess this year. Late roses, too. The iris don't sell much, so I'm letting 'em come or stay as they like."

"That should bring them out."

"Now isn't that the truth? You can coax and tickle all year and not get a bloom for thanks. Turn your back on 'em and they run you down."

Like love, she thought, and caught her tongue. But a splash of color took to her cheeks.

"Say, you're looking nice, Mrs. Shepherd, if you don't mind my saying it."

"Thank you. A touch of spring, I suppose."

"Don't it just send your blood racing? How would you like an armful of these?"

"I'd be very pleased, Mr. Joyce. But I'd like to pay you for them."

"Indeed not. I won't sell half of them—they come in a heap."

She watched his expert hand nip the blooms. He was already tanned, and he stooped and rose with a fine grace. In all the years he had lived next to them he had never been in the house, nor they in his except the day of his wife's funeral. He hadn't grieved much, she commented to Gerald at the time. And little wonder. The woman was pinched and whining, and there wasn't a sunny day she didn't expect a drizzle before nightfall. Now that Sarah thought of it, Joyce looked younger than he did when Mrs. Joyce was still alive.

"There. For goodness' sakes, Mr. Joyce. That's plenty."

"I'd give you the field of them this morning," he said, piling her arms with the flowers.

"I've got half of it now."

"And what a picture you are with them."

"Well, I must hurry them into water," she said. "Thank you."

She hastened toward the house, flying like a young flirt from her first conquest, and aware of the pleased eye following her. The whole morning glowed in the company she kept with the flowers. She snapped off the radio: no tears for Miss Julia today. At noon she heard Mr. Joyce's wagon roll out of the yard as as he started to his highway stand. She watched at the window. He looked up and lifted his hat.

At odd moments during the day, she thought of him. He had given her a fine sense of herself and she was grateful. She began to wish that Gerald was returning that night. Take your time, Sarah, she told herself. You don't put away old habits and the years like bric-a-brac. She had softened up, no doubt of it. Not a fat woman, maybe, but plump. Plump. She repeated the word aloud. It had the sound of a potato falling into a tub of water.

But the afternoon sun was warm and the old

laziness came over her. Only when Mr. Joyce came home, his voice in a song ahead of him, did she pull herself up. She hurried a chicken out of the refrigerator and then called to him from the porch.

"Mr. Joyce, would you like to have supper with me? Gerald won't be home, and I do hate cooking for just myself."

"Oh, that'd be grand. I've nothing in the house but a shank of ham that a dog wouldn't bark for. What can I bring?"

"Just come along when you're ready."

Sarah, she told herself, setting the table, you're an old bat trying your wings in daylight. A half-hour later she glanced out of the window in time to see Mr. Joyce skipping over the fence like a stiff-legged colt. He was dressed in his Sunday suit and brandishing a bottle as he cleared the barbed wire. Sarah choked down a lump of apprehension. For all that she planned a little fun for herself, she was not up to galloping through the house with an old Don Juan on her heels. Mr. Joyce, however, was a well-mannered guest. The bottle was May wine. He drank sparingly and was lavish in his praise of the dinner.

"You've no idea the way I envy you folks, Mrs. Shepherd. Your husband especially. How can he bear the times he spends away?"

He bears it all too well, she thought. "It's his work. He's a salesman. He sells spices."

Mr. Joyce showed a fine set of teeth in his smile—his own teeth, she marveled, tracing her bridgework with the tip of her tongue while he spoke. "Then he's got sugar and spice and everything nice, as they say."

What a one he must have been with the girls, she thought, and to marry a quince as he had. It was done in a hurry no doubt, and maybe at the end of a big stick.

"It must be very lonesome for you since Mrs. Joyce passed away," she said more lugubriously than she intended. After all the woman was gone three years.

"No more than when she was with me." His voice matched hers in seriousness. "It's a hard thing to say of the dead, but if she hasn't improved her disposition since, we're all in for a damp eternity." He stuffed the bowl of his pipe. "Do you mind?"

"No, I like the smell of tobacco around the house."

"Does your husband smoke?"

"Yes," she said in some surprise at the question.

"He didn't look the kind to follow a pipe," he said, pulling noisily at his. "No, dear lady," he added when the smoke was shooting from it, "you're blessed in not knowing the plague of a silent house."

It occurred to her then that he was exploring the situation. She would give him small satisfaction. "Yes. I count that among my blessings."

There was a kind of amusement in his eyes. You're as lonesome as me, old girl, they seemed to say, and their frankness bade her to add: "But I do wish Gerald was home more of the time."

"Ah, well, he's at the age when most men look to a last trot around the paddock," he said, squinting at her through the smoke.

"Gerald is only forty-three," she said, loosing the words before she knew it.

"There's some take it at forty, and others among us leaping after it from the rocking chair."

The conversation had taken a turn she certainly had not intended, and she found herself threshing around in it. Beating a fire with a feather duster. "There's the moon," she said, charging to the window as though to wave to an old friend.

"Aye," he said, "there's the moon. Are you up to a trot in it?"

"What did you say, Mr. Joyce?"

"I'd better say what I was thinking first. If I hitch Micky to the old rig, would you take a turn with me on the Mill Pond Road?"

She saw his reflection in the window, a smug, daring little grin on his face. In sixteen years of settling she had forgotten her way with men. But it was something you never really forgot. Like riding a bicycle, you picked it up again after a few turns. "I would," she said.

The horse ahead of the rig was a different animal from the one on the plow that morning. Mr. Joyce had no more than thrown the reins over his rump than he took a turn that almost tumbled Sarah into the sun frames. But Mr. Joyce leaped to the seat and pulled Micky up on his hind legs with one hand and Sarah down to her cushion with the other, and they were off in the wake of the moon. . . .

The sun was full in her face when Sarah awoke the next morning. As usual, she looked to see if Gerald were in his bed by way of acclimating herself to the

day and its routine. With the first turn of her body
she decided that a gallop in a rusty-springed rig was
not the way to assert a stay of youth. She lay a few
moments thinking about it and then got up to an
aching sense of folly. It remained with her through
the day, giving way at times to a nostalgia for her
bric-a-brac. She had never realized how much of
her life was spent in the care of it.

By the time Gerald came home she was almost the
person he had left the day before. She had held out
against the ornaments, however. Only the flowers
decorated the living-room. It was not until supper
was over and Gerald had settled with his book that
he commented.

"Sarah, what happened to the old Chinese philoso-
pher?"

"I put him away. Didn't you notice? I took all the
clutter out of here."

He looked about him vacantly as though trying to
recall some of it. "So you did. I'll miss that old boy.
He gave me something to think about."

"What?"

"Oh, I don't know. Confucius says . . . that sort of
thing."

"He wasn't a philosopher at all," she said, having
no notion what he was. "He was a farmer."

"Was he? Well, there's small difference." He
opened the book.

"Aren't the flowers nice, Gerald?"

"Beautiful."

"Mr. Joyce gave them to me, fresh out of his
garden."

"That's nice."

"Must you read every night, Gerald? I'm here all day with no one to talk to, and when you get home you stick your nose into a book . . ." When the words were half out she regretted them. "I didn't tell you, Gerald. I had Mr. Joyce to dinner last night."

"That was very decent of you, dear. The old gentleman must find it lonesome."

"I don't think so. It was a relief to him when his wife died."

Gerald looked up. "Did he say that?"

"Not in so many words, but practically."

"He must be a strange sort. What did she die of?"

"I don't remember. A heart condition, I think."

"Interesting." He returned to his book.

"After dinner he took me for a ride in the horse and buggy. All the way to Cos Corner and back."

"Ha!" was his only comment.

"Gerald, you're getting fat."

He looked up. "I don't think so. I'm about my usual weight. A couple of pounds maybe."

"Then you're carrying it in your stomach. I noticed you've cut the elastic out of your shorts."

"These new fabrics," he said testily.

"They're preshrunken," she said. "It's your stomach. And haven't you noticed how you pull at your collar all the time?"

"I meant to mention that, Sarah. You put too much starch in them."

"I ran out of starch last week and forgot to order it. You can take a size fifteen-and-a-half now."

"Good Lord, Sarah, you're going to tell me next I should wear a horse collar." He let the book slide

closed between his thighs. "I get home only three or
four nights a week. I'm tired. I wish you wouldn't
aggravate me, dear."

She went to his chair and sat on the arm of it.
"Did you know that I was beginning to wonder if
you'd respond to the poke of a hat-pin?"

He looked directly up at her for the first time in
what had seemed like years. His eyes fell away. "I've
been working very hard, dear."

"I don't care what you've been doing, Gerald. I'm
just glad to find out that you're still human."

He slid his arm around her and tightened it.

"Aren't spring flowers lovely?" she said.

"Yes," he said, "and so is spring."

She leaned across him and took a flower from the
vase. She lingered there a moment. He touched his
hand to her. "And you're lovely, too."

This is simple, she thought, getting upright again.
If the rabbit had sat on a thistle, he'd have won the
race.

"The three most beautiful things in the world,"
Gerald said thoughtfully, "a white bird flying, a
field of wheat, and a woman's body."

"Is that your own, Gerald?"

"I don't know. I think it is."

"It's been a long time since you wrote any poetry.
You did nice things once."

"That's how I got you," he said quietly.

"And I got you with an old house. I remember the
day my mother's will was probated. The truth,
Gerald—wasn't it then you made up your mind?"

He didn't speak for a moment, and then it was a

continuance of some thought of his own, a subtle twist of association. "Do you remember the piece I wrote on the house?"

"I read it the other day. I often read them again."

"Do you, Sarah? And never a mention of it."

It was almost all the reading she did any more. His devotion to books had turned her from them. "Remember how you used to let me read them to you, Gerald? You thought that I was the only one besides yourself who could do them justice."

"I remember."

"Or was that flattery?"

He smiled. "It was courtship, I'm afraid. No one ever thinks anybody else can do his poetry justice. But Sarah, do you know—I'd listen tonight if you'd read some of them. Just for old times' sake."

For old times' sake, she thought, getting the folder from the cabinet and settling opposite him. He was slouched in his chair, pulling at his pipe, his eyes half-closed. Long ago this same contemplativeness in him had softened the first shock of the difference in their ages.

"I've always liked this one best— *The Morning of My Days*."

"Well you might," he murmured. "It was written for you."

She read one piece after another, wondering now and then what pictures he was conjuring up of the moment he had written them. He would suck on his pipe at times. The sound was like a baby pulling at an empty bottle. She was reading them well, she thought, giving them a mellow vibrance, an old love's tenderness. Surely there was a moment coming when he would rise from the chair and come to her. Still he sat, his eyes almost closed, the pipe now in hand on the chair's arm. A huskiness crept into her voice, so rarely used to this length any more, and she thought of the nightingale's singing, the thorn against its breast. A slit of pain in her own throat pressed her to greater effort, for the poems were almost done.

She stopped abruptly, a phrase unfinished, at a noise in the room. The pipe had clattered to the floor, Gerald's hand still cupped in its shape, but his chin was now on his breast. Laying the folder aside, she went over and picked up the pipe with a rather empty regret, as she would pick up a bird that had fallen dead at her feet.

Gerald's departure in the morning was in the tradition of all their days, even to the kiss upon her cheek and the words, "Till tomorrow evening, dear, take care."

Take care, she thought, going indoors. Take care of what? For what? Heat a boiler of water to cook an egg? She hurried her chores and dressed. When she saw Mr. Joyce hitch the wagon of flowers, she locked the door and waited boldly at the road for him.

"May I have a lift to the highway?" she called out, as he reined up beside her.

"You may have a lift to the world's end, Mrs. Shepherd. Give me your hand." He gave the horse its rein when she was beside him. "I see your old fella's taken himself off again. I daresay it gave him a laugh, our ride in the moonlight."

"It was a giddy business," she said.

"Did you enjoy yourself?"

"I did. But I paid for it afterwards." Her hand went to her back.

"I let out a squeal now and then bending over, myself. But I counted it cheap for the pleasure we had. I'll take you into the village. I've to buy a length of hose anyway. Or do you think you'll be taken for a fool riding in on a wagon?"

"It won't be the first time," she said. "My life's full of foolishness."

"It's a wise fool who laughs at his own folly. We've that in common, you and me. Where'll we take our supper tonight?"

He was sharp as mustard.

"You're welcome to come over," she said.

He nodded. "I'll fetch us a steak, and we'll give Micky his heels again after."

Sarah got off at the post office and stayed in the building until Joyce was out of sight—Joyce and the gapers who had stopped to see her get out of the wagon. Getting in was one thing, getting out another. A bumblebee after a violet. It was time for this trip. She walked to the doctor's office and waited her turn among the villagers.

"I thought I'd come in for a checkup, Dr. Philips," she said at his desk. "And maybe you'd give me a diet."

"A diet?" He took off his glasses and measured her with the naked eye.

"I'm getting a little fat," she said. "They say it's a strain on the heart at my age."

"Your heart could do for a woman of twenty," he said, "but we'll have a listen."

"I'm not worried about my heart, Doctor, you understand. I just feel that I'd like to lose a few pounds."

"Uh-huh," he said. "Open your dress." He got his stethoscope.

Diet, apparently, was the rarest of his prescriptions. Given as a last resort. She should have gone into town for this, not to a country physician who measured a woman by the children she bore. "The woman next door to us died of a heart condition," she said, as though that should explain her visit.

"Who's that?" he asked, putting away the instrument.

"Mrs. Joyce. Some years ago."

"She had a heart to worry about. Living for years on stimulants. Yours is as sound as a bullet. Let's have your arm."

She pushed up her sleeve as he prepared the apparatus for measuring her blood pressure. That, she felt, was rising out of all proportion. She was ashamed of herself before this man, and angry at herself for it, and at him for no reason more than that he was being patient with her. "We're planning insurance," she lied. "I wanted our own doctor's opinion first."

"You'll have no trouble getting it, Mrs. Shepherd. And no need of a diet." He grinned and removed the apparatus. "Go easy on potatoes and bread, and on the sweets. You'll outlive your husband by twenty years. How is he, by the way?"

"Fine. Just fine, Doctor, thank you."

What a nice show you're making of yourself these days, Sarah, she thought, outdoors again. Well, come in or go out, old girl, and slam the door behind you . . .

Micky took to his heels that night. He had had a day of ease, and new shoes were stinging his hooves by nightfall. The skipping of Joyce with each snap of the harness teased him, the giggling from the rig adding a prickle. After the wagon, the rig was no more than a fly on his tail. He took the full reins when they slapped on his flanks and charged out from the laughter behind him. It rose to a shriek the faster he galloped and tickled his ears like something alive that slithered from them down his neck and his belly and into his loins. Faster and faster he plunged, the sparks from his shoes like ocean spray. He fought a jerk of the reins, the saw of the bit in his mouth a fierce pleasure. He took turns at his own fancy and only in sight of his own yard again did he yield in the fight, choking on the spume that lathered his tongue.

"By the holy, the night a horse beats me, I'll lie down in my grave," Joyce cried. "Get up now, you buzzard. You're not turning in till you go to the highway and back. Are you all right, Sarah?"

Am I all right, she thought. When in years had she know a wild ecstasy like this? From the first leap of the horse she had burst the girdle of fear and shame. If the wheels had spun out from beneath them, she would have rolled into the ditch contented.

"I've never been better," she said.

He leaned close to her to see her, for the moon had just risen. The wind had stung the tears to her eyes, but they were laughing. "By the Horn Spoon," he said, "you liked it!" He let the horse have his own way into the drive after all. He jumped down from the rig and held his hand up to her. "What a beautiful thing to be hanging in the back of the closet all these years."

"If that's a compliment," she said, "it's got a nasty bite."

"Aye. But it's my way of saying you're a beautiful woman."

"Will you come over for a cup of coffee?"

"I will. I'll put up the horse and be over."

The kettle had just come to the boil when he arrived.

"Maybe you'd rather have tea, Mr. Joyce?"

"Coffee or tea, so long as it's not water. And I'd like you to call me Frank. They christened me Francis but I got free of it early."

"And you know mine, I noticed," she said.

"It slipped out in the excitement. There isn't a woman I know who wouldn't of collapsed in a ride like that."

"It was wonderful." She poured the water into the coffee pot.

"There's nothing like getting behind a horse," he said, "unless it's getting astride him. I wouldn't trade Micky for a Mack truck."

"I used to ride when I was younger," she said.

"How did you pick up the man you got, if you don't mind my asking?"

And you the old woman, she thought; where did you get her? "I worked for a publishing house and he brought in some poetry."

"Ah, that's it." He nodded. "And he thought with a place like this he could pour it out like water from a spout."

"Gerald and I were in love," she said, irked that he should define so bluntly her own thoughts on the matter.

"Don't I remember it? In them days you didn't pull the blinds. It used to put me in a fine state."

"Do you take cream in your coffee? I've forgotten."

"Aye, thank you, and plenty of sugar."

"You haven't missed much," she said.

"There's things you see through a window you'd miss sitting down in the living-room. I'll wager you've wondered about the old lady and me?"

"A little. She wasn't so old, was she, Mr. Joyce?" Frank, she thought. Too frank.

"That one was old in her crib. But she came with a greenhouse. I worked for her father."

Sarah poured the coffee. "You're a cold-blooded old rogue," she said.

He grinned. "No. Cool-headed I am, and warm-blooded. When I was young, I made out it was the likes of poetry. She sang like a bird on a convent wall. But when I caged her she turned into an old crow."

"That's a terrible thing to say, Mr. Joyce."

The humor left his face for an instant. "It's a terribler thing to live with. It'd put a man off his nut. You don't have a bit of cake in the house, Sarah, to go with this?"

"How about muffins and jam?"

"That'll go fine." He smiled again. "Where does your old fella spend the night in his travels?"

"In the hotel in whatever town he happens to be in."

"That's a lonesome sort of life for a married man," he said.

She pulled a chair to the cupboard and climbed up to get a jar of preserves. He made no move to help her although she still could not reach the jar. She looked down at him. "You could give me a hand."

"Try it again. You almost had it that time." He grinned, almost gleeful at her discomfort.

She bounced down in one step. "Get it yourself if you want it. I'm satisfied with a cup of coffee."

He pounded his fist on the table, getting up. "You're right, Sarah. Never fetch a man anything he can fetch himself. Which bottle is it?"

"The strawberry."

He hopped up and down, nimble as a goat. "But then maybe he doesn't travel alone?"

"What?"

"I was suggesting your man might have an outside interest. Salesmen have the great temptation, you know."

"That's rather impertinent, Mr. Joyce."

"You're right, Sarah, it is. My tongue's been home so long it doesn't know how to behave in company. This is a fine cup of coffee."

She sipped hers without speaking. It was time she faced that question, she thought. She had been hedging around it for a long time, and last night with Gerald should have forced it upon her. "And if he does have an outside interest," she said, lifting her chin, "what of it?"

"Ah, Sarah, you're a wise woman, and worth

waiting the acquaintance of. You like me a little now, don't you?"

"A little."

"Well," he said, getting up, "I'll take that to keep me warm for the night."

And what have I got to keep me warm, she thought. "Thank you for the ride, Frank. It was thrilling."

"Was it?" he said, coming near her. He lifted her chin with his forefinger. "We've many a night like this ahead, Sarah, if you say the word." And then when she left her chin on his finger, he bent down and kissed her, taking himself to the door after it with a skip and a jump. He paused there and looked back at her. "Will I stay or go?"

"You'd better go," she choked out, wanting to be angry but finding no anger in herself at all.

All the next day Sarah tried to anchor herself from her peculiar flights of fancy. She had no feeling for the man, she told herself. It was a fine state a woman reached when a kiss from a stranger could do that to her. It was the ride made you giddy, she said aloud. You were thinking of Gerald. You were thinking of . . . the Lord knows what. She worked upstairs until she heard the wagon go by. She would get some perspective when Gerald came home. It seemed as though he'd been gone a long time.

The day was close and damp, and the flies clung to the screens. There was a dull stillness in the atmosphere. By late afternoon the clouds rolled heavier, mulling about one another like dough in a pan. While she was peeling potatoes for supper, Frank drove in. He unhitched the horse but left him in the harness, and set about immediately building frames along the rows of flowers. He was expecting a storm. She looked at the clock. It was almost time for Gerald.

She went out on the front porch and watched for the bus. There was a haze in the sweep of land between her and the highway, and the traffic through it seemed to float thickly, slowly. The bus glided toward the intersection and past it without stopping. She felt a sudden anger. Her whole day had been strung up to this peak. Since he had not called, it meant merely that he had missed the bus. The next one was in two hours. She crossed the yard to the fence. You're starting up again, Sarah, she warned herself, and took no heed of the warning.

Frank looked up from his work. "You'd better fasten the house," he said. "There's a fine blow coming."

"Frank, if you're in a hurry, I'll give you something to eat."

"That'd be a great kindness. I may have to go back to the stand at a gallop."

He was at the kitchen table, shoveling in the food without a word, when the heavy sky lightened. He went to the window. "By the glory, it may blow over." He looked around at her. "Your old boy missed the bus, did he?"

"He must have."

Frank looked out again. "I do like a good blow. Even if it impoverished me, there's nothing in the world like a storm."

An automobile horn sounded on the road. It occurred to Sarah that on a couple of occasions

Gerald had received a ride from the city. The car passed, but watching its dust she was left with a feeling of suspended urgency. Joyce was chatting now. He had tilted back in the chair and for the first time since she had known him, he was rambling on about weather, vegetables, and the price of eggs. She found it more disconcerting than his bursts of intimate comment, and she hung from one sentence to the next waiting for the end of it. Finally she passed in back of his chair and touched her fingers briefly to his neck.

"You need a haircut, Frank."

He sat bolt upright. "I never notice it till I have to scratch. Could I have a drop more coffee?"

She filled his cup, aware of his eyes on her. "Last night was something I'll never forget—that ride," she said.

"And something else last night, do you remember that?"

"Yes."

"Would you give me another now to match it if I was to ask?"

"No."

"What if I took it without asking?"

"I don't think I'd like it, Frank."

He pushed away from the table, slopping the coffee into the saucer. "Then what are you tempting me for?"

"You've a funny notion of temptation," she flared up, knowing the anger was against herself.

Joyce spread his dirt-grimed fingers on the table. "Sarah, do you know what you want?"

The tears were gathering. She fought them back. "Yes, I know what I want!" she cried.

Joyce shook his head. "He's got you by the heart, hasn't he, Sarah?"

"My heart's my own!" She flung her head up.

Joyce slapped his hand on the table. "Ho! Look at the spark of the woman! That'd scorch a man if there was a stick in him for kindling." He moistened his lips and in spite of herself Sarah took a step backwards. "I'll not chase you, Sarah. Never fear that. My chasing days are over. I'll neither chase nor run, but I'll stand my ground for what's coming to me." He jerked his head toward the window. "That was only a lull in the wind. There's a big blow coming now for certain."

She watched the first drops of rain splash on the glass. "Gerald's going to get drenched in it."

"Maybe it'll drown him," Joyce said, grinning from the door. "Thanks for the supper."

Let it come on hail, thunder, and lightning. Blow the roof from the house and tumble the chimney. I'd go out from it then and never turn back. When an old man can laugh at your trying to cuckold a husband, and the husband asking it, begging it, shame on you. She went through the house clamping the locks on the windows. More pleasure putting the broom through them.

An early darkness folded into the storm, and the walls of rain bleared the highway lights. There was an ugly yellow tinge to the water from the dust swirled into it. The wind sluiced down the chimney, spitting bits of soot on the living-room floor. She spread newspapers to catch it. A sudden blow, it would soon be spent. She went to the hall clock. The bus was due in ten minutes. What matter? A quick supper, a good book, and a long sleep. The wily old imp was right. A prophet needing a haircut.

The lights flickered off for a moment, then on again. Let them go out, Sarah. What's left for you, you can see by candlelight. She went to the basement and brought up the kerosene lamp and then got a flashlight from the pantry. As she returned to the living-room, a fresh gust of wind sent the newspapers out of the gate like scud. The lights flickered again. A sound drew her to the hall. She thought the wind might be muffling the ring of the telephone. When she got there, the clock was striking. The bus was now twenty minutes late. There was something about the look of the phone that convinced her the line was dead. It was unnerving to find it in order. Imagination, she murmured. Everything was going perverse to her expectations. And then, annoyed with herself, she grew angry with Gerald again. This was insult. Insult on top of indifference.

She followed a thumping noise upstairs. It was on the outside of the house. She turned off the light and pressed her face against the window. A giant maple tree was rocking and churning, one branch thudding against the house. There was not even a blur of light from the highway now. Blacked out. While she watched, a pinpoint of light shaped before her. It grew larger, weaving a little. A flashlight, she thought, and wondered if Gerald had one. Then she recognized the motion: a lantern on a wagon. Frank was returning.

When she touched the light switch there was no response. Groping her way to the hall she saw that all the lights were out now. Step by step she made her way downstairs. A dankness had washed in through the chimney, stale and sickening. She lit the lamp and carried it to the kitchen. From the window there, she saw Frank's lantern bobbing as he led the horse into the barn. She could not see man or horse, only the fading of the light until it disappeared inside. When it reappeared she lifted her kerosene lamp, a greeting to him. This time he came around the fence. She held the door against the wind.

"I've no time now, Sarah. I've work to do," he shouted. "He didn't come, did he?"

"No!"

"Is the phone working?"

She nodded that it was and waved him close to her. "Did the bus come through?"

"It's come and gone. Close the door or you'll have the house in a shambles." He waved his lantern and was gone.

She put the pot roast she had prepared for Gerald in the refrigerator and set the perishables close to the freezing unit. She wound the clock and put away the dishes. Anything to keep busy. She washed the kitchen floor that had been washed only the day before. The lantern across the way swung on a hook at the barn, sometimes moving toward the ground and back as Joyce examined the frames he was reinforcing.

Finally she returned to the living-room. She sat for a long time in Gerald's chair, watching the pattern of smoke in the lamp-chimney. Not even a dog or cat to keep her company. Not even a laughing piece of delft to look out at her from the mantelpiece; only the cold-eyed forebears, whom she could not remember, staring down at her from the gilt frames, their eyes fixed upon her, the last and the least of them who would leave after her—nothing.

It was not to be endured. She lunged out of the chair. In the hall she climbed to the first landing where she could see Joyce's yard. He was through work now, the lantern hanging from the porch although the house was darkened. It was the only light anywhere, and swayed in the wind like a will-o'-the-wisp.

She bounded down the stairs and caught up her raincoat. Taking the flashlight she went out into the storm. She made her way around the fence, sometimes leaning into the wind, sometimes resting against it. Joyce met her in his driveway. He had been waiting, she thought, testing his nerves against her own, expecting her. Without a word, he caught her hand and led her to his back steps and into the house. "I've an oil lamp," he said then. "Hold your light there till I fix it."

She watched his wet face in the half-light. His mouth was lined with malicious humor, and his eyes as he squinted at the first flame of the wick were fierce, as fierce as the storm, and as strange to her. When the light flared up, she followed its reaches over the dirty wall, the faded calendar, the gaping cupboards, the electric cord hanging from a naked bulb over the sink to the back door. There were dishes stacked on the table where they no doubt stood from one meal to the next. The curtains were stiff with dirt, three years of it. Only then did she take a full glimpse of the folly that had brought her here.

"I just ran over for a minute, Frank . . ."

"A minute or the night, sit there, Sarah, and let me get out of these clothes."

She took the chair he motioned her into, and watched him fling his coat into the corner. Nor could she take her eyes from him as he sat down and removed his boots and socks. Each motion fascinated her separately, fascinated and revolted her. He wiped between his toes with the socks. He went barefoot toward the front of the house. In the doorway he paused, becoming a giant in the weird light.

"Put us up a pot of coffee, dear woman. The makings are there on the stove."

"I must go home. Gerald . . ."

"To hell with Gerald," he interrupted. "He's snug for the night, wherever he is. Maybe he won't come back to you at all. It's happened before, you know, men vanishing from women they don't know the worth of."

Alone, she sat stiff and erect at the table. He was just talking, poisoning her mind against Gerald. How should she get out of here? Run like a frightened doe and never face him again? No, Sarah. Stay for the bitter coffee. Scald the giddiness out of you once and for all. But on top of the resolve came the wish that Gerald might somehow appear at the door and take her home. Dear, gentle Gerald.

She got up and went to the sink to draw the water for coffee. A row of medicine bottles stood on the window-sill, crusted with dust. Household remedies. She leaned close and examined a faded label: "Mrs. Joyce— Take immediately upon need."

She turned from the window. A rocker stood in the corner of the room. In the old days the sick woman had sat in it on the back porch, rocking, and speaking to no one. The stale sickness of her was still about the house, Sarah thought. What did she know of people like this?

He was threshing around upstairs like a penned bull. His muddy boots lay where he had taken them off, a pool of water gathering about them. Again she looked at the window-sill. No May wine there. Suddenly she remembered Dr. Philips's words: "Lived on stimulants for years." She could almost see the sour woman, even to her gasping for breath . . . "Take immediately."

Fix the coffee, Sarah. What kind of teasing is this? Teasing the dead from her grave before you. Teasing. Something in the thought disturbed her further . . . an association: Joyce watching her reach for the preserves last night, grinning at her. "Try it again, Sarah. You almost had it that time." And she could still hear him asking, "Which bottle?" Not which jar, but which bottle.

She grabbed the kettle and filled it. Stop it, Sarah. It's the storm, the waiting, too much waiting . . . your time of life. She drew herself up against his coming, hearing his quick steps on the stairs.

"Will you give us a bit of iodine there from the window, Sarah? I've scratched myself on those blamed frames."

She selected the bottle carefully with her eyes, so

that her trembling hand might not betray her.

"Dab it on here," he said, holding a white cuff away from his wrist.

The palm of his hand was moist as she bent over it and she could smell the earth and the horse from it. Familiar. Everything about him had become familiar, too familiar. She felt his breath on her neck, and the hissing sound of it was the only sound in the room. She smeared the iodine on the cut and pulled away. His lips tightened across his teeth in a grin.

"A kiss would make a tickle of the pain," he said.

Sarah thrust the iodine bottle from her and grabbed the flashlight. "I'm going home."

His jaw sagged as he stared at her. "Then what did you come for?"

"Because I was lonesome. I was foolish . . ." Fear choked off her voice. A little trickle of saliva dribbled from the corner of his mouth.

"No! You came to torture me!"

She forced one foot toward the door and the other after it. His voice rose in laughter as she lumbered away from him. "Good Lord, Sarah. Where's the magnificent woman who rode to the winds with me last night?"

She lunged into the electric cord in her retreat, searing her cheek on it. Joyce caught it and wrenched it from the wall, its splayed end springing along the floor like a whip. "And me thinking the greatest kindness would be if he never came home!"

The doorknob slipped in her sweaty hand. She dried it frantically. He's crazy, she thought. Mad-crazy.

"You're a lump, Sarah," he shouted. "And Mr. Joyce is a joker. A joker and a dunce. He always was and he will be till the day they hang him!"

The door yielded and she plunged down the steps and into the yard. In her wild haste she hurled herself against the rig and spun away from it as though it were something alive. She sucked in her breath to keep from screaming. She tore her coat on the fence hurtling past it, leaving a swatch of it on the wire. Take a deep breath, she told herself as she stumbled up the steps. Don't faint. Don't fall. The door swung from her grasp, the wind clamoring through the house. She forced it closed, the glass plate tingling, and bolted it. She thrust the flashlight on the table and caught up the phone. She clicked it wildly.

Finally it was the operator who broke through. "I have a call for you from Mr. Gerald Shepherd. Will you hold on, please?"

Sarah could hear only her own sobbing breath in the hollow of the mouthpiece. She tried to settle her mind by pinning her eyes on the stairway. But the spokes of the staircase seemed to be shivering dizzily in the circle of light, like the plucked strings of a harp. Even the sound of them was vibrant in her head, whirring over the rasp of her breath. Then came the pounding footfalls and Joyce's fists on the door. Vainly she signaled the operator. And somewhere in the tumult of her mind she grasped at the thought that if she unlocked the door, Joyce would come in and sit down. They might even light the fire. There was plenty of wood in the basement. But she could not speak. And it was too late.

Joyce's fist crashed through the glass and drew the bolt. With the door's opening the wind whipped her coat over her head; with its closing, her coat fell limp, its little pressure about her knees seeming to buckle them.

"I'm sorry," came the operator's voice, "the call was canceled ten minutes ago."

She let the phone clatter onto the table and waited, her back still to the door. Ten minutes was not very long ago, she reasoned in sudden desolate calmness. She measured each of Joyce's footfalls toward her, knowing they marked all of time that was left to her. And somehow, she felt, she wanted very little more of it.

For only an instant she saw the loop he had made of the electric cord, and the white cuffs over the strong, gnarled hands. She closed her eyes and lifted her head high, expecting that in that way the end would come more quickly . . .

The Crate at Outpost 1

MATTHEW GANT

The wind whistled through the valley, and the pyramidal tent that signified Outpost 1 quivered before the blast. As always, sentry Rudd placed his hand before the oil burner that feebly lit the interior of the tent, shielding the yellow flame from the stray gusts that whipped through the torn canvas. And, as always, he cast a quick, nearly guilty look at sentry Dennison, who lay fully dressed on a narrow cot in the rear of the tent.

"It won't fizz out," Dennison said. He lay on his back, his hands resting behind his head, and his eyes stared at the sloping ceiling. Occasionally he wiggled his fingers and watched with amusement the play of shadows on the canvas overhead.

"I know," Rudd said, biting his lip and looking away.

"Then why do you do it?" Dennison said.

"I don't know," Rudd said. He spread his hands.

Outside, the wind sank for a moment and from far off came the barking of dogs. Rudd shivered and drew the frayed collar of his parka close about him. He stole another quick look at Dennison, and then his eyes shifted to the corner of the tent just to the left of the doorway flap.

The crate was still there.

"What are you afraid of?" Dennison asked. "It won't move."

"I don't know," Rudd said, and then he flared for a moment. "It's our job. We must see the crate."

He stood up defiantly and strode to the crate. It squatted on the corner, four feet high, four feet long, four feet wide. It was of wood, nailed securely across the top.

Rudd remembered the last nailing detail. They had come in during the warm weather and ripped out the rusting nails with their hands. One of them had howled when a nail slipped and gashed his palm. The naildriver was the biggest man Rudd had ever seen. He pounded the new, shiny nails with the heel of his rifle, and soon the crate was nearly as good as new.

And while they had changed the nails, a two-striper had stood over the detail, with a rifle that shone dully in the flickering gloom of the tent.

Rudd had seen many nailing details come and go. The thought filled him with pride. Ever since they had landed on the island outpost, he and Dennison had been assigned to see the crate.

"You can see it from your bed," Dennison said, breaking the thoughts. "There's no rule about seeing it from your bed."

"I don't care," Rudd said. "It's easier to see from here."

Dennison said, "Ah-h-h," and the sound turned

into a yawn. "Wake me when the two-striper comes," he said.

Rudd flinched. He wanted to tell Dennison that he was not to sleep on duty. Rudd was not supposed to see the crate alone. When the two-striper had told them the order, this had been emphasized:

"Never see the crate alone. Always make sure you're both seeing it at the same time. One man alone can't be trusted."

And both Dennison and Rudd had nodded, gravely.

But it was always the same. Dennison would sleep until the two-striper reached the flap and, cursing, tried to find the tent buttons. And Dennison would be on his feet, gripping his rifle, when the two-striper finally strode to the tent's center and reviewed his sentries.

Once Dennison hadn't been lucky. The two-striper had found the buttons quickly and the soft mud outside had cushioned his steps, and he was inside before Dennison woke. Dennison had to stand on his feet for a very long time after that.

And the two-striper had lectured him about the crate.

"Do you know why you're here, soldier?" the two-striper had asked Dennison.

"Yes," Dennison said. "To see the crate."

"And why see the crate?" the two-striper persisted.

"So nobody gets it," Dennison answered, his face reddening under the softly-spoken questions.

"And why should nobody get it?" the two-striper probed.

Dennison had stammered then and Rudd wanted

to help him out, but he didn't want to have to stand for a very long time also. Besides, he did not know the answer.

"Because," the two-striper snapped. "That's why, you fool."

And Dennison repeated, "Because." And the two-striper imposed the sentence and left.

Later that night Rudd had whispered to Dennison, who stood there, his rifle clutched tight in his hands. "Are you awake?"

"Yes," Dennison had said.

"I was wondering," Rudd said. "I was wondering about something."

"You're always wondering about something," Dennison said. "What's it this time?"

"I was wondering because why," he said, his voice still a whisper in the pitch-black tent.

"Because why what?" Dennison asked harshly. "Because why what, you fool?"

"Nothing," Rudd said, and he turned to see the crate though it was too dark to make it out.

But gradually he found the nerve to ask, and Dennison, who had been in the service far longer than he, and who was once a two-striper himself, finally told him.

"Because the crate was once owned by the enemy, long, long ago," he had said, and even Dennison, who slept when he should have been seeing the crate, let his eyes creep to the flap in case the two-striper, or, even worse, the yellow-bar were near.

"The enemy," Rudd had said, involuntarily, his eyes bugging.

"Shut up, you fool," Dennison hissed.

And many, many seasons of warm to cold had gone by before Rudd had asked more questions and learned more about why the crate had to be seen.

Dennison did not know the whole story, for no man did, he said.

But the facts were these: the crate contained an enemy weapon, an old and very powerful weapon, which must never be allowed to fall into his hands again. And during bad times, such as now when the dogs were out barking in pursuit of enemy smell, the crate had to be seen all the time so that nobody got it away.

It was as simple as that.

And from that time on, Rudd had felt the pride of his job, and he wondered even more strongly how Dennison could sleep when he ought to be seeing.

Especially during bad times, when the dogs were barking.

Rudd had never heard so much barking as these past nights. He wished, sometimes, he were back with the others, not at Outpost 1. Once, last warmth, he had become ill and a doctor had visited him, a one-striper. Before he had left, the doctor had told him of the others.

"They are sick-afraid," he had said. "They say the enemy is nearer."

But though for a moment Rudd, too, was sick-afraid, he laughed at the doctor. Doctors knew so little, especially about the movement of soldiers.

But when he told Dennison of it, Dennison didn't laugh. He sat and stared through the open flap at the sun sinking behind the peaks.

And now, the dogs were barking as never before. And the two-striper had come in twice this night, instead of once, and even though their share of oil had been burned up, he had brought more. "See the crate," he said, shortly, as he left.

And Rudd saw the crate, and even Dennison lay there on his bed, his eyes wide open.

They were not relieved until the sun was high the next day.

And that night when they returned to the tent, the two-striper handed them each a bullet for their rifles. It was the first time either man had ever held a loaded rifle.

"See the crate," the two-striper had said fiercely before he left, "see the crate." And Rudd noticed the dark circles under the two-striper's eyes.

"These are bad times," Rudd said to Dennison, staring at him anxiously.

"Bad," Dennison repeated.

"Do you think—?" Rudd started.

"Do I think what, you fool?" Dennison said. But his voice was not sharp at all.

"Do you think the enemy is coming?"

Outside the wind howled again, howled loud, but even over the howl came the sound of the dogs.

"I don't know," Dennison had said, at last.

Rudd quickly put his hand over the oil burner to shield it from the wind, but this time Dennison didn't say anything. Things were bad, Rudd knew.

He stood straight and he thought: I will do my job. He walked to the crate and leaned on it.

"Don't touch it, you fool," Dennison said.

"But why?" Rudd asked, puzzled. He had touched it many times before, feeling the creaking wood and sometimes he had peeled splinters of wood from the crate and used them to make pictures in the mud outside.

"Ah-h-h," Dennison said. "Just don't."

And Rudd walked away, ashamed.

Suddenly the outside quivered with noise. The dogs were nearby now, and there must have been dozens of them, yapping and howling, and Dennison said, "Listen."

"The barking is loud," Rudd said.

"No, not the barking. I can hear them gnashing their teeth."

Rudd listened and he heard, too, and he thrilled to the sound. "The enemy will never get to us, not with those dogs of ours," he boasted.

And through the sound came the clomping of a man's heavy boots, running in thick mud.

"The enemy!" Rudd said, his hands tightening over the stock of the rifle, his hand reaching for the bolt.

But it wasn't the enemy. It was a one-striper, the runner from the others.

He stood swaying in the center of the tent, a huge man with a black beard, his eyes red-rimmed and circled with the same sort of black lines, though even deeper, as those about the two-striper's.

"Is this it?" he panted, pointing to the crate. It had been many seasons since Rudd had seen the runner, and he looked much older, and Rudd felt sorry that the runner didn't even remember the crate.

"Yes," he said. "That's it."

The runner stood there and the tent was still. He bent once and lightly moved his hand toward the crate, and then drew it back quickly. He spun on his heavy boots and faced the sentries.

"You must run," he said. "We are beaten."

"Beaten?" Rudd said. "I don't believe it."

Dennison stared at the runner and then he sat on his cot and started to pull on his boots. "Come on," he said to Rudd, "we don't have all night."

"But—"

"Beaten," the runner insisted.

"And the crate?" Rudd said. "The crate?"

"Destroy it," the runner said. "Quickly. You have no time. You must go to the hills when you have finished. Do you have enough oil?"

Rudd stared at the lamp which flared full and strong.

"No, you fool," Dennison said, "not for the lamp. For the crate. The enemy must not get the crate."

The runner handed Rudd a can of oil, and with his bayonet, ripped it open. He stood at the flap for a long moment, and then he raised his hand to his eyes. "Good-by," he said, "and hurry."

Rudd stared at the open can of oil, and then he started to pour it on the wooden slats across the top of the crate. The barking was frantic now, yards away it seemed.

Dennison tore the can from his hand. "No," he panted, "there must be something inside the wood that can't be destroyed this way, wet packing or metal or something. We'll have to remove the top." He reached for the wood and started to pull at the slats.

"No," Rudd said. "We're not allowed to. We must see the crate, not the inside."

But Dennison would not be stopped, and Rudd watched as the slats groaned and pulled up sharply. Some cracked in Dennison's hands as he clawed at them, and suddenly, the last two slats came up together and the top was off.

They moved back a pace and looked down. There was a sheet of yellowed paper, with five black marks on it, over the inside of the crate, and Dennison reached out and grabbed it away and they both leaned forward to see.

They looked up at each other, and there was a frown on each forehead. Inside the crate were box-like things, most of them the length of a man's hand span, maybe a little longer, not quite as wide, and two, three fingers deep. Each one was covered with cloth.

There were steps outside now, and the dogs were no longer near, their barking off down the valley.

Dennison screamed once, in rage and fear, and he sprinkled oil frantically on the top of the box-like things and he sprinkled oil on the yellowed paper with the five black marks, and he thrust the paper into the oil lamp until a corner caught fire.

Then he threw the burning paper on top of the crate, and they both raced from the tent for the hills.

And as Rudd ran, he was sick-afraid, and even many seasons later while he hid in the woods, he still remembered with cringing fear the crate, and sometimes when he found himself drawing in the mud, the thing he drew was the five black marks that had been on the yellowed paper covering the things inside—

BOOKS

My Unfair Lady

GUY CULLINGFORD

I was sitting in a nook in the woods reading a paperback, when this little girl parted the leaves and looked in at me. At first sight she seemed no better or worse than the usual run of small females, a set of indeterminate features framed in towy pigtails which had a long way to go to reach her shoulders. She was wearing a fairly clean dress, bare legs and sandals.

"Excuse me, mister," she said, staring at me good and hard.

"Certainly," I said amiably. "But the wood's big enough for both of us, and I daresay we'll get on better at a distance."

I went on with my reading. And though I kept my eyes on the printed word, I could feel hers like a pair of gimlets boring into me.

"How about leaving me in peace?" I said. "Be a good girl."

She made no attempt to move. She was following her own line of thought, not mine. After a moment, she said, "There's a gentleman being unkind to a lady under that tree." And she turned a bit and pointed.

I felt myself getting hot under the collar, and I said, "That's none of my business or yours either. Run away home, you nasty prying little girl. I don't want to know you."

She stayed put, not budging an inch. For a full minute she remained silent, twisting one ankle round the other.

Then she said, "How'd you like it if someone stuck a knife into you?"

"What!" I leapt to my feet, slamming the book shut. "Why didn't you say that in the beginning? Where's this? What—what tree'd you say?"

She was off like a shot with me right after her. We went about twenty feet down the slope, and then the tail of the girl's little dress vanished into a tangle of undergrowth. I scrambled after her. But when we got to the foot of the tree, I stopped short, silently staring.

There the woman lay, on last year's leaves with her head supported by a beech trunk. The knife must have found the heart, for she was just as dead as the leaves, although she hadn't been there as long. There's always something pretty shocking in sudden death, and she couldn't have been more than twenty. She must have been a good-looker, too. The haft of the knife was still in place, and suddenly I felt sick at my stomach. I turned away to throw up and realized with a start that the kid who'd brought me there had vanished; she must have melted away while I was busy taking in the situation. I hadn't time to be sick. It suddenly dawned on me that I was in a serious position. That wretched little girl was as valuable to me as her weight in diamonds; she was my one and only alibi that I'd visited the scene of the crime and nothing more. So I had to find her again as soon as possible.

I bolted down the slope, right to the bottom where there was a kind of paddling pond crammed full of children. But though I darted here and there, and there were dozens of little girls, there wasn't a trace of the one I wanted. I tell you, I stood still, and the sweat trickled down my face. I suppose ten minutes elapsed before I gave up the search. Then I had to ask myself a question. What do I do now? I was all for racing away as fast as my legs would take me. If I'd had a hat I could have pulled down over my eyes, I don't think I should have hesitated to do that. But I was bare-headed, and I'd been behaving, in the light of later events, in what might well have been described as oddly by any interested onlooker. There were several mothers who must have spared a moment from watching Bobbie get his pants splashed on to make a mental note of my interest in little girls, perhaps were even ready to have a word with a policeman. And, by heaven, there was a policeman ready made for them, standing in the shade of the trees, no doubt presiding benignly over the frolics of the young, and all set to prevent any casualty amongst the waders.

I had a horrid vision of myself on the run—the man the police wanted to interview in connection with the murdered girl. Well, in a choice of evils it's my motto to choose the lesser. I headed for the policeman, as if in his stalwart frame lay my only hope of salvation.

"Officer," I said in a voice that broke with uncertainty, "Officer, I want to report a crime."

That shook him. He was a youngish man, and he looked as if all his blood had suddenly drained into his boots. But he pulled himself together and asked me a few questions, and soon we were making it up the slope together, my heart pumping a great deal harder than was called for by the incline.

Of course, later on I got passed on to higher authority for questioning, first a detective sergeant and then an inspector, then both together. I stuck to my story, and they seemed to me to be decent fellows. They almost believed me.

What really rattled them was one of those fantastic coincidences which would be quite inadmissible in fiction. When the constable first bore me off to the police station, I was still clutching that confounded paperback, and when they took it off me, there on the cover, for them to see, was a blond with a dagger in her heart. I hadn't even noticed the subject of the luridly painted cover until I had it pointed out to me. In the absence of any more substantial clue, blood or strands of hair or incriminating fingerprints, they had to make the most of that. In defense, I stuck to the little girl who had drawn me into my predicament; she was all I had.

"Pity you don't know her name," commented the the inspector, a shade dryly I thought.

"I don't go round asking the names of strange little girls," I said. "I'm not fond enough of them for that."

The inspector nodded. "Mind you," he said, "if what you're telling us is the truth, there's no need to be alarmed. If the kid's above ground we'll find her, don't you worry."

"Then I'll not worry," I said.

"Lucky the schools haven't broken up," said the sergeant. "We'll go through them with a fine-tooth comb till we find her, that is . . ." He paused significantly and scratched his nose. I could see he wasn't convinced.

I got to know the sergeant quite well during the next twenty-four hours—and the local schools. As far as the children were concerned, our arrival was a welcome interruption, but the teachers were less approving. Finally, at Omega Road Girls' School we struck oil.

After a short talk with the head-mistress, we were shown into a classroom of the correct age group. There were about four and twenty little darlings present, with the one we were after practically indistinguishable from the rest—except to me. She was seated at a desk, second row from the front. We had been warned not to upset the little dears, so the sergeant in a voice flowing with milk and honey asked them if they'd any of them ever seen this gentleman (pointing to me) before anywhere. Up shot a forest of hands. Only one in the second row remained at desk level. You can guess whose.

"Where?" asked the sergeant.

"Pleasir, pleasir," they chanted in unison, and one being singled out by the head-mistress for a solo speech said, "Please, Ma'am, we all saw him at the paddling pool in Hammer Wood on the afternoon the young woman got done in."

The head-mistress shot me a frosty look, as if I

should be held responsible for any psychic damage done to these innocents. At once I asked the sergeant for the privilege of half a minute's private conversation. We cowered behind the blackboard, and I whispered into his ear that the one who hadn't put up her hand was the one we were after. He emerged brushing his moustache, first one side, then the other, and said, "I want to ask the little girl in the second row who didn't put up her hand if she has ever seen this gentleman before?"

"Speak up, Ruby Gant," said the head-mistress, cooing at the little wretch. "No one's going to hurt you, dear."

The child's indeterminate features registered no expression whatever. She took her time about it, studying me with a sort of vacant earnestness.

"I never seen him in me life, Miss Birch," she finally said. "I don't know that gentleman at all, and . . ." here the lips parted in a grin to disclose a set of tiny, regular teeth . . . "I don't know as I want to."

A giggle ran round the class, and Miss Birch did nothing to suppress it. Instead, she asked mildly, "You weren't at the pool with the others, then?"

"No, Miss Birch, Ruby wasn't at the pool with us," said a child who was seated behind Ruby Gant. "She said she had to go straight home."

"Is that right, Ruby?"

"Yes, Miss Birch. I wanted to look after me baby brother, so our mum could get a rest."

You could practically see the halo above that flaxen crown.

"I have always found Ruby a very truthful little

girl," remarked Miss Birch, sotto voce to the sergeant.

That was that. I ask you, what could I do about it?

They had to let me go in the end, for there wasn't a shred of real evidence. They couldn't trace any connection between me and the murdered girl, and it wasn't any good bringing a prosecution on the strength of a lurid book jacket. Although I was told dozens of women volunteered to give information on my personal appearance down at the pool that afternoon. You know, the usual thing, the wild and glaring eyes, the maniacal frenzy, etcetera, etcetera. I never varied my story, however much opportunity I was given, and there was nothing known against me, and I was in steady employment.

As far as I could see, they would never nail anyone else for the wood-killing either. Like most of those girls who are found murdered, she was not known to have had any men friends. Apparently, she ran to type, quiet and reserved and self-respecting. Well, she was now, anyway, poor thing. The knife was of a common sort which might be found in the possession of any boy scout. Although it had been sharpened to a fine edge, there were no fingerprints on it. As for fallen leaves, they don't measure up to flower beds when it comes to holding the impression of a distinctive shoe heel. If I'd done the murder myself, I couldn't have made a neater job of it.

Finally, the C.I.D. had to admit themselves beaten, and I left the police station for the last time without a stain on my character. Huh! I lost my job, I lost my place of residence, I lost my friends. And, in addition to all this, no girl in that district would be seen dead with me. Though for weeks afterwards, had girls permitted me to escort them, they would have been the safest girls in the world. I never took a step without police protection, very, very unobtrusive. The smallest squeak would have brought the man on my tail to my side.

All the same, I wasn't moving from the neighborhood, not yet awhile. I found a fresh dwelling with a deaf mute for a landlady, a fresh job at half the pay, and there I stuck, waiting for time to pass which is reputedly a great healer.

But I was waiting with a purpose. When three months were up, I found myself alone again—without police protection, that is. Then I thought it was safe to get busy. They say a child's memory is short, and I didn't want to leave it too long. I started to hang about the Omega Road Girls' School, at four o'clock when the kids were coming out. I marked my prey; three months had made very little difference to her, and I herded her off from the rest of the flock. As a matter of fact, it was as easy as pie because she left the others at a road junction and trailed off on her own. I guess it was like that the day at the pool; she was strictly an individualist. I had decided to use guile, and had been toting round with me for days a big bag of toffees.

"Hey, Ruby," I said, catching up with her and offering the bag. "Have a sweetie."

She recognized me at once. She didn't look scared

at all, but she shook her head and said, "My mum says I'm never to take sweets from strangers."

"I'm not a stranger. I'm the man you nearly put behind bars for life, don't you remember?"

"Serves yer right. You shouldn't have spoken nasty to me."

Then she showed her teeth in the famous grin. You could see she didn't bear me an ounce of spite.

"Besides . . ." she said.

"Besides what?"

"I didn't want to get meself in trouble. I didn't want to draw attention to meself, see."

My God, she'd got it all there in her little brain-pan at the age of eight or thereabouts. She didn't care a fig what became of me; it was her own skin she was intent on preserving.

She undoubtedly knew who had killed the girl . . .

I tried not to show any excitement, and I said as casually as I could, matching my step to hers: "Then you saw the chap who did it. I thought it was one of your lies!"

"Don't be saucy. Of course I saw 'im. Leastways, I saw his back. He was bending over."

"You mean you never saw his face at all. Well, that's no good, you couldn't pick him out."

"I could and all, if I wanted to. Wears a blue suit."

"So does my Uncle Bert. What the hell! Why every—"

"You shouldn't swear. My mum says it's not nice."

"You and your mum! I'll tell you what your mum is, she's as big a liar as you are if she says you were at home minding the baby when you were busy snooping at people in the wood."

"She can't keep her eye on the clock all the time, can she? Not with my young brother she can't. And I wasn't snooping, Mister Clever. I was playing 'ouses under the trees."

"And you say you know this chap?"

"I didden say I knew 'im. I said I could put my finger on 'im if I liked."

"Then why don't you?"

"It's none of my business." She brought it out with an air of secret triumph.

But it was my business all right, and my particular business to keep on baiting her until I got the response I wanted. I've often heard little girls doing it to each other, and nine times out of ten it works.

So I gathered my resources together, and packing all the scorn I could into my voice, said, "Huh! Ruby Gant, you don't know a thing!"

"I do."

"You're just making it up."

"I'm not."

"Yes you are. You never saw the chap at all, or if you did, you wouldn't know him from Adam."

"I told you 'e'd got blue clothes on."

"Well, where does he live?"

"I dunno where 'e lives, but I know where 'e is this minnit."

"You're a nasty story teller!"

"No I'm not."

"Yes you are."

I was thoroughly into the spirit of the thing, when she suddenly capitulated.

"If I take you to where he is, then will you believe me?"

"Now you're talking," I said. "You take me to him and I'll believe you."

She looked at me hard with that intent yet somehow vacant stare which was part of her make-up.

"If I do, will yer swear not to tell anyone?"

"Of course I will."

"Then say it after me."

"What is it? What have I got to say?"

She licked her grubby first finger and held it up in the air.

"See my finger's wet . . . go on and say it."

I licked my own finger and followed her instructions.

"See my finger's dry."

"See my finger's dry."

"Slit my throat if I tell a lie." Here she drew her finger ominously across her scraggy little throat.

I repeated the childish oath. I hadn't the faintest intention of sticking to it. I'd have been an outright fool if I considered I owed any allegiance to that child.

But my having taken the oath seemed to satisfy her. She said, "Come on, then."

She pranced off and I followed her as I'd done once before. The only difference was that now she wore a skimpy cloth coat and we were on the pavements and not in the path in the wood.

She led me from this by-road into another and yet another until at last we came out on the High Street. There were lots of people about shopping, but she didn't moderate her pace, but slipped between them like an eel, while I blundered after. I must have looked odd chasing after that scrap of a kid, as if life depended on it. But I wasn't conscious of making a fool of myself; my heart was thumping wildly, because I felt sure I was on to something important.

Finally, we came to the crossroads where the High Street joins the main arterial road coming from the city.

Ruby Gant came to a sudden standstill, which brought me right up on her heels.

She dropped back to my side, and looking up at me, gave the faintest flick to her thumb.

"There 'e is, then. What did I tell yer?"

There he was, with his back to us, blue suit, white gloves and all, directing the home-going traffic, the young cop I'd given myself up to that day in the wood, by the paddling pool.

I stood gazing stupidly at him, my mind in a whirl, for perhaps ten seconds. Then I turned to Ruby. You know what? The little devil wasn't there. She'd played the same trick on me as before. She must have moved like greased lightning.

It was hopeless to look for her amongst the crowd. A child as small as that could take cover anywhere. She might have darted into the nearest chain store for temporary refuge, or be halfway home already.

So there I was, up a tree. I turned about and began to walk slowly back along the High Street, mechanically dodging the busy shoppers while I mulled what had happened over in my mind. Was Miss Ruby Gant stringing me along in her own inimitable fashion? And was this last audacity—pure invention on the spur of the moment—a final thumb at the nose at me, for venturing to criticize her past conduct?

Did her fiendish ingenuity prompt her to select a policeman as the supreme example of improbability? Was she even now giggling away at the idea of it?

Did she really know who had murdered the girl in the wood? Was the blue suit merely a product of her fertile fancy, or had it some basis in fact?

It was a matter beyond dispute that the cop had been right on the spot, or as near as makes no difference. It would have taken him less than no time to have slipped down the slope from the fatal tree into position as guardian of the pool. Just because no motive had come to light for the murder of the girl, it didn't follow that there was none.

When I was a boy I was never keen to tangle with the forces of law and order, and I could therefore imagine what effect the idea of mixing it with a policeman would have on one of Ruby's age and environment. You notice that I don't say tender age. Still, it was nice to think that there might be some reason for what that kid had done to me, besides the mere gratification of a childish spite.

Now that I harked back, I had a vivid mental picture of the blood draining out of the policeman's face when I first reported to him my discovery of the crime. Was every cop so squeamish, however inexperienced?

But even if Ruby had made me a present of the killer, what good was it likely to do me? I shouldn't like to see the expression on the sergeant's face if

I'd be so foolish as to trot round to the police station with this new theory.

And suddenly I saw the whole thing from the point of view of the police, and knew myself that it was only a pack of lies, or rather, that mixture of truth and tarradiddle in which Ruby specialized.

Well, let bygones be bygones, I thought. Thanks to Ruby, I should always be a man with a past . . . no need to allow her to complicate my future.

I felt that I needed a drink to strengthen my resolution, even if it was only a strong black coffee, and as this feeling happened to coincide with my passing one of the local milk bars, I pushed the door and went in.

It was one of those narrow affairs like a tramcar, with tables in front and the works at the end. I was nearly up to the counter, when I saw something which pulled me up dead.

There, perched up on a stool, with her back three-quarters-wise to me, was that demon-child. She had her skinny elbows planted on the counter, and her monkey paws round a beakerful of something.

But she wasn't drinking. She seemed to be in a sort of ecstasy, gazing up with rapt adoration at the face of the Adonis presiding over the counter. The man was sleek and dark and as handsome as a rattlesnake. You know the type.

There was a loud sort of buzzing noise in my ears. I stood perfectly still, and deep down inside me I had that sudden hideous conviction of truth without proof such as a chap gets sometimes.

I added my stare to Ruby's.

The man must have just finished buttering some

slices of cut bread ready for sandwiches, because he still held the knife loosely in his right hand, whilst with the index finger of the left he was absent-mindedly testing the sharpness of the blade.

He was not interested in either of us.

All his attention was centered on the pair of young girls who sat at the table next to the counter, chattering away together in the animated way girls have if within ten yards of any personable male. His eyes, half-narrowed, feasted on them as on some delectable prospect.

Then, as if drawn by a magnet, he released the knife, and came forward, brushing past the entranced Ruby, to collect their empty cups.

As he bent over them in his regulation short white jacket, murmuring who knows what sweet inducements, he revealed to me the back view of a pair of pants of a peculiarly revolting shade. I decided not to stop for refreshment.

I did a rightabout turn, and was out of those surroundings in less time than it takes to say "Blue Murder."

Oh yes, I agree there are loose ends. There are several things I should like to know myself.

For instance, just when did Mistress Ruby catch up with him?

Did she track him down systematically by his choice in suiting? Had she known him before? Or was it one of those odd chances, beginner's luck, as you might say?

How long was he prepared to go on stuffing her up with free ice cream, hot chocolate and what have you, to keep her on his side?

And what was going to happen when he stopped?
Or when . . . well, never mind.

These questions, or any variants on same, are likely to go unanswered as far as I'm concerned.

When two tigers get together, that's no place for me.

New Murders for Old

CARTER DICKSON

Hargreaves did not speak until he had turned on two lamps. Even then he did not remove his overcoat. The room, though cold, was stuffy, and held a faintly sweet odour. Outside the Venetian blinds, which were not quite closed, you saw the restless, shifting presence of snow past street-lights. For the first time, Hargreaves hesitated.

"The—the object," he explained, indicating the bed, "was there. *He* came in by this door, here. Perhaps you understand a little better now?"

Hargreaves' companion nodded.

"No," said Hargreaves, and smiled. "I'm not trying to invoke illusions. On the contrary, I am trying to dispel them. Shall we go downstairs?"

It was a tall, heavy house, where no clocks ticked. But the treads of the stairs creaked and cracked sharply, even under their padding of carpet. At the back, in a kind of small study, a gas-fire had been lighted. Its hissing could be heard from a distance; it roared up blue, like solid blue flames, into the white fretwork of the heater; but it did little to dispel the chill of the room. Hargreaves motioned his companion to a chair at the other side of the fire.

"I want to tell you about it," he went on. "Don't

think I'm trying to be"—his wrist hesitated over a word, as though over a chesspiece—"highbrow. Don't think I'm trying to be highbrow if I tell it to you" —again his wrist hesitated—"objectively. As though you knew nothing about it. As though you weren't concerned in it. It's the only way you will understand the problem he had to face."

Hargreaves was very intent when he said this. He was bending forward, looking up from under his eyebrows; his heavy overcoat flopped over the sides of his knees, and his gloved hands, seldom still, either made a slight gesture or pressed flat on his knees.

"Take Tony Marvell, to begin with," he argued. "A good fellow, whom everybody liked. Not a good business man, perhaps: too generous to be a good business man; but as conscientious as the very devil, and with so fine a mathematical brain that he got over the practical difficulties.

"Tony was Senior Wrangler at Cambridge, and intended to go on with his mathematics. But then his uncle died, so he had to take over the business. You know what the business was then: three luxury hotels, built, equipped and run by Old Jim, the uncle, in Old Jim's most flamboyant style: all going to rack and ruin.

"Everybody said it was madness for Tony to push his shoulder up against the business world. His brother—that's Stephen Marvell, the former surgeon —said Tony would only bring Old Jim's card-houses down on everybody and swamp them all with more debts. But you know what happened. At twenty-five, Tony took over the business. At twenty-seven, he had the hotels on a paying basis. At thirty, they were hotels to which everybody went as a matter of course: blazing their sky-signs, humming with efficiency, piling up profits which startled even Tony.

"And all because he sneered at the idea that there could be any such thing as overwork. He never let up. You can imagine that dogged expression of his: 'Well, I don't like this work, but let's clean it up satisfactorily so that we can get on to more important things'—like his studies. He did it partly because he had promised Old Jim he would, and partly *because* (you see?) he thought the business so unimportant that he wanted to show how easy it was. But it wasn't easy. No man could stand that pace. London, Brighton, Eastbourne; he knew everything there was to know about the Marvell Hotels, down to the price of a pillow-case and the cost of grease for the lifts. At the end of the fifth year he collapsed one morning in his office. His brother Stephen told him what he had to do.

" 'You're getting out of this,' Stephen said. 'You're going clear away. Round the world, anywhere; but for six or eight months at the shortest time. During that time, you're not even so much as to think of your work. Is that clear?'

"Tony told me the story himself last night. He says that the whole thing might never have happened if he had not been forbidden to write to anybody while he was away.

" 'Not even so much as a postcard,' snapped Stephen, 'to anybody. If you do, it'll be more business; and then God help you.'

" 'But Judith—' Tony protested.

" 'Particularly to Judith,' said Stephen. 'If you insist on marrying your secretary, that's your affair. But you don't ruin your rest-cure by exchanging long letters about the hotels.'

"You can imagine Stephen's over-aristocratic, thin-nosed face towering over him, dull with anger. You can imagine Stephen in his black coat and striped trousers, standing up beside the polished desk of his office in Harley Street. Stephen Marvell (and, to a certain extent, Tony, too) had that over-bred air which Old Jim Marvell had always wanted and never achieved.

"Tony did not argue. He was willing enough, because he was tired. Even if he were forbidden to write to Judith, he could always think about her. In the middle of September, more than eight months ago, he sailed by the *Queen Anne* from Southampton. And on that night the terrors began."

Hargreaves paused. The gas-fire still hissed in the little, dim study. You would have known that this was a house in which death had occurred, and occurred recently, by the look on the face of Hargreaves' companion. He went on:

"The *Queen Anne* sailed at midnight. Tony saw her soaring up above the docks, as high as the sky. He saw the long decks, white and shiny like shoe-boxes, gleaming under skeins of lights; he saw the black dots of passengers moving along them; he heard the click rattle-rush of winches as great cranes swung over the crowd on the docks; and he felt the queer, pleasurable, restless feeling which stirs the nerves at the beginning of an ocean voyage.

"At first he was as excited as a schoolboy. Stephen Marvell and Judith Gates, Tony's fiancée, went down to Southampton with him. Afterwards he recalled talking to Judith; holding her arm, piloting her through the rubbery-smelling passages of the ship to show her how fine it was. They went to Tony's cabin, where his luggage had been piled together with a basket of fruit. Everybody agreed that it was a fine cabin.

"It was not until a few minutes before the 'all-ashore' gong that the first pang of loneliness struck him. Stephen and Judith had already gone ashore, for all of them disliked these awkward, last-minute leave-takings. They were standing on the docks, far below. By leaning over the rail of the ship he could just see them. Judith's face was tiny, remote and smiling; infinitely loved. She was waving to him. Round him surged the crowd; faces, hats, noise under naked lights, accentuating the break with home and the water that would widen between. Next he heard the gong begin to bang: hollow, quivering, pulsing to loudness over the cry: 'All ashore that's going ashore!'; and dying away into the ship. He did not want to go. There was still plenty of time. He could still gather up his luggage and get off.

"For a time he stood by the rail, with the breeze from Southampton Water in his face. Such a notion was foolish. He would stay. With a last wave to Judith and Stephen, he drew himself determinedly away. He would be sensible. He would go below and unpack his things. Feeling the unreality of that hollow night, he went down to his cabin on C Deck. And his luggage was not there! He stared round the stuffy cabin with its neat curtains at the portholes. There had been a trunk and two suitcases, gaudily labelled, to say nothing of the basket of fruit. Now the cabin was empty.

"Tony ran upstairs again to the purser's office. The purser, a harassed man behind a kind of ticket-window desk, was just getting rid of a clamouring crowd. In the intervals of striking a hand-bell and calling orders, he caught Tony's eye.

" 'My luggage—' Tony said.

" 'That's all right, Mr. Marvell,' said the harassed official. 'It's being taken ashore. But you'd better hurry yourself.'

"Tony had here only a feeling of extreme stupidity. 'Taken ashore?' he said. 'But why? Who told you to send it ashore?'

" 'Why, *you* did,' said the purser, looking up suddenly from a sheet of names and figures.

"Tony only looked at him.

" 'You came here,' the purser went on, with sharply narrowing eyes, 'not ten minutes ago. You said you had decided not to take the trip, and asked for your luggage to be taken off. I told you that at this date we could not, of course, refund the—'

" 'Get it back!' said Tony. His voice sounded wrong. 'I couldn't have told you that. Get it back!'

" 'Just as you like, sir,' said the purser, smiting on the bell, '*if* there's time.'

"Overhead the hoarse blast of the whistle, that mournfullest of all sounds at sea, beat out against Southampton Water. B Deck, between open doors, was cold and gusty.

"Now Tony Marvell had not the slightest recollection of having spoken to the purser before. That was what struck him between the eyes like a blow, and what, for the moment, almost drove him to run away from the *Queen Anne* before they should lift the gang-plank. It was the nightmare again. One of the worst features of his nervous breakdown had been the conviction, coming in flashes at night, that he was not real any longer; that his body and his inner self had moved apart, the first walking or talking in everyday life like an articulate dummy, while the brain remained in another place. It was as though he were dead, and seeing his body move. Dead.

"To steady his wits, he tried to concentrate on familiar human things. Judith, for instance; he recalled Judith's hazel eyes, the soft line of her cheek as she turned her head, the paper cuffs she wore at the office. Judith, his fiancée, his secretary, who would take care of things while he was away; whom he loved, and who was so maddeningly close even now. But he must not think of Judith. Instead, he pictured his brother Stephen, and Johnny Cleaver, and any other friends who occurred to him. He even thought of Old Jim Marvell, who was dead. And—so strong is the power of imaginative visualisation—at that moment, in the breezy lounge-room facing the purser's office, he thought he saw Old Jim looking at him round the corner of a potted palm.

"All this, you understand, went through Tony's mind in the brief second while he heard the ship's whistle hoot out over his head.

"He made some excuse to the purser, and went below. He was grateful for the chatter of noise, for the people passing up and down below decks. None of them paid any attention to him, but at least they were there. But, when he opened the door of his cabin, he stopped and stood very still in the doorway.

"The propellers had begun to churn. A throb, a heavy vibration, shook upwards through the ship; it made the tooth-glass tinkle in the rack, and sent a series of creaks through the bulkheads. The *Queen Anne* was moving. Tony Marvell took hold of the door as though that movement had been a lurch, and he stared at the bed across the cabin. On the white bedpread, where it had not been before, lay an automatic pistol."

The gas-fire had heated its asbestos pillars to glowing red. Again there was a brief silence in the little study of the house in St. John's Wood. Hargreaves—Sir Charles Hargreaves, Assistant Commissioner of Police for the Criminal Investigation Department—leaned down and lowered the flame of the heater. Even the tone of his voice seemed to change when the gas ceased its loud hissing.

"Wait!" he said, lifting his hand. "I don't want you to get the wrong impression. Don't think that the fear, the slow approach of what was going to happen, pursued Tony all through his trip round the world. It didn't. That's the most curious part of the whole affair.

"Tony has told me that it was a brief, bad bout, lasting perhaps fifteen minutes in all, just before and just after the *Queen Anne* sailed. It was not alone the uncanny feeling that things had ceased to be real. It was a sensation of active malignancy—of hatred, of danger, of what you like—surrounding him and pressing on him. He could feel it like a weak current from a battery.

"But five minutes after the ship had headed out to

open sea, every such notion fell away from him. It was as though he had emerged out of an evil fog. That hardly seems reasonable. Even supposing that there are evil emanations, or evil spirits, it is difficult to think that they are confined to one country; that their tentacles are broken by half a mile's distance; that they cannot cross water. Yet there it was. One moment he was standing there with the automatic pistol in his hand, the noise of the engines beating in his ears and a horrible impulse joggling his elbow to put the muzzle of the pistol into his mouth and—

"Then—snap! Something broke: that is the only way he can describe it. He stood upright. He felt like a man coming out of a fever, shaken and sweating, but back from behind the curtain into the real world again. He gulped deep breaths. He went to the porthole and opened it. From that time on, he says, he began to get well.

"How the automatic had got into his cabin he did not know. He knew he must have brought it himself, in one of those blind flashes. But he could not remember. He stared at it with new eyes, and new feeling of the beauty and sweetness of life. He felt as though he had been reprieved from execution.

"You might have thought that he would have flung the pistol overboard in sheer fear of touching it. But he didn't. To him it was the part of a puzzle. He stared much at it: a Browning 38, of Belgian manufacture, fully loaded. After the first few days, when he did keep it locked away out of sight in his trunk, he pondered over it. It represented the one piece of evidence he could carry back home with him, the one tangible reality in a nightmare.

"At the New York Customs-shed it seemed to excite no surprise. He carried it overland with him—Cleveland, Chicago, Salt Lake City—to San Francisco, in a fog, and then down the kindled sea to Honolulu. At Yokohama they were going to take it away from him; only a huge bribe retrieved it. Afterwards he carried it on his person, and was never searched. As the broken bones of his nerves knitted, as in the wash of the propellers, there was peace, it became a kind of mascot. It went with him through the blistering heat of the Indian Ocean, into the murky Red Sea, to the Mediterranean. To Port Said, to Cairo in early winter. To Naples and Marseilles and Gibraltar. It was tucked away in his hip-pocket on the bitter cold night, a little more than eight months after his departure, when Tony Marvell —a healed man again—landed back at Southampton in the S.S. *Chippenham Castle.*

"It was snowing that night, you remember? The boat-train roared through thickening snow. It was crowded, and the heat would not work.

"Tony knew that there could be nobody at Southampton to meet him. His itinerary had been laid out in advance, and he had stuck to the bitter letter of his instructions about not writing even so much as a postcard. But he had altered the itinerary, so as to take a ship that would get him home in time for Christmas; he would burst in on them a week early. For eight months he had lived in a void. In an hour or two he would be home. He would see Judith again.

"In the dimly lighted compartment of the train, his fellow-passengers were not talkative. The long voyage had squeezed their conversation dry; they almost hated each other. Even the snow roused only a flicker of enthusiasm.

" 'Real old-fashioned Christmas!' said one.

" 'Ha!' said another appreciatively, scratching with his fingernails at the frosted window.

" 'Damn cold, *I* call it,' snarled a third. 'Can't they ever make the heat work in these trains? I'm damn well going to make a complaint!'

"After that, with a sympathetic grunt or mutter, each retired behind his newspaper; a white, blank wall which rustled occasionally, and behind which they drank up news of home.

"In other words (Tony remembers that he thought then), he was in England again. He was home. For himself, he only pretended to read. He leaned back in his seat, listening vaguely to the clackety-roar of the wheels, and the long blast of the whistle that was torn behind as the train gathered speed.

"He knew exactly what he would do. It would be barely ten o'clock when they reached Waterloo. He would jump into a cab, and hurry home—to this house—for a wash and brush-up. Then he would pelt up to Judith's flat at Hampstead as hard as he could go. Yet this thought, which should have made him glow, left him curiously chilly round the heart. He fought the chill. He laughed at himself. Determinedly he opened the newspaper, distracting himself, turning from page to page, running his eye down each column. Then he stopped. Something familiar caught his eye, some familiar name. It was an obscure item on the middle page.

"He was reading in this paper the news of his own death. Just that.

" 'Mr. Anthony Dean Marvell, of Upper Avenue Road, St. John's Wood, and owner of Marvell Hotels, Ltd., was found shot dead last night in his bedroom at home. A bullet had penetrated up through the roof of the mouth into the brain, and a small-calibre automatic was in his hand. The body was found by Mrs. Reach, Mr. Marvell's housekeeper, who . . .'

"A suicide!

"And once again, as suddenly as it had left him aboard ship, the grasp fell on him, shutting him off from the real world into the unreal. The compartment, as I told you, was very dimly lighted. So it was perhaps natural that he could only dimly see a blank wall of upheld newspapers facing him; as though there were no fellow-passengers there, as though they had deserted him in a body, leaving only the screen of papers that joggled a little with the rush of the train.

"Yes, he was alone.

"He got up blindly, dragging open the door of the compartment to get out into the corridor. The confined space seemed to be choking him. Holding his own newspaper up high, so as to catch the light from the compartment, he read the item again.

"There could be no possibility of a mistake. The account was too detailed. It told all about him, his past and present . . .

" '. . . His brother, Mr. Stephen Marvell, the eminent Harley Street surgeon, was hurriedly summoned. . . . His fiancée, Miss Judith Gates . . . It is understood that in September Mr. Marvell suffered a nervous breakdown, from which even a long rest had not effected a cure. . . .'

"Tony looked at the date of the newspaper, afraid of what he might see. But it was the date of that day: the twenty-third of December. From this account, it appeared that he had shot himself forty-eight hours before.

"And the gun was in his hip-pocket now.

"Tony folded up the newspaper. The train moved under his feet with a dancing sway, jerking above the click of the wheels; and another thin blast of the whistle went by. It reminded him of the whistle aboard the *Queen Anne*. He glanced along the dusky corridor. It was empty except for someone, whom he supposed to be another passenger, leaning elbows on the rail past the windows and staring out at the flying snow.

"He remembers nothing else until the train reached Waterloo. But something—an impression, a subconscious memory—registered in his mind about that passenger he had seen in the corridor. First it had to do with the shape of the person's shoulders. Then Tony realized that this was because the person was wearing a greatcoat with an old-fashioned brown fur collar. He was jumping blindly out of the train at Waterloo when he remembered that Old Jim Marvell always used to wear such a collar.

"After that he seemed to see it everywhere.

"When he hurried up to the guard's van to claim his trunk and suitcases, the luggage-ticket in his hand, he was in such a crowd that he could not move his arms. But he thought he felt brown fur press the back of his shoulders.

"A porter got him a taxi. It was a relief to see a London cab again, in a coughing London terminus, and hear the bump of the trunk as it went up under the strap, and friendly voices again. He gave the address to the driver, tipped the porter, and jumped inside. Even so, the porter seemed to be holding open the door of the taxi longer than was necessary.

"'Close it, man!' Tony found himself shouting. 'Close it, quick!'

"'Yessir,' said the porter, jumping back. The door slammed. Afterwards, the porter stood and stared after the taxi. Tony, glancing out through the little back window, saw him still standing there.

"It was dark in the cab, and as close as though a photographer's black hood had been drawn over him. Tony could see little. But he carefully felt with his hands all over the seat, all over the open space; and he found nothing."

At this point in the story, Hargreaves broke off for a moment or two. He had been speaking with difficulty; not as though he expected to be doubted, but as though the right words were hard to find. His gloved fingers opened and closed on his knee.

For the first time his companion—Miss Judith Gates—interrupted him. Judith spoke from the shadow on the other side of the gas-fire.

"Wait!" she said. "Please!"

"Yes?" said Hargreaves.

"This person who was following Tony." She spoke also with difficulty. "You aren't telling me that it was—well, was—?"

"Was what?"

"Dead," said Judith.

"I don't know who it was," answered Hargreaves, looking at her steadily. "Except that it seemed to be somebody with a fur collar on his coat. I'm telling you Tony's story, which I believe."

Judith's hand shaded her eyes. "All the same," she insisted, and her pleasant voice went high, "even supposing it was! I mean, even supposing it was the person you think. *He* of all people, living or dead, wouldn't have tried to put any evil influence round Tony. Old Jim loved Tony. He left Tony every penny he owned, and not a farthing to Stephen. He always told Tony he'd look after him."

"And so he did," said Hargreaves.

"But—"

"You see," Hargreaves told her slowly. "You still don't understand the source of the evil influence. Tony didn't, himself. All he knew was that he was bowling along in a dark taxi, through slippery, snowy streets; and whatever might be following him, good or bad, he couldn't endure it.

"Even so, everything might have ended well if the taxi-driver had been careful. But he wasn't. That was the first snowfall of the year, and the driver miscalculated. When they were only two hundred yards from Upper Avenue Road, he tried to take a turn too fast. Tony felt the helpless swing of the skid; he saw the glass partition tilt, and a black tree-trunk rush up, huge at them until it exploded against the outer windscreen. They landed upright against the tree, with a buckled wheel.

"'I *'ad* to swerve,' the driver was crying. 'I *'ad* to! An old gent with a fur collar walked smack out in front of—'

"And so, you see, Tony had to walk home alone.

"He knew something was following him before he had taken half a dozen steps. Two hundred yards don't sound like a great distance. First right, first left, and you're home. But here it seemed to stretch out interminably, as such things do in dreams. He did not want to leave the taxi-driver. The driver thought this was because Tony doubted his honesty about bringing the luggage on when the wheel was repaired. But it was not that.

"For the first part of the way, Tony walked rapidly. The other thing walked at an equal pace behind him. By the light of a streetlamp Tony could see the wet fur collar on the coat, but nothing else. Afterwards he increased his pace to what was almost a run; and, though no difference could be seen in the gait of what was behind him, it was still there. Unlike you, Tony didn't wonder whether it might be good or evil. These nice differences don't occur to you when you're dealing with something that may be dead. All he knew was that he mustn't let it *identify* itself with him or he was done for.

"Then it began to gain on him, and he ran.

"The pavement was black, the snow dirty grey. He saw the familiar turning, where front gardens were built up above the low, stone walls; he saw the street sign fastened to one of those corners, white lettering on black; and, in sudden blind panic, he plunged for the steps that led up to his home.

"The house was dark. He got the cold keys out of his pocket, but the key-ring slipped round in his fingers, like soap in bath-water, and fell on the tiled floor of the vestibule. He groped after it in the dark—just as the thing turned in at the gate. In fact, Tony heard the gate creak. He found the keys, found the lock by a miracle, and opened the door.

"But he was too late, because the other thing was already coming up the front steps. Tony says that at close range, against a streetlamp, the fur collar looked more wet and moth-eaten; that is all he can describe. He was in a dark hall with the door open. Even familiar things had fled his wits and he could not remember the position of the light-switch.

"The other person walked in.

"In his hip-pocket, Tony remembered, he still had the weapon he had carried round the world. He fumbled under his overcoat to get the gun out of his pocket; but even that weak gesture was no good to him, for he dropped the gun on the carpet. Since the visitor was now within six feet of him, he did not stop. He bolted up the stairs.

"At the top of the stairs he risked a short glance down. The other thing had stopped. In faint bluish patches of light which came through the open front door, Tony could see that it was stooping down to pick up the automatic pistol from the carpet.

"Tony thinks—now—that he began to switch on lights in the upper hall. Also, he shouted something. He was standing before the door of his bedroom. He threw open this door, blundered in, and began to turn on more lamps. He had got two lamps lighted before he turned to look at the bed, which was occupied.

"The man on the bed did not, however, sit up at the coming of noise or lights. A sheet covered him from head to feet; and even under the outline of the sheet you could trace the line of the wasted, sunken features. Tony Marvell then did what was perhaps the most courageous act of his life. He had to know. He walked across and turned down the upper edge of the sheet, and looked down at his own face; a dead face, turned sightlessly up from the bed.

"Shock? Yes. But more terror? No. For this dead man was real, he was flesh and blood—as Tony was flesh and blood. He looked exactly like Tony. But it was now no question of a real world and an unreal world; it was no question of going mad. This man was real; and that meant fraud and imposture.

"A voice from across the room said: '*So you're alive!*' And Tony turned round, to find his brother Stephen looking at him from the doorway.

"Stephen wore a red dressing-gown, hastily pulled round him, and his hair was tousled. His face was one of collapse.

"'I didn't mean to do it!' Stephen was crying out at him. Even though Tony did not understand, he felt that the words were a confession of guilt; they were babbling words, words which made you pity the man who said them.

"'I never really meant to have you killed aboard that ship,' said Stephen. 'It was all a joke. You know I wouldn't have hurt you; you know that, don't you? Listen—'

"Now Stephen (as I said) was standing in the

doorway, clutching his dressing-gown round him. What made him look round towards the hall behind, quickly, Tony did not know. Perhaps he heard a sound behind him. Perhaps he saw something out of the corner of his eye. But Stephen did look round, and he began to scream.

"Tony saw no more, for the light in the hall went out. The fear was back on him again, and he could not move. For he saw a hand. It was only, so to speak, the flicker of a hand. This hand darted in from the darkness out in the hall; it caught hold of the knob on the bedroom door, and closed the door. It turned a key on the outside, locking Tony into the room. It kept Stephen outside in the dark hall—and Stephen was still screaming.

"A good thing, too, that Tony had been locked in the room. That saved trouble with the police afterwards.

"The rest of the testimony comes from Mrs. Reach, the housekeeper. Her room was next door to Stephen's bedroom, at the end of the upstairs hall. She was awakened by screams, by what seemed to be thrashing sounds, and the noise of hard breathing. These sounds passed her door towards Stephen's room.

"Just as she was getting out of her bed and putting on a dressing-gown, she heard Stephen's door close. Just as she went out into the hall, she heard, for the second time in forty-eight hours, the noise of a pistol-shot.

"Now, Mrs. Reach will testify in a coroner's court that nobody left, or could have left Stephen's room after the shot. She was looking at the door, though it was several minutes before she could screw up enough courage to open the door. When she did open it, all sounds had ceased. He had been shot through the right temple at close range; presumably by himself, since the weapon was discovered in a tangle of stained bed-clothing. There was nobody else in the room, and all the windows were locked on the inside. The only other thing Mrs. Reach noticed was an unpleasant, an intensely unpleasant smell of mildewed cloth and wet fur."

Again Hargreaves paused. It seemed that he had come to the end of the story. An outsider might have thought, too, that he had emphasised these horrors too much, for the girl across from him kept her hands pressed against her eyes. But Hargreaves knew his business.

"Well?" he said gently. "You see the explanation, don't you?"

Judith took her hands away from her eyes. "Explanation?"

"The natural explanation," repeated Hargreaves, spacing his words. "Tony Marvell is not going mad. He never had any brain-storms or 'blind flashes.' He only thought he had. The whole thing was a cruel and murderous fake, engineered by Stephen, and it went wrong. But if it had succeeded, Stephen Marvell would have committed a very nearly perfect murder."

The relief he saw flash across Judith's face, the sudden dazed catching at hope, went to Hargreaves' heart. But he did not show this.

"Let's go back eight months," he went on, "and take it from the beginning. Now, Tony is a very wealthy young man. The distinguished Stephen, on the other hand, was swamped with debts and always on the thin edge of bankruptcy. If Tony were to die, Stephen, the next of kin, would inherit the whole estate. So Stephen decided that Tony had to die.

"But Stephen, a medical man, knew the risks of murder. No matter how cleverly you plan it, there is always *some* suspicion; and Stephen was bound to be suspected. He was unwilling to risk those prying detectives, those awkward questions, those damning postmortem reports—until, more than eight months ago, he suddenly saw how he could destroy Tony without the smallest suspicion attaching to himself.

"In St. Jude's Hospital, where he did some charity work, Stephen had found a broken-down ex-schoolmaster named Rupert Hayes. Every man in this world, they say, has his exact double. Hayes was Tony's double to the slightest feature. He was, in fact, so uncannily like Tony that the very sight of him made Stephen flinch. Now, Hayes was dying of tuberculosis. He had, at most, not more than a year to live. He would be eager to listen to any scheme which would allow him to spend the rest of his life in luxury, and die of natural causes in a soft bed. To him Stephen explained the trick.

"Tony should be ordered off—apparently—on a trip round the world. On the night he was to sail, Tony should be allowed to go aboard.

"Hayes should be waiting aboard that same ship, with a gun in his pocket. After Stephen or any other friends had left the ship conveniently early, Hayes should entice Tony up to the dark boat-deck. Then he was to shoot Tony through the head, and drop the body overboard.

"Haven't you ever realized that a giant ocean-liner, just before it leaves port, is the ideal place to commit a murder? Not a soul will remember you afterwards. The passengers notice nothing; they are too excited. The crew notice nothing; they are kept too busy. The confusion of the crowd is intense. And what happens to your victim after he goes overboard? He will be sucked under and presently caught by the terrible propellers, to make him unrecognizable. When a body is found—if it is found at all—it will be presumed to be some dock-roysterer. Certainly it will never be connected with the ocean-liner, because there will be nobody missing from the liner's passenger list.

"Missing from the passenger list? Of course not! Hayes, you see, was to go to the purser and order Tony's luggage to be sent ashore. He was to say he was cancelling the trip, and not going after all. After killing Tony he was then to walk ashore as—"

The girl uttered an exclamation.

Hargreaves nodded. "You see it now. He was to walk ashore *as Tony*. He was to say to his friends that he couldn't face the journey after all; and everybody would be happy. Why not? The real Tony was within an ace of doing just that.

"Then, Hayes, well coached, would simply settle down to play the part of Tony for the rest of his natural life. Mark that: his natural life; a year at most. He would be too ill to attend to the business, of course. He wouldn't even see you, his fiancée, too often. If ever he made any bad slips, that, of course, would be his bad nerves. He would be allowed to 'develop' lung trouble. At the end of a year, amid sorrowing friends . . .

"Stephen had planned brilliantly. 'Murder'? What do you mean, murder? Let the doctors examine as much as they like! Let the police ask what questions they like! Whatever steps are taken, Stephen Marvell is absolutely safe. For the poor devil in bed really has died a natural death.

"Only—well, it went wrong. Hayes wasn't cut out to be a murderer. I hadn't the favour of his acquaintance, but he must have been a decent sort. He promised to do this. But, when it came to the actual fact, he couldn't force himself to kill Tony: literally, physically couldn't. He threw away his pistol and ran. On the other hand, once off the ship, he couldn't confess to Stephen that Tony was still alive. He couldn't give up that year of sweet luxury, with all Tony's money at his disposal to soothe his aching lungs. So he pretended to Stephen that he had done the job, and Stephen danced for joy. But Hayes, as the months went on, did not dance. He knew Tony wasn't dead. He knew there would be a reckoning soon. And he couldn't let it end like that. A week before he thought Tony was coming home, after writing a letter to the police to explain everything, Hayes shot himself rather than face exposure."

There was a silence. "That, I think," Hargreaves said quietly, "explains everything about Tony."

Judith Gates bit her lips. Her pretty face was working; and she could not control the twitching of her capable hands. For a moment she seemed to be praying.

"Thank God!" she murmured. "I was afraid—"

"Yes," said Hargreaves; "I know."

"But it still doesn't explain everything. It—"

Hargreaves stopped her.

"I said," he pointed out, "that it explains everything about Tony. That's all you need worry about. Tony is free. You are free. As for Stephen Marvell's death, it was suicide. That is the official record."

"But that's absurd!" cried Judith. "I didn't like Stephen; I always knew he hated Tony; but he wasn't one to kill himself, even if he were exposed. Don't you see, you haven't explained the one real horror? I must know. I mean, I must know if you think what I think about it. Who was the man with the brown fur collar? Who followed Tony home that night? Who stuck close by him, to keep the evil influences off him? Who was his guardian? Who shot Stephen in revenge?"

Sir Charles Hargreaves looked down at the sputtering gas-fire. His face, inscrutable, was wrinkled in sharp lines from mouth to nostril. His brain held many secrets. He was ready to lock away this one, once he knew that they understood each other.

"You tell me," he said.

Terrified

C. B. GILFORD

Paul Santin had a good day. Small town doctors and drug stores were doing a thriving business, and, therefore, so was Paul Santin, pharmaceutical salesman. But it had been a long day, and now it was past eleven. Santin was driving fast on the country back road, trying to make it home before midnight.

He was tired, sleepy, fighting to stay awake for another half hour. But he was not dozing. He was in complete control of his car. He knew what he was doing.

He'd passed few other cars. Right now the road seemed deserted. He'd chosen this route just for that reason. Light traffic. And that's the way it was—an almost empty road—when he saw the other car.

He saw it first as a pair of headlights rounding the curve a quarter mile ahead. The lights were fantastically bright, and the driver failed to dim them. Santin cursed him, whoever he was. He dimmed his own lights, but received no answering courtesy. He cursed again, vindictively switched his own lights back to highway brightness. But he sensed no real danger in it.

He was vaguely aware that the other car was rocketing toward him at high speed. Too much speed for the kind of road they were on. Mechanically, he slacked off on the accelerator, concentrated on stayin on his own side of the road, and on not looking directly at those oncoming lights.

But it was much too late when he realized the other car was hogging the center of the road. And he had to make his decision too quickly. Whether to bore right in, perhaps leaning on his horn, hoping the other driver would pull aside. Or to hit the shoulder and take his chances with gravel and dirt.

He took the second choice, but not soon enough. He saw the other car wasn't going to concede an inch; so he swerved to the right. The blow was delivered against his left rear fender and wheel. The rear of his car skidded ditchward ahead of the front. Then the whole car seemed to defy gravity. It rolled sideways, leaped into the air, throwing Santin clear of itself at the top of the leap.

He didn't see or hear the final crash of the machine. All his consciousness was in the impact of his body against the hillside that met him like a solid wall; then he slid downward in the midst of a miniature avalanche of small stones and dirt. Afterwards he lay still, and so was all the world around him.

In that first moment, he felt no pain. The shock had numbed him. But he knew he was alive. He knew he was somehow conscious. He was also distantly, vaguely aware that his body was broken and beginning to bleed.

The blinding lights were gone. He was lying on his back in a patch of weeds. Above him were the stars and a bright full moon. They seemed closer to him than they had ever seemed before. Perhaps it was that optical illusion that first gave him the idea he was going to die.

At that moment, he felt no anger about it. He could remember his anger before the crash, but it was a distant, unreal thing to him. Again the thought of dying flitted across his mind. The dying feel nothing toward other creatures. They are completely concerned with themselves.

Then he heard the voices. A renewal of contact with the world. There'd been people in that other car. He wondered about them, calmly, without fury, without sympathy. But he gave all his attention to the listening.

"He isn't here." A masculine voice a bit young.

The other car had been hit too. It had been stopped. Or perhaps the driver had stopped the car without being forced to. Anyway, the people from that car, whoever they were, had walked back to his car and were looking for him.

To help him? His first instinct was to call out, guide them to where he lay. They'd been selfish in hogging the road, but now they were charitable, wanting to aid. But then another instinct rose to fight against the first. Would they really be friendly? Suddenly he felt terrified of them. Without knowing why. Surely everybody wants to help accident victims. Don't they?

"He must have been thrown out." A girl's voice answering. Frightened.

"I guess so. What'll we do?" The same masculine voice. So there must be only two of them.

"Look for him," the girl said.

A hesitation. "Why?"

Another hesitation. "Don't you want to know what happened to him . . . or her?"

"I don't know." The masculine voice trembled. "I don't know . . ."

"I think we ought to look around and find him."

"Okay . . . It's dark though."

"You've got a flashlight, haven't you?"

"Sure. I'll get it."

Footsteps up on the road. The boy returning to his own car for the flashlight. And then silence again.

Santin waited, trembling in sweat of new fear. He hadn't liked the sound of those voices. That boy and girl weren't people who would care. If he was dying, they weren't people who would be of much help.

If he was dying? He was certain of it. The pain was beginning now. He could identify it in several places. His face, his chest, both his legs. And somewhere deep inside him, where nobody could reach but a doctor. That was the area of pain that made him certain of death.

So it didn't matter, did it? Whether or not they found him with their flashlight?

"Okay, I've got it." The boy's voice. "Where do we look?"

"In the ditch, I guess."

Scuffling footsteps, disturbing gravel, crunching through grass and brush. Then a winking light, sweeping back and forth. Both the light and the footsteps getting nearer. Inevitably, they would find him. He could speed their search by calling to them. But he didn't. He waited.

"Hey!"

The light was in his face. Paralyzed, he couldn't

seem to turn away from it. The footsteps hurried.
And then they were there. Two forms standing over
him, outlined against the sky. And the light shining
in his eyes. He blinked, but they didn't seem to
understand that the light bothered him.

"He's alive." The girl. "His eyes are open."

"Yeah, I see . . ."

"But he's hurt." The figure who was the girl knelt
down beside him, mercifully shielding him from the
flashlight. Because of the brightness of the moon, he
could see her face.

She was young, terribly young, sixteen maybe. She
was pretty too, her hair dark, her skin pale, perhaps
abnormally so, her made-up mouth lurid in contrast.
But there was no emotion in her face. She was in
shock possibly. But as her eyes roved over his in-
juries, no sympathy lighted in her eyes.

"You're pretty badly hurt, aren't you?" The ques-
tion was right at him.

"Yes . . ." He discovered he could speak without
great difficulty.

"Where? Do you know?"

"All over, I guess. Inside especially."

The girl was thoughtful over his reply. Her next
question seemed cold, calculated. "Do you think you
could pull through if we got help?"

He thought too, gave himself time to answer. But
even so, he made a mistake. "I think I'm going to
die," he said, and knew he had made a mistake as
soon as he'd said it.

The girl's face changed somehow, imperceptibly.
Santin couldn't fathom the change. He only knew it

had happened. She pulled away from him, rose to her feet, rejoining the boy.

"He's going to die," she said. As if she knew it as certainly as Santin himself.

"There's no use trying to find a doctor then, is there?" The boy sounded relieved, as if his responsibility for this whole thing had ended now.

"I guess not."

"What'll we do then?"

"Nothing, I guess. Just wait here. A car's bound to come along sometime."

"We can ride back to town then, huh?" The boy seemed to depend completely on the girl for leadership.

"Sure. We can send a doctor or somebody back. But this guy will probably be dead by then. And we'll have to report to the police."

"The police?"

"We'll have to. You killed a man."

There was silence then. Santin lay at their feet, looking up at the two silhouetted figures. They were talking about him as already dead. But somehow it didn't anger him yet. Maybe because he considered himself dead too.

"Arlene . . . what'll they do to me?"

"Who, the police?"

"Yes . . . You said I killed a man."

"Well, you did, didn't you?"

The boy hesitated. "But it was an accident," he managed finally. "You know it was an accident, don't you, Arlene? I mean, it just happened . . ."

"Sure."

They were talking softly, but Santin could hear every word they said. And he felt compelled somehow to speak. "Every accident is somebody's fault," he told them.

They were startled. He could see them look at each other, then down at him again. "What do you mean by that, mister?" the boy asked after a moment.

"This accident was your fault. That's what I mean." He still wasn't angry. That wasn't why he argued. But he felt the blame should be established.

"How was it my fault?"

"First of all, you didn't dim your lights . . ."

"Well, neither did you."

"I did at first."

"But you switched back to highway lights again."

"Only after you refused to dim."

The boy was silent again for a moment. Then he said, "But when we hit, you had your lights on bright."

Santin had to admit it. "I got mad," he said. "But that's not the most important thing. You were driving over on my side of the road."

The boy's face went around to the girl. "Arlene, was I on his side of the road?"

It seemed she giggled. Or something like it. "How do I know? We were—"

She didn't finish the sentence, but Santin guessed the rest of it. They'd been necking, or petting, or whatever young people called it these days. That was why the boy hadn't dimmed his lights. And that was why he'd had poor control of his car. And now he, Santin, had to pay the price of their good time.

It angered him, finally. With a curious sort of

anger. Detached somehow, separate from himself. Because now in the long run it didn't really matter to him. Since he was going to die.

But also Santin felt a certain satisfaction. He could speak vindictively, and with assurance. "You see, you were on the wrong side of the road. So it was your fault."

The boy heard him, but he kept looking at the girl. "What will they do to me?" he asked her. "The police, I mean. What will they do to me?"

"How do I know?" she snapped at him. She'd been so calm. Now maybe the initial shock was wearing off. Now maybe she was becoming frightened, nervous.

"Even if I was on the wrong side of the road," the boy said, "it was still an accident. I didn't try to run into this guy's car. I didn't try to kill him."

"That's right . . ."

"You read about these things in the paper. Nothing much happens to the driver. Maybe he gets fined. But my dad can pay that. And even if I had to go to jail, it wouldn't be for long, would it, Arlene? What do you think it would be? Thirty days?"

"Or maybe sixty. That wouldn't be so bad."

Santin listened to them. And slowly the anger welled higher in him. Or maybe even ninety days, he could have added. Some insurance company would pay. But the killer himself wouldn't pay nearly enough. Ninety days for murder.

"There's just one thing," the boy said suddenly.

"What?"

"It'll be called an accident. And maybe it'll be called my fault. A little bit anyway. That is, if this guy here doesn't spout off to anybody."

"About what?"

"About who dimmed lights and who didn't. And who was on whose side of the road. But of course he can't spout off if he's dead."

"That's right." There was suddenly something strange in the girl's voice, an awareness.

"So he's got to be dead. Do you see what I mean, Arlene?"

"He said he was going to die . . ."

"Yeah, but he doesn't know. And neither do we. But he's got to die. We've got to make sure he dies." The boy's voice went up suddenly, toward the pitch of hysteria.

Santin saw the girl clutch the boy's arm and look up into his face. The whole posture of her body denoted fear.

"There's another thing too." The boy spoke swiftly, almost babbling. "My dad has told me about insurance. They have to pay more for a guy who's just crippled than for a guy who's dead. They pay big money to cripples. I don't know whether our insurance is that big. If this guy doesn't die, and is just hurt real bad, it might cost us a lot more than the insurance we got. And, man, what my dad would do to me then."

The girl was terrified now. "But he's going to die," she whispered hoarsely.

"How do we know that, Arlene? How do we know?"

Santin felt no pain now. Only fury. They hadn't offered to help him. They wanted him dead. They were selfish, unbelievably selfish. And they were cruel enough to discuss all this right in front of him.

Suddenly, the boy was kneeling, and the flashlight was probing Santin's face again. Santin blinked in the glare, but despite it, he got his first look at the boy. Young. Young like the girl. But not calm like she'd been. Panic was in his eyes. And he was hurt too. An ugly scalp wound marred the left side of his head, and blood was matted in his hair.

"How do you feel, mister?" the boy asked.

Santin disdained to answer. He wouldn't give them the same satisfaction again. He wouldn't tell them of the hot flood of pain that washed over him in ever-growing waves. He wouldn't tell them he'd already heard death whispering in his ear, cajoling him to let go of life.

But he saw the desperation in the boy's face. The boy searched farther with the flashlight, playing it up and down Santin's body. Then he stood up.

"He doesn't look like he's hurt bad enough to die," he told the girl.

No, it doesn't look like that, Santin thought. The damage is inside. But it's just as fatal. Don't tell them though. Let them sweat. And you might stay alive till somebody comes.

A sudden eruption of pain blotted out his thoughts, leaving him barely conscious.

The girl screamed, and it was as though she was screaming for him. The boy had apparently struck him in some way. "What are you doing?" she demanded.

The boy's answer was almost a scream too. "He's got to die. I've got to make him die."

There was a strain of decency in the girl somewhere. Or a woman's compassion. "But you can't kill him," she told the boy fiercely.

"What difference does it make?" he argued back, with hysteria in his voice again. "I've already killed him, haven't I? He's just got to die quick, that's all. Don't you understand, Arlene?"

Obviously she didn't. She clung to him, holding him back.

"Nobody will ever know the difference," he told her. There was logic in his argument. "He's hurt already. They'll think it's from the accident."

They were silent for a little while. By twisting his head as far as he could, Santin could see them. They were two dark shadows against the lighter background of the sky, so close together that they merged. Santin could sense the desperation in their embrace. The girl with her feminine instinct for mercy. The boy nothing more than a brute, mad with the desire for self-preservation. Yet somehow the girl could love him. And because she loved him, she was in this together with him.

"All right, Vince," he heard her say finally.

And still all Santin could do was to lie there. Probably he was going to be beaten and kicked to death. Murdered deliberately, logically, to protect a weak, vicious kid. Somehow he hadn't been so afraid of that other death. But he was afraid of this one. This death had a quality of horror about it.

"No!" he yelled at them with all his strength. "No!"

His cry broke up their embrace. The flashlight in the boy's hand probed his face again. Santin had been proud before, but he wasn't now. He didn't turn away from the light. He let them see his terror.

"Do you think you can do it, Vince?" the girl asked. Her voice was steady. Now that she'd been convinced, she'd be the stronger of the two.

"I don't know," he said. "But I've got to."

Santin saw him coming and closed his eyes.

"Wait a minute," he heard the girl say, as from the far end of a long tunnel. He existed in a red haze of agony now, and her voice seemed far away.

"What's the matter?"

"You're getting blood on yourself, aren't you?"

"I don't know."

"Look and see."

"Yes, I am. But what difference does it make?"

"Vince, Vince, are you crazy? They'll see the blood. And maybe somebody will get suspicious. They can analyze blood, and tell who it belonged to."

A spark of hope, and Santin dared to open his eyes again. The boy was poised above him for another onslaught, but now he hesitated.

"I know what to do," he said finally.

He left suddenly, exited from Santin's view. But Santin could hear him thrashing around in the weeds. And then finally his shout.

"Arlene, come over and help me lift this."

More thrashing among the weeds. The girl joining the boy.

And the boy's excited voice. "The guy was thrown out of the car, wasn't he? Okay then, he just hit his head on this, that's all. We'll rearrange the body a little. Come on now, let's lift it together."

A slow returning of the footsteps. Wildly, Santin

searched for them. Saw them. They were coming toward him together, their backs bent, straining. Between them they carried a wide flat object that seemed to be very heavy.

He didn't scream this time. He couldn't. Even his vocal cords were paralyzed. But he could watch them. They walked slowly, with great effort. They stopped, one on each side of him, and the huge, heavy, flat object they held blotted out the sky above his face.

Then, at the very last moment of his life, he became aware of something. A soothing calm flooded over him. I was going to die anyway, he thought. This is quicker, of course, maybe even merciful. But it's also murder.

He prayed. A strange prayer. He prayed for a smart cop.

Sergeant Vanneck of the State Highway Patrol was a smart cop. In the gray light of dawn, he studied tire marks on the road. They were hard to see on the dark asphalt, and he couldn't be entirely sure.

He was a little surer how he felt about the pair who stood by his car and watched him as he went about his work. The boy called Vince and the girl called Arlene. They were like most other youngsters who got involved in fatal accidents, and they were also different. So, as the dawn grew brighter, he continued his search.

He found more than he'd expected to find. The body had been removed and the area was pretty well trampled. But he found the evidence nevertheless. It was clear, unquestionable.

He climbed back out of the ditch and walked over

to the girl and the boy. There must have been something terrifying in his face, because it made the boy ask nervously, "What's the matter, Sergeant?"

"There are two sides to a rock," Sergeant Vanneck said. "The top side stays clean, washed by the rain. The bottom side is dirty from contact with the ground. Now you tell me, sonny, how Mr. Santin was thrown from his car so that he hit his head on the bottom side of that rock?"

The Duel

JOAN VATSEK

When Janine stopped talking, sometimes as now she seemed to stop breathing also, as if to listen. The silence came in through the walls of the old Virginia house and pressed itself between them.

"Are you sure this place isn't too lonely for you?" Laurence asked again.

"I'm all right, really I am," Janine said with a fleeting smile. "Stop worrying. Everything's fine. Besides," she added reasonably, "we had to come here. There wasn't any place else to go, was there, now that we've spent all our money on me? I mean was there, darling?"

"No," Laurence agreed after a brief pause. "But I'd forgotten how isolated it was. If you think—"

"It's fine. It's a wonderful old house. Perhaps I'll even try my painting again."

She turned to gaze through the window, her slender arms resting on the sill. It was a high window, and round, like a porthole. From it there was nothing to be seen but woods, stretching away unbroken up the hills to the west.

After a while, her mouth constricted, she turned brightly toward him again.

"You'll have lots of ideas here," she said. "And I'll try to let you alone when you're writing. Really."

She came gracefully toward the kitchen table where he was sitting, resting. While he went on with the unpacking, she managed supper. It came out of cans, but she served the food on fine china set on white damask cloth. She had unpacked and washed the china first of all, while Laurence got sheets and blankets out and made their bed and set the kitchen in working order.

They were surrounded by unpacked boxes in the dining room, but the good dishes were all aglow with pastel color and gold, and Janine glanced at them from time to time, satisfied.

She brought with her always this touch of luxury. It was a part of her being, a part of the aura that made her a unique and lovely woman.

Her gaze drifted around the room, uncarpeted, and bare, and hesitantly to the rooms beyond, in which their apartment furniture would leave echoing spaces.

She avoided looking at the windows now that the blue dusk was sifting down into the solitary valley.

The house was all that remained of an old Virginia estate. It had been left to Laurence by his father, who had gone bankrupt in gentlemanly fashion a generation earlier, raising thoroughbred horses. The acres that surrounded the house had been long since sold. The house and the grounds around it were unsalable; it was too remote. So now, after being away from it since his boyhood, he had returned.

Half hidden in the long grass behind the house

one could still find the remains of stables and slave quarters—tumbled foundation stones and unexpected pits.

A stream ran through the far part of the field, which could be crossed on a homemade plank bridge, and on the other side of the stream was an old burying ground with stones half sunk in the earth and hidden by weeds and grass. Beyond the forgotten headstones a tangle of woods had taken over.

In the evening silence they could hear the gurgling of the stream more loudly than when they had been busy with unpacking.

For an instant Laurence caught from Janine, from the tilt of her head and her look of vague dread, the ominous undertones of the gurgling water over stones. He sensed too the eeriness for her of the mist rising from the stream, which he had been accustomed to from childhood as part of a summer evening.

"We'll leave as soon as we have a little money," he promised flatly into the silence and the holding of her breath.

"Good," she whispered.

Later in the big bed she lay shivering beside him.

"Cold?" he asked. "Come closer."

"I'm fine," she denied. "Just sleepy. Goodnight, Laurence."

"Goodnight, my darling."

She watched the moonlight stalk with grim shadows across the uncurtained room and fall across the counterpane. With a fierce intake of breath she rolled away from it, toward her husband, with superstitious dread remembering that moonlight must not shine upon one's bed.

"I can't sleep," she whispered desperately. "Cover the window, Laurence—cover the window. Keep the moon out. Please keep the moon out!"

In an instant he was wide awake and half across the room. He hung his robe over the curtain rods and said in an ordinary voice, "Better, Janine?"

"Better," she said, relaxing. "Much, much better. Thank you, darling."

"Can you sleep now? Want your eau de cologne? Anything?"

"No, dearest," she said with a low laugh, now that she was safe again in the darkness. "Just come back and let me put my arms around you, and we'll both drift off."

By the end of the week their belongings were all put away, the furniture arranged, the curtains hung. Their nearest neighbor was a farmer a mile away. Laurence hired one of his sons to cut the lawn, and his daughter, Trisa, a girl of seventeen, to come in for daily straightening and housecleaning. He and Janine drove to town twice a week to get groceries, and their mail and milk was delivered.

Everything had settled down to an orderly routine, and Laurence began to work again regularly. Janine kept to her promise. She no longer sought excuses to interrupt him; she brought his lunch on a tray and left it at his door.

Late one afternoon he went downstairs. It had been raining steadily all day long; he had scarcely seen Janine. He found her in the living room sitting cross-legged on the old Oriental rug before the fireplace.

It gave him a momentary start to see her there. How often he'd sat like that himself as a boy, while his mother read to him of Robin Hood and King Arthur's knights, and a fire crackled on the hearth. But there was no fire now, only a few cold ashes.

Janine did not hear him but remained absorbed in something on the floor in front of her. In the strange half-light she looked more than ever like a Dürer drawing. She was not beautiful in the ordinary sense of the word, she was simply arresting and unforgettable.

Puzzled, he became aware of what preoccupied her. On the floor she had placed an old inlaid chessboard that had been in the house since he could remember. She had turned it over and on the polished back had placed a crystal wine glass, upside down.

Two fingertips of her right hand rested lightly on the base of the glass. As he watched, the glass seemed to glide across the board of its own volition in slow, swooping arcs, carrying her hand with it.

"What are you doing, Janine?" he asked.

She started, screamed, struck the glass a sidelong blow and sent it rolling off the board to the floor.

"No, no!" she cried.

He came into the room carefully, as if someone were asleep.

"I startled you," he said. "Forgive me. I just couldn't imagine what you were doing."

"Oh," she said, collecting herself, her breath coming unevenly. She picked up the glass and put it back. He saw now that she had carefully traced the letters of the alphabet on the back of the chessboard in ink.

"Haven't you ever received messages this way?" she asked with pretended carelessness. "Mother and I used to do it by the hour, when I was a girl, before she died."

"Messages from whom?" Laurence asked, careful to keep his tone casual.

"Oh, from beyond," Janine told him, looking surprised that he needed an explanation. "Mother and I used to talk to Father this way, and he brought all sorts of odd friends. Mother said it was just like him —when he was alive he was always bringing home the strangest people."

"But Janine—" Laurence began.

"I suppose," Janine added, watching him, "you and the doctor would say it was just Mother's way of escaping reality."

Fleetingly he thought of Janine's mother, gallant and pathetic. Gently brought up, left with nothing when her husband drowned sailing on the Charles River, she had opened a boarding house for students. Somehow she had sent Janine to the best schools, instilling in her daughter her own dream of the day when Janine, with her beauty and intelligence, would make a splendid success of some undefined kind—as a singer perhaps, or an actress, or a painter.

She had died, worn out but serenely satisfied with her handiwork, shortly before Janine and Laurence married.

Janine was watching him now with a hint of challenge in her smile.

"Try it," she said. "This is a wonderful old house. It was built in 1690—think of all the people who have lived and died here since then. And some of them are still around. I don't know why some stay and some don't, but it's always that way. Try it and see if any of them will talk to you."

"All right," he said, and forced a smile. He dropped to the rug beside her and took her hand. It slipped away from him, so he picked up the board and put it in front of him.

"Just place two fingers on the glass," she explained. "Relax and wait and when the glass moves, let it take your hand with it."

He did so, prepared when nothing happened to smile and suggest having an early dinner and seeing a movie. But as he waited with his fingers lightly touching the crystal, it was as if the unnatural stillness he had been aware of as he watched Janine were gathering again.

The glass began to move. He was not aware of any conscious muscular effort, but the glass slid in a smooth arc across the board to the letter N. It paused, then swept on to the letter O. From there it went back even more swiftly to N. To O once more. To N. To O. Then the glass with a violent jerk dragged his hand straight across the board and off the edge.

"*No, no, no,*" Janine read out. "I guess he doesn't want to talk to you, darling."

With an effort remaining calm, Laurence took out a cigarette and lit it.

"Who doesn't want to talk to me, Janine?"

"Roderick Jamieson," she said. "Major Roderick Jamieson. He once lived here. I was just talking to him when you came in. He was killed during the Revolution, he told me, at the Battle of Yorktown. He's buried in the little burying ground out back. I'm going to look for his tombstone tomorrow."

Laurence caught his breath. He had left the grass long in the little cemetery, and hadn't told Janine it was there.

But she must have found it and scraped the moss off the marble stone that did have the name Roderick Jamieson on it, though no one in the family had ever known just who Roderick Jamieson was.

"I see," Laurence said, feeling a weight lowering on his shoulders. "Of course you know, Janine"—he spoke as carefully as if to a child—"the glass is moved by your own unconscious muscular actions. And any message it might spell out comes from inside your own mind."

"Perhaps," Janine said. "But that doesn't make the message any the less real, darling. Because who puts it there? Answer me that!" Abruptly her manner changed. "Don't worry, darling. I've nothing to do and Major Jamieson is fun, that's all. He's so boastful of his exploits. According to him he's fought so many duels and made love to so many women!"

She gave a ripple of excited laughter.

"No one could believe *all* his stories. It drives him into a rage when I tell him he's making them up. Sometimes he flings the glass across the room."

To his surprise she leaned into his arms, against his chest. They could both feel his heart pounding.

"I love you," he said tensely, summoning her back.

"I know." She turned to him and lifted her face to be kissed. Her lips were warm and yielding. There seemed to be no transition necessary for her. She could live in the real and the unreal world at one and the same time. He took her in his arms and held her convulsively, feeling her closeness for the first time in months.

"You've no idea," she murmured, "how furious this makes him."

He lay awake that night after Janine had fallen asleep and was breathing regularly, her breath soft and warm upon his cheek.

He racked his brains for something to interest her, to draw her away from this game with the board and the glass and the imaginary rival. And with anguish he recalled the happiness of their first four years together, when he and Janine had lived in a tiny apartment overlooking Washington Square, and he had written two books, both quite successful.

Janine had been so undaunted and gay about her own career, going the rounds of the Broadway theatrical producers' offices, carrying her scrapbook of notices praising her performances in summer stock productions . . . then the year slavishly studying art . . . the short-lived practical period in an advertising agency writing copy . . . the brief enthusiasm for avant-garde poetry, and the thin sheaf of verses, never published.

Then her repudiation of New York, her longing for the country and isolation. They had moved to New Hampshire for her sake, so that she could really paint. As for Laurence, he could write anywhere.

In the lovely old colonial house overlooking the ocean Janine had produced half a dozen creditable landscapes. After endless hesitation she had entered them in a local art show. When none of them received even an honorable mention, she had in unfeigned tedium put away her paints and canvases.

Then, during the long New England winter, had come the first of those spells of apathy which had led them to one specialist after another, in Boston, New York, Washington . . .

And now, their money gone, they were here.

Laurence tried to get Janine to call on people; she refused. They drove thirty miles to see the movies twice a week, until she balked and begged him to go alone.

She assured him she was happy. As if to prove it, she at last unpacked her paints and canvases and began some desultory sketching. He expected her to abandon them at any moment, but she did not. Instead, she became abruptly absorbed in her painting. She began work on a canvas which she would not let him see, which she made him promise not to look at until it was finished.

Happy to see her occupied, though he knew she still used the board and glass daily, he went back to work. He determined to treat her preoccupation with the messages lightly, until she should have enough of it. He even asked about Roderick Jamieson from time to time, his manner jesting.

But Janine took no notice of the jesting, and answered as naturally as if Roderick Jamieson were real.

One Sunday when Janine was washing the fine china after dinner—a task she never left to Trisa—Laurence said casually that he was going for a stroll, and made directly for the little bridge and the burying ground on the other side. He found the stone, right at the edge of the cemetery where he remembered it. The long grass beside it had been trampled. Janine must have been there. But the moss on the headstone now made the name quite illegible. How could she have known? To satisfy himself, he scraped off enough moss to verify the letters JAMIE . . .

Monday he drove the fifteen miles to town alone for groceries. "Trisa, stay here until I get back," he told the sloe-eyed, sleepy farm girl in the kitchen. "If your mistress wants to send you home, find some excuse to stay. I'll pay you double when I get back."

In town he stopped at the local Historical Society, a musty room where a pleasant, elderly woman kept the records of the town and its environs, going back to pre-Revolutionary days.

After looking around in a happy fluster, for hardly anyone ever came, the librarian found a brief biography cut from some older record book and pasted into an album with other yellowed prints.

"Major Roderick Jamieson," she said. "I knew I remembered the name. He came from around here. A famous duelist, it says here, killed in action at Yorktown. Decorated by Lafayette."

So Roderick Jamieson had been real enough. But how had Janine known he was buried behind the house when the moss on the headstone was untouched? And certainly she had never visited the Historical Society—she had never been to town alone.

There was only one other possibility. Among the ancient books and papers in the attic, Laurence decided, she must have found some records that mentioned Roderick Jamieson. He had never come across any such reference himself, but then, it was years since he had been up there and he had never rummaged very deeply into the moldering old newspapers and letters that had gathered dust there for perhaps two hundred years.

But he put off checking in the attic, not admitting to himself that he was afraid he would find no record of Jamieson there.

"Roderick is growing fantastically jealous of you, darling," Janine said one afternoon, as she swung idly in the hammock. Laurence had brought out some lemonade flavored with mint he had found in a patch run wild.

"Mmmm," he said. "Had a letter from my agent today. He likes the new book but he wants me to work on it some more."

"What a bore."

"It means we have to stay put for the moment."

"Oh, that. I wouldn't want to leave."

"You wouldn't?" he asked uneasily.

"No. It's delightful simply to have time. I've never known anything like this place for time. I could just drift along forever."

"Lotus eater," he smiled, relieved.

She turned to him a look full of mysterious sorrow. "Yes," she said. "I'm not fighting it any more. I'm an idle and useless woman."

"Janine, you're nothing of the sort."

"But I am." She started the hammock swinging by lacing her fingers into the ropework. Her fingers were strong, bone-strong. The nails were long and polished. She was always immaculately groomed. She spent hours in front of the little dressing table in the dressing room he had fitted up for her.

"You should have told me years ago," she said half-accusingly. "Roderick claims a woman doesn't need to be useful. At least not a woman like me. He says her only duty is to be ornamental."

"He does, eh?" Laurence was not the least bit amused. "What else does he say?" He sought to understand the new role she was playing.

"Oh, he talks interminably about himself, as I told you. He tells me about his duels and his love affairs. I accuse him of having the love affairs simply because he had such a zest for polishing off the husbands. He doesn't deny it."

"Did he use sword or pistol?" Laurence asked, watching her face closely without seeming to do so.

She hesitated. "He's a little bit vague about that—he doesn't specify what weapons he used. Once he went into a tantrum and wouldn't speak to me for days, when I suggested he wasn't always a gentleman about these 'duels.' When he came out of his miff, he informed me that he had been fabulous with his pistols, and that he had killed six men single-handed, before he was killed in action at Yorktown. He was only twenty-seven, and he seems, sometimes, ever so much younger than that—much younger than you've ever been, darling."

"Six men? All husbands?" he asked dryly. This was a familiar theme with Janine—only a new twist. She didn't really like husbands, or being a wife: essentially she wanted a state of romantic tension, indefinitely sustained.

"Three or four were husbands," she said carelessly.

"But when I ask him what became of the ladies afterwards—all presumably free to marry him—he distracts me by complimenting me on my eyebrows, or something equally silly."

"Why? You have very nice eyebrows," Laurence said. "I suppose he's in love with you?"

"Oh, madly. He spends a lot of time brooding over how he can manage a duel with you. It's a great frustration to him not to be able to fling a glove in your face."

"He might fling the glass," Laurence suggested.

"That's not bad, darling," she said, as though she had not expected so much wit from him. "I'll suggest it. Would you like to see what he looks like?"

"See what he looks like?" He was momentarily startled.

She took him by the hand and led him into the living room. On an easel by the window was the canvas she had never let him see. Now, as she removed the covering and turned the picture toward him with the smile of a mischievous child, he understood.

It was the head and shoulders of a young man. His blond hair was long, and it curled down over his ears and to his collar. His face was thin and aristocratic, his lips twisted in a slight smile that might have been pleasing except for his eyes.

His eyes were an intense blue that was almost black. They seemed to catch and hold Laurence's gaze as if he were giving some command. There were depths to the painted eyes, depths of darkness, and when Laurence looked into the eyes, he saw that

Janine hadn't painted Roderick Jamieson smiling.

It was undoubtedly the best thing she had ever done.

"It's superb," Laurence exclaimed. Then, trying to appear unconcerned, "So this is Major Roderick Jamieson."

"He says it's a perfect likeness"—laughter bubbled on Janine's lips—"except that it doesn't make him handsome enough. I told him his insufferable vanity begins to bore me."

"You must try another oil," Laurence said, choosing his words. "This is really very fine."

"Perhaps I will." Abruptly she covered the picture. Her voice was flat and uninterested. "It was fun."

That evening after Janine was asleep, Laurence wrote at last to the doctor in Washington who had treated her:

Janine's neurosis in this lonely place has taken a new turn. She spends her time dreaming. She has imaginary conversations through a homemade ouija board. She seems to be going gently

His pen tore through the sheet of paper, penetrating to the green blotter beneath. He burned the letter over the kitchen stove.

"Roderick says I should leave you," Janine said at breakfast, yawning and smiling at him. "He claims you don't understand me. He says you don't believe a word of what I tell you about him, and that you think I am going mad. Do you?"

Laurence concentrated on stirring his coffee, not trusting the expression of his eyes. His hands trembled. Had Janine watched him struggling with the letter, seen him burn it, guessed its contents?

"He does, eh? What else does he say?"

"Oh, never mind him, he's always making up things." She shrugged. She got up and kissed him. The rest of the day she put herself out to be sparkling, gay, witty—and she refused to be drawn back to Roderick Jamieson.

That night Laurence woke and found she had stolen downstairs. He got out of bed and crept down the stairs to the living room, where he paused in the doorway, drawn back and hidden by darkness.

Janine had lit a fire with a bit of paper and some kindling wood. This was the only light in the room. She was laughing and talking to herself, and the glass lay idle by the board.

He could make out no word of what she was saying, for she was speaking in a voice so low it sounded almost like someone else talking. The faint murmur could even have been the wind. But he could see her lips moving and her eyes shining with an animation she had not displayed for a long, long time. Unlike her pretense of gaiety all day, this was genuine.

She was dressed in a diaphanous nightgown and matching loose robe. It had big sleeves tight at the wrist, and it was closed at the throat with a blue ribbon. Once she caught at her throat with a look of confusion, as if someone there beside her had reached up to unfasten it.

Then she said something teasingly, shaking her head from one side to the other in negation.

Laurence had a premonition that she was about to rise and turn, so he went stealthily to bed, his heart throbbing and his head aching intolerably.

Janine came drifting back a few moments later, all

her languor returned. As she lay beside him he could feel her exhaustion.

Whatever it had been, it hadn't been play-acting. It had taken a lot out of her.

In her sleep, later, she spoke. "Run! Run! Run!" she whispered. Then she gave a little moan and her head fell sideways on the pillow.

Laurence wrote the doctor the next morning, telling him the whole story, and not trusting the letter to Trisa, mailed it himself.

The doctor wrote to bring Janine at once for further treatment. He reminded Laurence sternly that he had been unwilling to let Janine go: he had not considered her cured. Laurence had asked desperately for advice; the doctor gave none. He said simply to come to Washington at once.

Laurence spent an hour staring at his bank book. He did not need to open it to read the figures.

He looked out the window at Janine. Around the house was a smooth carpet of lawn, but she preferred always to walk in the long grass, rustlingly, on the other side of the stream. Sometimes she vanished for hours in the woods. Did she meet Roderick Jamieson there?

He started, his fists clenched. Was her nonsense infecting him too? Yet it was true that she acted as though she had a lover.

He had never seen her so lovely. An inner wholeness seemed to possess her whole being. She was no longer torn apart as before by self-questionings, self-accusations, and abortive ambitions that were soon dispelled and left her limp and defeated.

She walked proudly now, almost with arrogance,

and there were none of the nervous gestures and starts and stops that had marked her earlier illness.

He got out the doctor's letter to answer it, put it away again hopelessly, and began working, shutting out from his mind the seductive Virginia summer, the blue hot sky, the scent of honeysuckle, and his wife in its tangles, walking.

He worked all afternoon and sat down exhausted to the supper that Janine served by candlelight on fragile china, dreamily.

With a start Laurence noticed that she was drinking from the crystal glass she used for the ouija board, and that her hand was clasped around its stem almost constantly. She hardly ate, but drank lingeringly, her lips moving tenderly against the edge of the glass.

The wine, on top of a day of concentrated effort, made Laurence sleepy. He watched Janine through half-closed eyes.

She served brandied peaches in rose-crystal bowls, her every gesture fastidious and serene, as though she served a lover: but he knew that he was not the one she was thinking of.

As they went to bed, rain began to fall with a metallic patter on the copper roof gutters, and a soft whispering on the windowpanes. Thunder grumbled in the sky and lightning flashed, coming closer.

Janine fell asleep quickly and peacefully, but he was too weary. Sleep would not come. He turned and tossed, he lit cigarettes and put them out. He lay and stared into darkness illuminated at intervals by the reflected glare of lightning, and heard the storm draw nearer.

The shutter began to bang as the wind rose. Irritated, he got up to fasten it. As he reshut the window and turned back he saw Janine standing, facing him.

He did not move or speak, frozen by her expression. She seemed to be looking directly at him with malevolent hatred.

After an electric moment she turned and went downstairs in the dark. He looked about for a flashlight, found none, and afraid to wait, gropingly followed her.

She did not turn even when he stepped upon the two creaking stairs, one after the other, hard. Then he was sure she was walking in her sleep.

The front door was open. He followed her out, shivering in the slashing rain. Ahead of him, Janine seemed to feel nothing. Her hair and her diaphanous gown blew back in the wind as the fitful lightning revealed her.

Laurence thought of the pits and foundation stones left of the old slave quarters and stables, toward which she was going. However great the shock, he must wake her.

"Janine!" he cried, his voice blending with the keening wind. "Janine!"

She heard her name, stopped in mid-flight, and must have made out the motion of his hurrying form, just as he could see only the erratically elusive white gown.

"Wait!" he called imperatively.

"You're slow, Roderick!" she called back. Then she gave a ripple of excited laughter and triumph. "Catch me!" she cried, coquetry in her voice. Starting away from him, she began to run. "Run, run, run!" she called. He remembered the compulsive words of her dream.

He ran. But she fled before him lightly, skirting the dangerous pits with amazing surefooted speed. She cut across the fields and Laurence followed, already sure of her destination. She raced across the little bridge, perhaps remembering vaguely some tale that spirits could not cross a stream.

Safe on the other side, she laughed exultantly. There was now nothing between her and the tangled woods, in which she might hide from him all night. He was soaked to the bone, and so must she be. She would catch pneumonia.

"Janine!" he called desperately. "Wait for me!"

"Too slow, too slow!" she called back. But she paused an instant. Lightning flared across the sky. In the brilliant white light he saw Janine looking toward him, her lips parted, her eyes wide with what seemed like dawning recognition, her hair and her thin gown plastered to her by the rain.

Laurence took the planks in three flying strides. He must get to her before she started off again. He must—he stretched his arm toward her, and then it seemed as if a vicious hand had treacherously seized his ankle. He felt himself flying through the air as if lifted bodily, and as he plunged forward he could see the marble slab sunken and tilted in the long grass. By the flare of lightning he could even see the letters from which he had scraped away the moss:

J A M I E . . .

Then his forehead came down full force on the edge of the marble.

When Trisa, the hired girl, came the next morning, she found Janine crouched on the living room floor in her still damp nightgown, crooning to Laurence, whose body she had somehow dragged into the house and whose bloody head was cradled in her lap. In the cold fireplace was a half-burnt chessboard, and the pieces of a broken glass were on the hearth.

Janine looked up slowly as Trisa entered.

"He didn't love me," she said, in a voice so hoarse Trisa could hardly understand her. "He never cared at all for me. He never cared for any woman. He just wanted to kill. To kill!"

It was the last coherent sentence she ever spoke.

Four O'Clock

PRICE DAY

The hands of the alarm clock on the table in front of Mr. Crangle stood at 3:47, on a summer afternoon.

"You're wrong about that, you know," he said, not taking his eyes from the face of the clock. "You're quite wrong, Pet, as I have explained to you often enough before. The moral angle presents no difficulties at all."

The parrot, in the cage hanging above him, cocked her head and looked down with a hard, cold, reptilian eye, an ancient eye, an eye older by age upon age than the human race.

She said, "Nut."

Mr. Crangle, his eye still on the clock, took a peanut from a cracked bowl at his elbow and held it above his head, to the bars of the cage. Pet clutched it in a leathery claw. The spring-steel muscles opened the horny beak. She clinched the peanut and crushed it, the sound mingling in the furnished room with the big-city sounds coming through the open window—cars honking, feet on the sidewalk, children calling to each other, a plane overhead like a contented, industrious bee.

"It is quite true," Mr. Crangle said at 3:49, "that only someone above all personal emotions, only someone who can look at the whole thing as if from the outside, can be trusted morally to make such a decision." As the big hand reached 3:50, he felt a sense of power surge deeply through him. "Think, Pet. In ten minutes. In ten little minutes, when I say the word, all the evil people all over the world will become half their present size, so they can be known. All the uncaught murderers and the tyrants and the proud and sinful, all the bullies and the wrongdoers and the blackmailers and nicotine fiends and transgressors." His eyes blazed with omnipotence. "All of them, every one."

Pet said, "Nut."

Mr. Crangle gave her one.

"I know you don't agree fully with the half-size solution," he said, "but I do believe it to be the best one, all things considered."

He had studied over the alternatives day and night since that morning three weeks ago when, as he sat on a bench in the park, looking at the pictures in the clouds across the lake, it came to him that he had the power to do this thing, that upon him at that moment had been bestowed the gift of putting a mark on all the bad people on earth, so that they should be known.

The realization surprised him not at all. Once before, such a thing had happened. He had once held the power to stop wars. That was when the radio was telling about the big air raids on the cities. In that case the particular thing he could do was to take the stiffness out of airplane propellers, so that some morning when the crews, bundled like children against cold, went out to get in their planes, they would find the props hanging limp, like empty banana skins.

That time, he had delayed too long, waiting for just the right time and just the right plan, and they had outwitted him, unfairly. They had invented the jet, to which his power did not apply.

Then, too, there had been the thing about wheels. The thing about wheels came to him in a coffee place as he was looking at a newspaper photograph of a bad traffic accident, three killed. The power, that was, to change all the wheels in the world from round to square, or even to triangular if he wished, so they would stub in the asphalt and stop. But he wasn't allowed to keep that power. Before he could work out a plan and a time, he had felt it taken from him.

The power over bad people had stayed. It had even grown stronger, if power like that could grow stronger. And this time he had hurried, though of course there were certain problems to be thought through.

First, who was to decide what people were evil? That wasn't too hard, really, in spite of Pet's doubts. An evil person was a person who would seem evil to a man who held within himself the knowledge of good and evil, if that man could know all the person's innermost secrets. An evil person was a person who would seem evil to an all-knowing Mr. Crangle.

Then, how to do it, the method? Mark them on the forehead, or turn them all one color, say purple? But then they would simply be able to recognize each other the more readily, and to band together in their wickedness.

When at last he hit upon the idea of a change in size, what came to him first was the thought of doubling the height and bulk of all the bad people. That would make them inefficient. They couldn't handle delicate scientific instruments or typewriters or adding machines or telephone dials. In time they would expire from bigness, like the dinosaurs in the article in the Sunday paper. But they might first run wild, with their great weight and strength, and hurt other people. Mr. Crangle wouldn't have liked that. He hated violence.

Half-size people, it was true, might be able to manipulate some of the machines. They could also be dangerous. But it would take them a long time to develop tools and weapons to their scale, and think how ridiculous they would be, meanwhile, with their clothes twice too big and their hats falling down over their ears.

At 3:54, Mr. Crangle smiled at the thought of how ridiculous they would be.

"Nut," Pet said.

He reached up and gave her one, his eyes still on the clock.

"I think," he said, "that the most interesting place to be would be at a murder trial where nobody knew whether the accused was guilty or not. And then at 4 o'clock, if he was guilty—"

Mr. Crangle's breath was coming faster. The clock hands stood at 3:56.

"Or watching the drunkards in a saloon," he said.

"Nut," Pet said, and he gave her one.

"Oh," he said, "there are so many places, so many places to be. But I'd rather be with you when it happens, Pet. Right here alone with you."

He sat tense in his chair. He could actually see the big hand of the clock move, in the tiniest little jerkings, leaving a hairline of white between itself and the black 3:57 dot, and moving to the 3:58 dot, narrowing the space, until it touched that dot, and then stood directly on it, and then moved past toward the 3:59 dot.

"At first," Mr. Crangle said, "the newspapers won't believe it. Even though some of it will happen right in the newspaper offices, they won't believe it. At first they won't. And then when they begin to understand that it has happened to a lot of people everybody knows are evil, then they'll see the design."

The clock said 3:59.

"A great story," Mr. Crangle said. "A great newspaper story. And nobody will know who did it, Pet, nobody but you and me."

The point of the big hand crept halfway past the 3:59 dot. Mr. Crangle's heart beat hard. His eyes were wide, his lips parted. He whispered, "Nobody will know."

The tip of the big hand touched the dot at the top of the clock face. The alarm went off. Mr. Crangle felt a great surge of strength, like water bursting a dam, and a great shock, as of a bolt of lightning. He closed his eyes.

"Now!" he said softly, and slumped exhausted.

By going to the window and looking down at the crowd in the street, he could have seen whether it had worked or not. He did not go to the window. He did not need to. He knew.

The alarm bell ran down.

Pet cocked her head and looked at him with an eye like polished stone.

"Nut," she said.

His hand, as he stretched it up, failed by a full foot and a half to reach the cage.

Too Many Coincidences

PAUL EIDEN

The funeral service was in an ancient, dark little Catholic church on Washington Street in the Village. Starbuck watched Kathy carefully throughout the unfamiliar requiem, following her up and down from the kneeler in the back pew, although he was certain she knew little more about the service than he did. Starbuck's religion was mathematics.

He sensed the Mass was nearing its end when the priests and servers in their black vestments were down at the far end of the aisle opposite them, bearing a heavy book and a crucifix-tipped staff. It was then Starbuck took his first good look at the short, blond man on his left.

He had become aware of him when the man first slid into the pew, his hat in his hand, bowing hesitantly, a tentatively introductory smile on his lips. Starbuck knew at once that he had seen him somewhere before. Perhaps, he hazarded, at one of the wakes for Kathy's old room-mates. He darted looks at him throughout the Mass, now and then catching a half-smile on his thick, mobile lips, wishing he could tap Kathy on the arm and nod at her for her quick, remembering smile and the artful re-introduction.

Starbuck hated unresolved problems of any sort. Now, sensing imminent escape from the church, he tried to concentrate on the man. A faint odor clung to him. It reminded Starbuck of hospitals. A doctor perhaps? A friend of this dead nurse, or one of the others?

It was hopeless. Starbuck was used to doing his thinking in a nearly soundless, air-conditioned office. The priest just beyond Kathy was chanting in Latin and an altar boy swung a censer filled with burning incense that overcame and banished the smell that seemed to cling to the blond man's clothes. Starbuck was left wondering if he had imagined it, as the priests and servers went up the nave and into the chancel.

The pallbearers—six, solemn, hulking Irish youths —brought the casket down to the foot of the aisle then. He could feel Kathy begin to sob beside him, as it was borne out into the sudden sunlight of the opened doors and the undertaker began calling out the carloads for the procession to the cemetery. Starbuck took his young wife's arm and led her out through a side door. The blond man followed them out.

Kathy had not seen the dead girl in more than a year. Even last night at the wake, the coffin had been sealed. *I don't blame them,* Starbuck had thought. *Four days in the water.* He had felt nothing at all at the wake or the funeral. He never did. Now, vaguely embarrassed, he wondered how Kathy could be so emotional.

He saw with irritation that the blond man had not

left them. Starbuck watched, as, still smiling faintly, the man touched his wife's forearm.

Kathy withdrew the tiny handkerchief with which she had been dabbing under her veil. Her eyes still wet, she smiled promptly at him. "Why, Mr. Carlson!"

Carlson ducked his head. "Very sad, very sad," he said.

Not a doctor, Starbuck's mind registered. "You've met my husband," Kathy was saying. "John Carlson, Alfred. Mr. Carlson was Pat Phelan's fiancé."

Starbuck shook his hand. Pat Phelan, one of the two that had been killed by the hit-and-run driver. "I wondered," Carlson was asking, in a voice with a faint linguistic accent, "are you going out to the cemetery . . . ?"

"Yes," Starbuck told him. "But we have our own car."

"That's what I wanted to ask," Carlson said, speaking to Kathy. "Could you drive me out?"

"Why, of course," Kathy said with her quick friendliness, taking his arm.

The last of the rented limousines was pulling away from the church. Starbuck led them down Sixth Avenue to where he had parked the car, repressing a frown of annoyance. After the burial, he had a long drive back across Brooklyn to the Battery Tunnel. He couldn't be in the office much before one as it was, and he was sure Kathy would quickly volunteer a side trip to drop this stranger off anywhere he asked.

He had wanted Kathy, for her outgoing friendliness and fresh red-haired beauty, the first moment he saw her in the hospital; after eight years of marriage, her emotionalism and sentimentality were a constant reproof and minor annoyance to Starbuck's own closely-reasoned sense of order and convenience. She could have been satisfied with the church service this morning, he thought; but she had insisted on the trip out to the graveside, and, even after he got her back downtown, she would have another hour's cab ride back up to Riverdale.

She was chatting volubly with Carlson in the back seat as Starbuck swung the Lincoln into the line of the cortege. The blond man leaned forward to offer them cigarettes from his pack. In the rear vision mirror, Starbuck saw his faint smile become pronounced as Kathy accepted one from him. He decided he didn't like Carlson much.

Kathy chattered effortlessly with Carlson as Starbuck followed the limousines out over the Williamsburg Bridge and down Meeker to New Calvary. No, Carlson hadn't married since they saw him last. Yes, he was still working for the pharmaceutical firm as a detail man, contacting physicians. *Unsuccessful,* Starbuck catalogued him, and all but forgot him. Kathy touched the blond man's hand sympathetically. "You have to forget Pat, you know. You'll meet someone else, just as nice. Wait and see."

No one had ever had to reassure him he would marry someone as desirable as Kathy, Starbuck reflected. He had known it all through his long bachelorhood, just as he had known he would make himself a wealthy man. The matter of a wife could wait until he had the money. Long ago, he had read

Voltaire's words: "A woman is never more sincere than when she is telling a millionaire: 'I love you.'" That had been the only reassurance Starbuck needed.

It was a cynical bit of wisdom which served Starbuck as a minor article of faith. The major article was that hard work and a cold faith in the logic of arithmetic would give him everything else that he wanted out of life. He had been right. Kathy was his wife. And for six years, he had been president of the fourth largest insurance company in America.

Mathematics was Starbuck's religion and logic its dogma; a sturdy staff, it supported him through all the storms and doubts of his career. It was to numbers and probabilities that Starbuck turned for strength. Take the question of Kathy's faithfulness to him. Or take the matter of her dead room-mates, for instance . . .

That poor bloated corpse in the hearse up ahead (Eileen. Eileen Something, wasn't it?) was the fourth one of Kathy's old nursing school room-mates to die in a little over two years. All young girls, under thirty. Five, if you counted back to the first one, years ago. The one whose death Kathy always referred to as "that horrible accident."

Starbuck remembered the consternation last summer when Kathy had mentioned the rate at which her old room-mates were dying off. They had a group of their friends out to their place on the Cape for a week-end—mostly Starbuck's fellow executives from the company, with their wives and young Quinlan from the legal department.

Smiling inwardly, Starbuck remembered his amusement. Really, it was amazing, but most people couldn't grasp the simplest equations in mathematical probabilities. Quinlan had become as excited as the women.

"My God!" he demanded accusingly, "aren't you worried at all? Four of her room-mates have died! Suppose something happens to her!"

Starbuck grinned at him tolerantly. "Isn't that silly, coming from an insurance man, Ed? Even one in the law office? Suppose all four had died of cancer. Would that increase Kathy's chances of dying of cancer?"

"But they've all died violently!" Quinlan exploded. "This first girl burned to death. Then the other was strangled to death in bed. And now two more run over by a hit-and-run driver!"

"Well?" Starbuck asked. "It's just a string of coincidences. Unlikely, of course, but the unlikely thing often happens in life." He looked around the group, an apostle expounding his gospel. "Their deaths don't alter Kathy's chances of living to a ripe old age. That would be like saying the chances of a roulette wheel stopping on red are increased because it has stopped on red four times in a row. Actually red's chances of turning up on the next spin are exactly the same as they ever were."

Starbuck smiled, warming at this chance to lecture. "In that example you are running into the principle of statistical independence—"

Behind their guests, Kathy smiled fondly and shook her head at him, the perfect hostess. Starbuck played to the older men for his laugh. "You draw dangerous—fatal—conclusions when you reason from too small a sample."

He got his laugh from the men, and even the wives seemed to relax, but young Quinlan was still in a flap. *"You're not worried?* Suppose— Suppose . . . ?"

"Suppose there's a curse on them?" Starbuck suggested urbanely, enjoying himself. Really, Quinlan must read mystery novels. "Like the one on the men who opened King Tut's tomb?"

Quinlan had subsided then, but not without a fretful look at Kathy. Starbuck grinned reminiscently, turning the car onto Laurel Hill in the procession. It had been ridiculous, just another example of the way undisciplined thinkers jumped to conclusions from insufficient facts. Starbuck never let his judgment or his emotions run away from him like that. He kept them firmly in check.

Take this marital fidelity thing, for instance. After all, he was fifty-three and Kathy was only twenty-nine. What was more natural than that she should one day choose a lover? It was right there in Kinsey —although he had some reservations about Kinsey's data-gathering and his disdain of the probability sample. Starbuck ran the IBM machine of his mind for the card bearing the statistic he wanted. Accumulative Incidence: Extra-Marital Coital Experience, By Decade Of Birth. Twelve per cent of the married women born between 1920 and 1929 had betrayed their husbands by the age of twenty-five.

Of course, the book had been compiled in 1953 and the findings did not extend beyond the age of twenty-five, but it seemed reasonable to extrapolate a percentage twice as large by age twenty-nine. The chances that Kathy would remain faithful to even a younger husband were, at best, no better than three out of four. There was a fact, and Starbuck liked to think that he had never grown emotional about a fact in his life.

He watched Kathy as the casket was lowered into the grave. Her face went white and she bit her lips, but no tears came. She was generally beyond the crying stage when they reached the cemetery.

All you could ask of a wife was that she be discreet about it when the time came. Starbuck rather suspected that Kathy had begun to cheat on him already. In his secret heart, he was proud of her for giving him not even the shadow of proof.

He had the Lincoln back on the highway, already thinking ahead to the work at the office, before Starbuck remembered Carlson. "Mr. uhh—uhh— Where can we drop you?"

The thick, flexible lips formed a deferential smile and Carlson ducked his head and said in his polite, faintly accented voice: "Anywhere at all. I am taking the rest of the day off."

The fool couldn't even make up his mind where he was going. "Well, I'm taking the car back down to Wall Street," Starbuck said curtly, conscious of Kathy's still white, troubled face. "I'm leaving it there, and then Mrs. Starbuck will be going back uptown by cab. Any place that's convenient for you."

Carlson raised his eyebrows. "Oh? You don't drive?" he asked Kathy. She shook her head absently. "Then, perhaps—a suggestion—I could drive you home in this fine car? It would save your husband trouble, too."

Kathy smiled broadly, instantly cheerful again. "Oh, wonderful! That's wonderful!"

Even Starbuck felt something like gratitude. He never brought the car to the office when it was avoidable. He hated the drive up or down in rush hour traffic. "Nice of you," he murmured.

He kissed Kathy and turned the keys over to Carlson at the corner of Wall and Broadway.

A thick sheaf of real estate reports on the company's properties across the nation waited on his desk. Starbuck turned from them in an oddly dilatory mood. He stood at the window for a long time, treasuring its panoramic view of the harbor, watching a rusty tramp plow toward the Narrows.

This had been his office since fifty-two; he had worked toward it for twenty-five years before that. Nearly two-thirds of Starbuck's life had been spent in this building. In the beginning there had been the long subway rides uptown to Columbia for that all-important first degree, then years more of nights afterwards at NYU, City College, mastering law, investment banking, real estate.

There was no ulcer. And he was eight years into the coronary bracket, Starbuck reminded himself smugly, without a first attack. Seven more years and he was past even that hurdle. In twelve he would be retired, moved up to chair the board. Kathy would be forty-one then, a dutiful, artfully unfaithful wife. He had everything he wanted.

Starbuck took an irritable turn around the office on the thick Persian rug, unable to attack the work on his desk. Something about today nagged at his mind, some danger signal. Angrily, hating it for the distraction, he assaulted it, free-associating.

The girl just buried, her swollen body crammed

into her coffin? Supposedly, she had slipped off the ferry returning her from the night shift at the Staten Island Hospital. Starbuck snorted. If the company holding her policy paid off on that without the suicide clause first becoming effective they were criminal fools.

Nobody fell off the Staten Island ferry, unless they were pushed, and the girl had been alone. If he were the emotional, excitable type like Ed Quinlan, Starbuck knew, he could blame his disquiet on these successive deaths of Kathy's old friends. But there was nothing there but a simple chain of coincidences.

Six girls, strangers, randomly assigned an apartment by a hospital personnel director. One commits suicide. Two others, the closest friends in the group, are smashed down by a hit-and-run driver, who is never apprehended. One slain in bed by a strangler, also never found. But the husband had been held a long time, hadn't he? Starbuck's mind challenged the coincidences. The police knew their business. The husband must have been guilty, even if they never found enough evidence to go into court.

And the first girl—that was nothing but a tragic, unforeseeable accident. Some of the girls sharing the apartment—it was never made quite clear just which ones—had doused her with ether.

Starbuck remembered the joke from his high-school science days. A drop of ether on the bare flesh, or even on the clothes, gave the body a freezing chill, far more intense than the one you experienced when a masseur spills rubbing alcohol on your back.

The girls had failed to notice though, that their

victim held a lit cigarette. The ether had caught instantly. The girl burned to death in the kitchen. A tragic, horrible accident.

Starbuck caught himself in midstride. *Ether?* That faint smell that had hung about Carlson when he first came into the church this morning, that had been overcome by the burning incense. It had reminded him somehow of hospitals. It could have been . . . It *was* ether! Starbuck felt the heavy stroke of his heart.

Now, wait a minute. This was the kind of lurid imagining that Ed Quinlan would supply. For this hypothesis to fit, Carlson would have to be some mad avenger out of a paper-back thriller, bent on executing Kathy in an ether immolation the same way the first girl had died.

There must be some other explanation. Too many implausibilities had to be explained. Carlson would have to be the murderer of four other girls. He would have to have known the first girl, loved her. Starbuck clawed his cheeks in an agony of recall. What did he remember of *her?*

Kathy had said she was shy, stand-offish, the butt of the group's teasing. There had been no family. But a fiancé, yes! Someone the other girls had never met, just a portrait on her dresser.

Starbuck sank into his chair, his disciplined, card-index memory racing. The fiancé? He had been a refugee. The last surviving member of a gypsy family that had disappeared into Hitler's concentration camp ovens. That could unhinge a mind. And, then, to have his girl die in the same way. It could start him on a mad search for vengeance against her killers—the whole group, whether guilty or innocent. Was it possible?

Starbuck remembered Carlson's accent, and panicked. He reached for the phone on his desk. But a gypsy. Carlson was blond. *A blond gypsy?* Starbuck sighed and settled back in the chair, shamefaced. Well, possible, of course, but just barely possible.

And what about the girl who was murdered? The husband had done that. Of course, the police couldn't prove it, and they released him, but that was no proof of innocence.

There was an implausibility for you: A *blond* gypsy, who *had to be driven insane* by an accidental murder to give him a motive, strangles a girl who was *probably murdered* by her husband.

But how do you explain the ether smell on him? Starbuck looked longingly at the phone. He could reach Kathy at home now. He wanted to call her.

To warn her? Of what? That a mad man with a bottle of ether in his pocket was about to murder her?

He knew Kathy. She would have chatted gaily with Carlson, all the way up the West Side Drive, glad of his company, as she was always glad of anyone's company. She wouldn't let him escape. He would have to come upstairs for coffee, tea, a drink. *And if he did have that ether . . .*

Suddenly, chillingly, Starbuck remembered the enigmatic smile on Carlson's face when Kathy accepted the cigarette from him. He had been so weirdly, unexplainably happy that she smoked!

"Are you all right, Mr. Starbuck?"

Mrs. Enlow, his secretary, was standing in the door, a soft, motherly frown on her face.

Starbuck's mind raced like a rat in a maze. This was insane. He had to convince himself that this wild speculation could not be true, that Kathy was safe at home, mixing a cocktail for Carlson.

"Would you like your coffee now?" Mrs. Enlow prodded him.

"Uh, yes." He had to talk to someone. Mrs. Enlow? No. "Would you ask young Quinlan, in Law, if he's not— Would you just tell him I'd like a word with him right away?"

There had to be some flaw in this mad hypothesis, Starbuck told himself. It broke every law of mathematical probability.

Carlson. Carlson. But, of course! Carlson had been the fiancé of one of those two girl friends who were run down by the hit-and-run driver. That was where Kathy knew him from. Surely, if he had been the first girl's fiancé, the fact would never have been hidden. They all would have certainly known him.

Starbuck smiled and leaned back in his chair. For a moment there, he had been on the point of calling the police, sending them rushing with sirens to his apartment. Wouldn't that have been a gorgeous mess!

This wild theory was certainly collapsing under a dead-weight of implausibilities. A *blond* gyspy, who *had to be driven insane,* who strangled a girl *murdered by another man,* and then ran down his own fiancée!

That exploded the Mad Avenger hypothesis, of

course, but it didn't explain why Carlson should be so pleased to see Kathy take a cigarette, or why he should smell of ether.

Raggedly, Starbuck's mind went back to the problem. This fool theory had to crumble before a scientific, dialectical approach. None of the room-mates had ever *seen* the first girl's boy friend, Kathy said. Just a picture in her room. They could have forgotten his face. His appearance could have changed in a few years. He could have arranged to meet the other girl, make love to her, run her and the other down in a car.

But what about the last girl? The one buried today. She was a suicide. How could that fit in? But was she a suicide? There were no witnesses. *She could have fallen.*

But nobody falls off the Staten Island ferry.

She could have been pushed. Starbuck's hand snatched up the phone.

At his barked command, Mrs. Enlow, in the outer office, got his home number. He counted twelve rings before he dropped it back on the hand-set. Thursday, the maid's day off. There was no one there to answer until Kathy arrived. Unless she already was there, dead. Sweating, Starbuck glanced at his watch. She'd had time to get up to Riverdale. Barely.

"Good afternoon, sir." Quinlan stood in the door, blond and handsome and youthful in beautifully cut flannels.

"Of course," Starbuck said, and almost giggled. "Oh, of course." Carlson had said he was a contact man for a drug outfit, calling on doctors. That accounted for the smell of ether about him. And the pleasure when Kathy accepted his cigarette? Well, just put it down to nervous relief. After all, Carlson was a man without much social poise, an unsuccessful foreigner riding in the car of a man like Starbuck.

"I beg your pardon?" Quinlan said.

Starbuck regretted the impulse that had caused him to send for this young fool. He felt shaken. He was aware of sweat on his palms and upper lip, a nervous trembling in his thighs and biceps. Were his nerves going? Was he losing his grip on a mind he had trained to function like a precision machine? Never, since he was a child, had Starbuck spent such a half-hour of fearful fantasying as this one just past.

At least he hadn't done anything foolish about summoning the police. It was a blessing he hadn't been able to reach Kathy on the phone. He had betrayed his lapse to no one. He set himself to chatting politely with Quinlan while they drank the coffee, already thinking of the work on his desk. Actually, Quinlan wasn't a bad young fellow. Pretty good lawyer.

Starbuck reached avidly for the stack of real estate reports when Quinlan left, and Mrs. Enlow had cleared off the cups. He should phone Kathy now. Husbandly check-up to see that she was home safe.

He listened to twenty unanswered rings before he disconnected.

"Mrs. Enlow," Starbuck said into the phone when her voice came back, "there's a Mrs. Kyle in my building. They have the other apartment on the floor. Would you ring her up for me, please? Mrs. Charles Kyle, I believe it is. And hurry, please."

Unreasonably, the fear was creeping back, but he was proud of the steadiness of his voice.

It took a long time for the woman's phone to be answered. Then Starbuck found himself talking to a soft, Negro maid's voice, tense and hard to understand because of a volume of unidentifiable background noise. It took a long time for Starbuck to make her understand who he was, and to whom he wanted to talk.

When Mrs. Kyle finally came to the phone, her voice was almost comically tearful. "Oh, Mr. Starbuck! That I should have to be the one to tell you!"

"What? Tell me what, for God's sake!"

"Can't you hear the sirens? There's a terrible fire in your apartment, Mr. Starbuck!"

Starbuck set the phone down. The expression on his face was that of a saint whose God had denied him.

THE GARGOYLE CONSPIRACY

A novel by
Marvin H. Albert

A bomb explodes in the Rome airport, leaving shreds of human flesh strewn about the wreckage. But it was nothing compared to what was to come. It was only the first step of a master terrorist who combined irresistible sexual seduction, all-powerful Arab oil money, an army of terrorist assassins and the latest in sophisticated weaponry in a plot to assassinate the American Secretary of State.

A great new thriller guaranteed to hold you on excitement's edge from the first explosive page to the ultimate shattering shock.

A Dell Book $1.95   (5239-02)

BESTSELLERS
FROM DELL
fiction